Nov. 1, 2011

The White Assassin

THE NIGHTSHADE CHRONICLES

BOOK I
Nightshade City

BOOK II
The White Assassin

The White Assassin

HILARY WAGNER

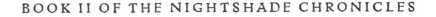

Holiday House / New York

Text copyright © 2011 by Hilary Wagner
Illustrations copyright © 2011 by Omar Rayyan
All Rights Reserved
HOLIDAY HOUSE is registered in the U.S. Patent and Trademark Office.
Printed and Bound in October 2011 at Maple Vail, York, PA. USA.
www.holidayhouse.com

1   3   5   7   9   10   8   6   4   2

Library of Congress Cataloging-in-Publication Data
Wagner, Hilary.
The white assassin / Hilary Wagner.—1st ed.
p. cm.
Sequel to: Nightshade City
Summary: Snakes, bats, and rats join forces to save Nightshade from Billycan and
his horde of brutal swamp rats, aided by an antidote to the drug that made Billycan
the way he is, but the revelation of secrets proves an even more powerful weapon
in the fight for peace.
ISBN 978-0-8234-2333-0 (hardcover)
[1. Fantasy.   2. Rats—Fiction.]   I. Title.
PZ7.W12417Whi 2011
[Fic]—dc22
2011009579

For Lenny Lee,
a very brave young writer
"Rats Rule!"

Contents

Acknowledgments

The rats of Nightshade are family to me and would not exist without my own family. Many thanks to my husband, Eric, who gives me extraordinary ideas, inspiring me to lead my rats to places they never expected to go. My son, Vincent, gives me the outlook of a growing boy—what interests him, what makes him happy, and what drives him nuts—which is a lot! Thanks, V! My daughter, Nomi, inspires me to keep wondering about everything and keep learning about the world around me with wide-eyed amazement on all the things I still don't know about. Thanks, Chip Chop!

Thanks to my agent, Marietta Zacker, who has the good grace to put up with me on a regular basis—and *still* keep talking to me! Heaps of thanks to my editor, Julie Amper. Once again, she worked tirelessly with me, making *The White Assassin* the very best it could possibly be. Billycan thanks you too and is glad you liked the brownies he made.

Last but not least, thank you to everyone who supported *Nightshade City*. I never thought so many people would read my books. Please don't stop! The rats have a lot more to say!

The White Assassin

CHAPTER ONE

A Gathering in a Chapel

GAINST A FULL ORANGE MOON that seemed to punch the night sky, eight members of the Mastiff County brown bat colony silently wheeled through the dark, each clutching a Nightshade rat in its claws. The rats, airborne for the first time, tightly gripped the legs of their bat escorts, staring nervously at the swamp below. Lofty white oaks and cypress trees, steeped in hanging moss, smothered the ground, curling under the rats' feet like ancient beings too aged to stand erect, their spidery branches beckoning the newcomers into their secret world.

Vincent bristled as they swept over the plantation manor, a ghostly whitewash against the black, its broken windows like rotting teeth, flaunting a ghoulish grin. Fitting, he thought. Where else should the rat dwell—the White Assassin, as the creatures of the swamp had so aptly named him. He glanced over at Victor, who gazed wide-eyed at the vast swamplands, then over at Carn, who suddenly twisted in the bat's grip, jolting as an owl screeched from the shadows.

Carn grunted as his escort squeezed him tighter, the bat warning him that it was not the time for such fidgeting, not unless Carn wished to be dropped into the bog and quickly consumed by whatever lurked below. Vincent knew well why Carn was so nervous, and it had little to do with their treacherous journey across the swamp. Carn faced a far more dangerous mission, one that would have even the toughest of rats quaking in fear.

Chief Elder Dresden soared down to the chapel at breakneck speed, his oversized wings unfurling as he prepared to land. Dangling precariously in Dresden's grasp, Juniper examined the bats' swamp-land home. It was a crumbling chapel, rotted by time and the elements to a deathly black. Its steeple leaned at an exaggerated angle, held upright only by the towering trees around it. All the windows and doors had long since disappeared. Fat, gnarled tree limbs and creepers grew through the openings, rambling endlessly across the chapel floor and up the crumbling walls.

One by one, the bats carried the rats into the chapel through a gaping hole in the steeple. Vincent's skin prickled as he took in the bizarre scene. The walls were adorned with peculiar symbols and massive paintings of ferocious fanged snakes in luminescent colors being flung into fire and chopped to pieces by swords wielded by black-cloaked humans. A secret sect once lived in the chapel, Dresden had explained, using snakes as part of their religious sacrifice.

Swooping up a staircase, Dresden flew to a round oak podium overlooking the chapel's pews. A lone torch stood on the podium, resting crookedly in its rusted iron stand, its flames illuminating the painted serpents. Dresden released Juniper as he landed on the podium. The rest of the bats followed, dropping off the other rats behind Juniper, and then flying to the ceiling in one smooth motion. While the rats were relieved to be back on land—or close to it—they remained edgy, unsettled by the flickering images of hideous writhing snakes all around them.

Dresden gave a shrill cry. The rats covered their ears, the sound excruciating. Within seconds, tiny eyes popped out from the darkness. Wings opened from their cocoon-like closures, and bat after bat softly fell from the rafters, easily navigating the web of tangled branches, elegantly plunging to the pews below and landing one next to the other as if waiting for a Sunday sermon. Juniper was awed by the speed and precision of the colony. If only we Nightshade rats could organize so swiftly, he thought.

Dropping from the ceiling, Cotton and Telula, Dresden's children, took position behind their father while the others continued to gather.

"They're here," whispered Cotton to his father. "Our borders are secure. As agreed, they have come alone." Dresden nodded. He looked at the Council and motioned to the chapel's entrance.

Two huge snakes entered, rolling down the center aisle, winding up and twisting down the trees and vines that grew through the floorboards, finally reaching the front row of pews. With an inquisitive gaze they eyed the bats and rats, then glided up the side of the pew where they abruptly stopped, staring intently at the freakish snake paintings on the wall—grim reminders of why no snake had dared venture into the chapel for generations. The pair exchanged glances, gliding from the railing onto the pew. Droppings fell from anxious young bats still up in the rafters, petrified by the slithering creatures their parents had always warned them about.

Juniper approached, cautious but undaunted. The mission was far too vital to give in to any dread a snake could inspire. "Greetings, new allies," he said, "thank you for coming tonight. I'm aware this chapel is not a welcome sight for your kind, but there was no other place for us to safely gather. I am Juniper, Chief Citizen of Nightshade City, and these others are all members of our esteemed Council. We have traveled to your swamp from the north based on information from our old friend Dresden."

Dresden, whose feet weren't meant to walk on land, came forward in an awkward spider-like crawl that made him the most vulnerable to the snakes. He stood between Juniper and Carn, the closest he had ever been to a snake, the bats' sworn enemy. "Welcome, snake leaders. I am Dresden, Chief Elder of the Third Chapter of the Mastiff County brown bat colony."

The banded snake spoke first, a large female, bigger than her companion. She was striped in wide segments of red, black, and yellow, her scales glistening like colored glass in the torchlight. She turned her head from side to side. "Thank you for your welcome, one and all," she said in a raspy tenor. "I am Silt, leader of the scarlet king snakes."

Victor nudged Vincent. "I thought snakes couldn't hear," he whispered.

"That's a myth," answered Vincent. "They hear—just in a different way. They feel the vibrations from our voices and translate them into speech."

"He's right," said the other snake in a throaty voice. "Why, I heard you just fine, young rat!" The snake laughed, causing his buttery skin to pulsate. His black, forked tongue, flanked by glowing white fangs, sputtered wildly from his mouth. Victor twisted uncomfortably, wincing at the sight of shiny, sharp teeth. "I am Wicker, leader of the rat snakes. Ironic, I know." He slowly coiled his long body around itself. "We wish you no harm. As you are well aware, snakes have long preyed on your kind—rats, bats, any meat we can safely digest. But now we must cease this practice. We must join forces with you against a common enemy." The snake's eyes narrowed. "Over the last three years, the white rat has killed vast numbers of our kind, slipping into our nests under cover of night. We've found many of our brothers' and sisters' bodies in the woods, gutted, his stench all over them. He is the only rat who has ever had the power and cunning to kill us. Never have we seen a rat so fast, so sly, so strong. We have tried to catch him, but he is a shrewd one. He has no business in this swamp. His tactics are dissolute—unnatural." Wicker glanced at the wall, snorting at the painted snake that glared back at him. "He is as unnatural as this chapel."

Silt twisted toward Dresden. "Is this the one your sentinels speak of? The one who knows the white rat well?" she asked, sticking out her blood-red tongue at Juniper.

"Yes," answered Dresden. "I'd say he knows him better than most. Juniper..."

"I won't waste your time," said Juniper to the snakes. "Billycan is everything you say and more. Thanks to Dresden's intelligence reports, we know Billycan is planning a grand-scale attack, using his brutal horde of swamp rats to invade Nightshade, to slaughter us and any rat who stands in the way of what he wants—and what he wants is our city." He looked at his Council and then back to the bats and snakes, his voice filling the chapel. "With your help, we can save our city. With our help, you can save yourselves. If we work together, we can capture him and stop his bloody reign forever."

Cocking her head, Silt stared fixedly at Juniper. "*Capture* him? Why not *kill* him?"

"We Nightshade rats have sworn an oath not to kill another creature unless absolutely necessary, not even Billycan. In our investigations we have discovered a serum created by human scientists, military scientists—one that forces their enemies to reveal the truth."

"And how will this *truth* serum help us?" asked Silt skeptically.

"Soon after we've injected him, Billycan will reveal all. We can find out if he's planning a major attack on the swamp snakes. Are there other proposed targets? Has he spies hidden in Nightshade, other allies with troops ready to attack even without Billycan? So you see, this cure will not only neutralize him, it will give us information vital to our safety, to our peace."

"Peace," said Silt with a sigh. "Something we haven't felt in three wearing years. Chief Citizen, how do you intend to capture the White Assassin and bring us such peace?"

Juniper put a paw on Carn's shoulder. "This one knows Billycan better than anyone in Nightshade." Vincent and Victor watched hopelessly, knowing there was nothing they could say to change their friend's mind. "Carn was a Kill Army soldier, working directly under Billycan's command for eleven years. He knows his ways, his habits—his malice—firsthand. Carn will go undercover to infiltrate the horde."

An unnatural sound erupted from the bowels of the rusty phonograph, forcing out the old human's theatrical sermon, his grainy voice sounding through the halls of the manor. "We come here tonight to celebrate de snake, under whose help gather all who share dis faith."

The cat fell to the floor. Billycan lifted its limp orange chin. The white rat cocked his head, examining the dead animal. The thing didn't appear to have much flesh on it, but it would do. Other than fish, turtles, and frogs, the swamp didn't have much to offer in the way of food. Poachers had killed off the gator population decades ago. He was told there were packs of wild boars that roamed the swamp, but he had yet to see one. Billycan was sick to death of turtles, and loathed the briny taste of frogs. After so many meals of oily fish, the thought of them was beyond stomach-turning. Cat meat was a welcome reprieve, no matter how meager.

Three years he'd been in the swamp now. After escaping the Nightshade rats, Billycan hadn't planned to end up here, but here he was, lord of the swamp rats, who found him so intriguing with his snow-white fur and neon-red eyes. They hailed him as a mystic sent to guide them. He grinned devilishly at the thought—him a sage, a spiritual leader. How pitifully funny!

The swamp rats were slow-witted and simple, making them easy to control, at least when they weren't acting like spoiled children. They had nowhere near the intellect of Trillium-born rats.

Slapping his ivory tail against the rotting floor of the manor, Billycan yelled to Cobweb and Montague to light the fire pit in the back of the plantation.

The fervor in the priest's voice grew louder, and the phonograph trembled as if terrified by his words. "Papa Twilight say don't fear the fiend that come to kill ya. Look him in those red devil eyes and let him know *you* gonna win!"

Dragging the cat by the tail, Billycan smiled broadly as he made his way to the back door of the manor. That was his favorite part of the sermon.

The flames licked the skinned cat as Cobweb and Montague turned the spit. The swamp rats sat in a crooked circle around the bonfire, staring at the searing carcass like tongue-wagging jackals. Billycan sat above them in a crude throne that Cobweb had carved for him out of a fallen bald cypress.

The lord of the swamp rats stared vacantly at the flames, his red eyes lightening to a cool orange. Lazily he scratched his snout, feeling the raised trail of blackened skin that traveled across his face—a souvenir of his clash with Juniper, who had anchored his claw at the corner of Billycan's eye, snagging it like a fishhook and creating a deep scar across his muzzle. He watched the cat meat brown. What a grisly way to die burning must be, he thought. How merciful of me to have killed the thing first.

Despite the fact that Billycan had managed to inflict more damage on Juniper—gouging out his eye—he vowed revenge on his mortal enemy. He would exact his pound of flesh. Juniper had done more than scar Billycan. He'd taken everything from him. Soon Billycan would take it all back.

Ravenously hungry, Billycan rapped four hard claws against the side of his crude wooden throne. The swamp rat horde could sit still no longer. He watched with little interest as a young female hurled a rock at the head of another. Her victim, a male, went down instantly, smacking the ground, blood trickling from his temple. The rat eventually pulled himself to his feet, wobbled a bit, and then laughed hysterically. Still dizzy from the blow, he fell back to the earth and lost consciousness. A gaggle of young females, including his attacker, gathered around him, giggling wildly and jumping up and down with glee.

"Imbeciles," muttered Billycan to himself. He knew if he didn't get back to Trillium soon he would surely lose all patience, taking out his rage on the swamp rats, tearing the lot to shreds. He was not meant to stay in this wretched swamp, with its swarms of insects and unrelenting heat, king to a mob of mindless fools.

At least he had Cobweb and Montague, his seconds-in-command. They were smart and they, too, were transplants. The two brothers had come by train when they were small boys—possibly from Trillium, for all they knew. Soon after they arrived, their entire family had been eaten by a pack of corn snakes. Cobweb and Montague were the only ones who'd escaped, finding sanctuary with the swamp rat horde.

When Billycan arrived in the swamp, they immediately took to him. He understood them. The brothers found that living with the horde was like dealing with children who never grew up. One after another they'd wander off, getting themselves eaten by snakes.

Snakes had always been a huge threat to the swamp rats. Billycan quickly put a stop to it. One night he crept into a nest of twenty rat snakes and slashed the family to pieces. He left just one of them alive, telling her that he spared her so she could warn the other snakes of the vicious White Assassin.

Billycan issued an ultimatum: the plantation and its grounds were now off-limits to the snakes. If a snake was caught on the premises, Billycan would kill it and then a dozen more of its kind as punishment. If a swamp rat was foolish enough to leave the plantation, the snakes could have at it. After seeing the carnage left by the oversized white rat, the snakes grudgingly agreed.

A week after the truce, an indigo snake slinked in, ignoring the warning and unconvinced of Billycan's lethal skills. No indigo has ever been seen since.

When it was finally ready, Cobweb and Montague ripped off a huge serving of cat meat and set it before Billycan. Drool gathered in his jaws as the scent hit his snout. He addressed his dim subjects, all slobbering, fiendish with hunger. "You may eat!" he called from his throne.

The swamp rats swiftly engulfed the cat, tearing at its smoked flesh, climbing on top of one another, a frenzy of teeth, claws, and tails. The horde was just as fanatical in its loyalty to him. Grinning at the spectacle, Billycan picked a string of meat from his yellowed incisors. Soon his horde would be in Nightshade.

The swamp rats had slept in a pile, snoring and snorting, lying limply on top of each other like dirty socks in a basket. Billycan had slept outside with the horde, too full from the late-night feast to drag himself inside the manor house. He rubbed the crust from his eyes and looked down from his throne, having been awakened by jeers and scuffling below him.

The horde had circled around two of their kind who were fighting it out in a makeshift arena. The swamp rats were all shades of toast, varying levels of brown. There were a few brutes, but for the most part everyone was roughly the same size. It was as if one brainless rat had been duplicated over and over again, forming a massive army of identical creatures.

Billycan watched the fight. It was Stono, one of the bigger males, and Thicket, a young but rough female who loved to pick on everyone. The mass of rats snorted and cheered as Thicket seized Stono by the scruff of his neck and pushed his snout into the mud.

Dizzily, Stono pulled himself up. He teetered to the left and then to the right, trying in vain to catch his balance. Everyone laughed riotously as he stumbled into Thicket, grabbing her by the middle, forcing them both to the ground.

Straddling him, Thicket pulled his ears. Using his hind legs against her chest, Stono flung her through the air and into the crowd. The onlookers giggled wildly as she crashed into them, landing on another rat, who fell to the ground unconscious—or maybe dead, it was hard to tell. The laughing grew almost psychotic when Thicket kicked the lifeless rat in the side.

Billycan leaped to his feet, slapping his tail against his throne. He looked down at the horde scornfully. "Enough!" he hollered. "What new stupidity is this? Stono, Thicket, you're my best fighters. I will not have you dead or knocked senseless for no good reason!" He pointed to the motionless rat lying on the ground. "If that one does not wake up by sunset, toss him over the border. Let the snakes eat him. I will not have him rotting in my midst!"

He looked at Stono, still panting from the fight, his tongue hanging from his mouth. "Where are Cobweb and Montague?"

Stono pushed his lolling tongue back into his mouth and wiped the mud from his muzzle. "Not sure, said they going on patrol— back in an hour," he answered.

"How long ago was that?"

Stono looked confounded. He gnawed on a claw, trying to think of when he saw them.

Billycan snarled in frustration. "Thicket, how long?" he demanded.

Picking gnats from her coat, Thicket shrugged.

"Oh, never mind!" snapped Billycan. "I'll find them myself!" Seething, he bounded off his throne and tramped into the manor, reminding himself that such idiocy ensured blind devotion.

It was time. Juniper, Vincent, and Carn sat in a cypress tree with Dresden and his children, looking down at the plantation.

Cotton and Telula had been keeping their eyes on the swamp rats' comings and goings for months now, tracking them throughout the grounds of the plantation, watching their every move.

Cotton extended a wing, pointing it at Stono. "That one," he said, "he's a real bruiser, always at the center of things, him and that female." He motioned to Thicket. "Nasty little thing, she is. I've seen her maul her own siblings, grinning as she knocks them out cold."

Spying a milkweed leaf beetle, Telula jutted forward, quickly snatching it up in her teeth, crunching sharply as she crushed its red-and-black shell. Vincent and Carn winced in disgust. "Billycan always has the two gray fellows in tow," she said, swallowing the beetle, "his seconds-in-command, Cobweb and Montague. They talk like him—like us—not at all like the horde. They're different, cinder from head to toe, not brown like the others."

The screen door leading to the backyard slammed shut. Dresden nudged Juniper. "There he is—there's your Billycan."

Juniper's neck bristled as he watched the white rat stroll out from the manor and leap nimbly atop his throne. Billycan looked younger, the warm climate apparently treating him well. He seemed heartier—bigger.

Closing his eyes for a moment, Juniper let out a heavy sigh. The stakes were higher than ever—more than anyone knew. "So there's the White Assassin, *lord* of the swamp rats. I thought the sight of him would make me seethe with rage, but I don't quite know how I feel."

Vincent sneered, suddenly angry. "I still don't understand why you insist on doing this, Juniper. Just eliminate him."

"Vincent, I'm aware of your stance on the matter," said Juniper calmly. "You clearly have your reasons—"

"I have seven *reasons!*" he shouted back at Juniper. "He murdered my parents, my brothers, my sisters. Get rid of him once and for all. Why must we capture him and run the risk he'll only manage to escape *again?*"

"Keep your voice down!" barked Juniper. "Are you trying to get us all killed? Upon founding Nightshade we all took an oath, and it's *not* a selective one. As a member of the Council, you must set an example. We don't kill—not even our enemies, no matter how deadly they are. We have the serum. We can find out the truth and be sure there are no others waiting in the wings, ready to pounce should his life end." He motioned to the horde. "He is going to set those wild fiends upon us like rabid wolves. He could have operatives all over Trillium, just waiting for their chance to take power. Do you really want to risk that? This is our only answer. We can find out *everything*. After that, he can rot alongside his high majors in Nightshade's prison corridor."

Vincent glowered at Billycan as he stretched leisurely in his throne. "I still don't agree with your decision—and for the record, much of the Council does not agree." Slowly he exhaled. "You have done a great deal for me and Victor. You have given us a future and have become our family. My father's dream—Nightshade—was realized because of *you*. So I do this for you, and for young Julius. He's the only good thing to come from that fiend who dares call himself a rat. No matter who gave him life, Julius is *your* boy through and through—a true Belancort."

Juniper set a paw on Vincent's shoulder. "Fair enough," he said.

Carn sat on the branch, his brown feet dangling in the air as he watched the swamp rats swoon and slobber over Billycan. Billycan had killed Carn's family, too, then forced the orphaned rat to serve as his Kill Army aide. He, too, was uneasy with Juniper's decision to leave Billycan unharmed, but he would abide by it. Working eleven years under Billycan, constantly surrounded by him, Killdeer, and the high majors, Carn had seen enough carnage for a lifetime.

He inspected his dirtied coat. He hadn't groomed himself since he made his decision to infiltrate the horde. A clean rat would surely stick out among the grubby swamp rats, but his filthy brown fur would help him fit in seamlessly. "It's time," he said. Carn was edgy but self-assured. This was his moment. He could not fail Juniper, who would surely blame himself should things end badly.

"I suppose the front yard, then," said Carn, referring to a drop-off point.

"Agreed," said Juniper. He sighed heavily. "Carn, are you absolutely sure you want—"

"Yes," said Carn, with a reassuring grin. "I want to do this. I *can* do this. No one will notice me in that sea of dirty brown rats. Besides, I've been around long enough to learn a thing or two." He winked. "Maybe even from old Billycan himself." He looked down at the horde. "With any luck, I'll get reliable information from someone. Being one of the horde, talking with them, maybe I'll get details the bats haven't learned just eavesdropping. I want Billycan captured just as much as you do, and I'll do anything to finally bring him to justice." He scanned the area surrounding the manor. "Telula, that rotting pile of firewood at the side of the manor—that can be our rendezvous point. We'll meet up every day, just after sunset, so I can report what I've learned."

"I'll be there without fail," said Telula. She pointed a wing toward Stono and Thicket, who were now wrestling in the grass. "You'll want to get near them, but be wary. They meet with Billycan often, so listen for information, but for Saints' sake stay on the fringes of things. I can't stress it enough. Remain unremarkable."

"Telula is right," said Vincent. "The moment Billycan catches a hint of your scent or a glimpse of your face, he'll—"

"I know," said Carn, smiling at Vincent reassuringly. "I know what he'll do to me."

Grabbing Carn by the shoulders, Juniper stared at him intently. "Never let your guard down, not even for a moment. Nightshade would never be the same if something happened to you—nor would I."

"You better return," said Vincent, a bleak expression on his face.

"Both of you, quit worrying," said Carn. "I'll be fine." He watched as Billycan walked back into the manor. He nodded at Telula. "Let's go."

Telula rose from the branch. She swiftly grabbed Carn by the scruff of his neck. With a broad swoop, she made her way around to the back of the mansion, smoothly setting Carn down in the boggy grass just inside the plantation borders. "Remember," Telula said as she flew back into the trees, "stay on the fringes of things—*unremarkable!*"

Juniper watched as Carn faded into the horde. No one seemed to notice his arrival, but Juniper worried. What would become of Carn?

CHAPTER TWO
The Horde

NIGHT HAD FALLEN. Carn crept under a rusted-out jalopy in the front yard and tried to get some sleep. It was an intermittent slumber, filled with half-conscious dreams, intensified by strange scents, garbled voices, and faint snarls all around him. The swamp rats had gathered just outside the car, sleeping peacefully in a tangled heap on the grass.

Carn awoke suddenly. He swallowed, his mouth dry, his paws trembling. What was he *thinking*? It had all seemed so different when they'd hatched the plan. Why did he offer himself up like that?

Maybe the swamp rats weren't so slow-witted after all. Maybe they were just callous fiends who preferred to live in squalor, too keen on killing to care about cleanliness. If they found him out, would he be torn to ribbons? Would they bring him screaming in terror to Billycan?

Carn cautiously poked his head out from under the car, trying to muster up courage—the same courage he'd mustered when he stood beside Juniper and denounced Billycan to the entire Kill Army. Be that rat, he thought. Be *that* rat.

He peered out from behind a tire. "Summon your mettle," he whispered to himself, struggling not to panic. Dense or not, *all* rats could smell fear. He clenched his teeth and rambled casually to the outskirts of the horde. His eyes wandered to Stono and Thicket, already awake, shaking themselves from their sluggishness.

Right away the pair spotted Carn eyeing them.

Bouncing up from the grass, Thicket bounded over to him. "Who you be?" she shouted, forcing her snout into his face, growling. She shoved Carn aggressively, knocking him on his back.

Carn stared up at Thicket in amazement. He'd never been hit by a female—and with such force! She was as powerful as any male he'd been in scrapes with back in the Catacombs.

"Who you be?" she demanded again, baring her teeth.

Carn had not thought about a name. He certainly couldn't use his own...and what about the horde's dialect? His refined speech would be a dead giveaway that he did not belong. He thought quickly, jumping to his feet. "Corn!" he blurted loudly. He growled forcefully, shoving Thicket backward.

Thicket hissed at him. The larger rat, Stono, was standing just behind her now.

"Corn!" he yelled again, thrusting his face into hers. It was a risky move, but if anything it would show he wasn't to be pushed around. "That who I be!"

Thicket took a step back. She crossed her arms and nibbled on the tip of her tail, looking the foreigner up and down. She was actually quite striking, with a bright and determined face and angular features. She pursed her mouth as she inspected him, looking almost demure. Carn thought perhaps she was toying with him, about to attack. Stono hung behind her like an overgrown child, ready to follow her lead. She was unquestionably in control.

Her tone became less confrontational. "Why I never seen you before?" she asked.

Carn searched his brain. Use as few words as possible, he thought. "I been out," he said indifferently, "hunting the woods for snakes and such."

Thicket looked surprised. Hunting snakes was dangerous, unheard of among the horde. Only Billycan was capable of killing them. "We don't kill snakes! They kill us!" she snapped indignantly, as if Carn had carried out some grave offense. "Ain't you scared of them?"

Telula had told him to stay on the fringes, and here he was talking to Thicket, the obvious ringleader of the horde, which had slowly wrapped around them in a circle as though a schoolyard tussle were about to break out. *Unremarkable*, Telula had told him. At this rate, he'd be dead before lunch.

Despite the growing number of spectators, Carn stayed in character. "Corn ain't scared a nothing," he sneered. "Not snakes, not nobody."

Thicket marched around him in a circle. "How many snakes you kill out there?"

"Don't know," he replied. "Lots, I guess. I break their bones and eat 'em up."

Thicket looked impressed. The swamp rats never lied, so they were unable to grasp the concept of deception. Thicket had no reason not to believe him. She stuck out her snout, sniffing his face and neck again. "How long you been hunting out there?"

"Real long time—years, I reason."

Thicket looked satisfied with his answer. That would explain

a new face. Rats were easily forgotten in the horde. A few years away
might as well have been an eternity.

"Corn," she said, turning to her male counterpart, "this be
Stono."

Carn nodded. Stono grunted in response, not sure if he wanted
another male sniffing around Thicket.

Thicket turned to Stono and glared at him. "What you rumbling
'bout back there?" she asked brusquely.

Stono grumbled something unintelligible and kicked the ground.
Thicket's voice suddenly grew mild, almost sweet. "Aw, don't go
fussing now. Corn just another rat. He ain't *you*, Stono. Nobody's
you." Thicket punched Stono's arm, her crude way of showing affection. Stono stopped pouting and gave her a shy smile, which looked
odd coming from such a brute of a rat.

Carn wouldn't have believed it had he not seen it with his own eyes,
not after what he'd heard from the bats. The swamp rats clearly felt gen-
uine emotion, not just the base instincts to kill and mate—even Thicket,

who by all accounts was an utter menace. Carn watched as Thicket tugged playfully at Stono's ear. He plucked her off her feet, throwing her to the ground. The two starting wrestling in the grass. They didn't play nice or even fair, but it was obvious they cared for each other.

This was not at all what Carn had expected. It made him think about Billycan. What lurked behind those swirling eyes of red? Who was *he*?

Picking up the rough country dialect of the swamp rats didn't require too much effort. Their drawl was thick, to be sure, their tongue crude, but Carn had little trouble understanding them. Their vocabulary was lacking, but their thoughts were well formed, not the mishmash of nonsensical words the bats had described.

As much as Carn wished to stay anonymous, after his first encounter with Thicket and Stono there was zero likelihood of that. Thicket had taken a shine to him, and unbelievably Stono was warming up, realizing Thicket had no romantic interest in the snake-killing Carn.

Since their meeting two days before, Thicket and Stono had quickly turned their twosome into a trio. Thicket was awed by his snake-killing prowess. She hoped Corn would impress Billycan, so he'd be allowed to go with them when they attacked Nightshade City.

Carn had yet to see his former commander up close. He'd managed to stay out of sight so far, but with Thicket and Stono so attached to him, his odds of staying undetected were slim.

On the upside, his new station should prove fruitful to the Council. Staying on the periphery as Telula suggested would surely put him at less risk, but he'd learn little information that Dresden's colony didn't already know.

Carn had been unable to meet with Telula as planned. Thicket stuck to him like glue. Even at night she'd get up often, making sure all was safe, stirring at the slightest noise. After two days the Council must think him already dead. He'd try again tonight.

Carn sat tensely with Thicket and Stono. It was hotter than usual, and they were leaning against the back wall, taking advantage of the afternoon shade the manor provided. Carn's heart suddenly jumped as the rickety screen door swung open. Clutching the damp ground, he dug his claws in, anchoring himself to the earth so that he couldn't be ripped away upon discovery. Through the rusty screen he saw a rat—a gray. It was Montague, one of Billycan's seconds. Cobweb tagged behind him. Carn's whole body went limp with relief, exhausted as though he'd been running uphill.

Thicket turned to him. "What be wrong with you, Corn?" she demanded. "You sick?"

Carn reclaimed his wits. He had promised he would not be governed by fear, yet here he was gripping the ground in sheer terror. "The heat," he panted. "Hot today."

Thicket stared at him skeptically. "It always be hot, nothing new 'bout that."

"Cooler in the woods, is all," he said, trying to give a rational excuse. "More shade."

Turning their gaze to the back of the manor, Cobweb and Montague spotted the rats they'd been searching for.

"Thicket, Stono, there you are," said Montague. He spoke properly, like a Trillium rat. "Billycan wants to see you two."

Grabbing Carn's arm, Thicket pulled him to his feet. "This here be Corn," said Thicket, shoving him in front of the seconds. "Just back from the woods, killed lots a snakes out there!"

Montague looked at him strangely—not suspiciously, just surprised to see a face he did not recognize. "Corn, you say? How long have you been gone? I don't seem to recall your face."

Carn wished he didn't have to talk like an idiot, but knew his life was more valuable than his pride. "Don't know for sure, been a long while now," he said, "real long."

Cobweb looked at Thicket. "Did you say he was killing *snakes*?"

"Yep," said Thicket proudly, "just like Billycan!"

Tapping his chin, Cobweb sized up Carn. "Billycan will want to know of this. Another rat who can take on the snakes. I'm sure he'll be interested in speaking to you, Corn."

"He can come with us right now," said Thicket, pulling Carn toward the door.

"Now, Thicket," said Montague, "you know no one can go inside without Billycan's approval. You'll fall into bad favor, and you wouldn't want that, now, would you? I'm sure Billycan will be quite intrigued with Corn's skill, but it will have to keep for now."

Thicket jutted out her chin. Her expression turned into a sulk. "Fine," she said, folding her arms.

Smiling, Cobweb patted Thicket's shoulder. "Don't pout, now," he said softly. "We'll be off to Nightshade in a matter of days, all of us getting a whole new life—a better one."

Carn's body stiffened at the news. Mere days! This changed everything.

"Off you go," said Montague, motioning to the door. "He's waiting for you in the parlor."

Thicket and Stono bounded up the back stairs and into the manor. Carn stood uneasily with Montague and Cobweb, hoping they'd just move along and go about their business. It seemed nothing had gone as planned since he entered the horde. The two seconds immediately started questioning him.

"So, Corn," said Cobweb, "how do you go about killing snakes? How do you do it?"

"Uh…first I stomp on 'em," said Carn, thinking fast, "breaking some bones, and then I grab their skulls from the back, before they even sees me. Crack their jaws apart."

"You're brave," said Cobweb. "Our whole family was killed by snakes, and much of the horde as well. I can't think of more vicious creatures."

"I'll be sure to tell Billycan about your special ability," said Montague. "You could be of real help to our cause. If you can kill snakes, you can surely kill rats. Billycan needs our help to reclaim his city, his kingdom that was stolen from him by treacherous Nightshade rats. Billycan says we can all live there, away from the snakes and this accursed heat. Well, we have our duties to attend to. Carry on, then." The seconds walked off to do a check of the perimeter.

Relieved, Carn leaned against the manor. But he had to get to Telula tonight. He had to get word to Juniper that the attack on Nightshade was now only days away.

Billycan crouched on the stained settee in the front parlor of the manor. He was furiously writing on a piece of parchment, constantly dipping his feather pen into the pot, loading up more ink. A drop had trickled down the feather and onto his paw, staining his white fur black.

Staring at his blackened digits, he wondered for a moment what it would be like to be someone else, to start over with a completely new identity. The thought quickly passed. He had starting writing again when the heady reek of body odor hit his nostrils. Stono's scent was particularly pungent.

Thicket and Stono had been standing in silence on the tattered parlor rug, waiting for Billycan to address them.

"Stono," said Billycan, not looking up, "bathing is not a crime, you know. You could bring down a herd of oxen with that rancid stench." He finally looked up from his papers. "We'll be leaving for Nightshade shortly. A truck is scheduled to be here in a matter of days. You'll have your orders as soon as I've finished going over the last of the city's blueprints. Stay out of trouble. I can't risk one of you getting injured because of your continuous roughhousing. Do you understand me?"

"Yes sir," answered Thicket.

"That's all, you may go," said Billycan, waving them away.

"Uh, sir," said Thicket timidly, "we found a snake killer—just like you."

Billycan cocked his head. "Did you say a snake killer?"

"Yep, a new rat, Corn. He kill the snakes, just like you."

"New," said Billycan guardedly. "What do you mean, new? How did you not know of him before?"

"Corn been out hunting all this time," replied Thicket. "A few years, he say."

"Well, Miss Thicket, why don't either of you remember him if it has been only a few years?"

Thicket looked at Stono. They didn't have an answer. They both shook their heads and shrugged.

Billycan rolled his eyes in frustration. "Oh, never mind," he said, "you two can't seem to remember yesterday, let alone last year. Regardless, Thicket, Billycan is glad to know about this rat. He may prove to be quite helpful. Now I've plans to work on, so off with you both." He brandished his pen at Stono. "Oh, and Stono, you *will* bathe tonight. Billycan can see the fleas on your hide from here. I will not have you festering in front of me."

Stono frowned resentfully, stomping his foot.

"Am I to have a problem with you, Stono?" asked Billycan with a flinty glare.

After a brief hesitation, Stono spoke. "No sir," he grumbled.

"Good," snapped Billycan. "Now get out."

The swamp rats ambled out of the manor. From the corner of his eye, Billycan watched as a wolf spider slowly traveled up a leg of the settee. Suddenly he pounced on it, crushing it violently with his ink-blackened fist before it had a chance to flee.

With a flick of his wrist he flung the crippled spider to the ground, its broken legs twitching on the Oriental rug. He stared at it intently until the thing finally stopped moving. He found all creatures' deaths quite fascinating.

Thicket had dragged Stono off by his ear to the plantation's murky pond to get clean, or at least to get the stink off him, finally giving Carn some breathing room.

His stomach knotted, he had been unable to eat the last two days' rations. He was now achingly hungry. He was watching a pair of grub worms squirming in the grass, seriously considering them, when he noticed a rat watching him, utterly transfixed—a female.

Their eyes locked. She was brown like the rest, but her coat was dark, like his. She was dainty, fine-boned. Gazing at him, she batted her eyes, tilting her head coyly. She edged nearer, flashing a surprisingly elegant smile.

"She's flirting with me," said Carn to himself, as though the world had ended. "Of all the times—she fancies me for a mate!"

Carn tried to ignore her, but she kept taking petite steps closer. "Oh, for Saints' sake," he muttered. In normal circumstances, Carn would never rebuff the advances of such a pretty girl, but given his situation, not to mention the fact that she was a swamp rat, their union was plainly not in the cards.

Never did he think he'd be thankful to see Thicket proudly marching back to him with a clean, or at least less offensive, Stono on her arm. "See?" she said. "Don't Stono look fine?"

"Real fine," said Carn, turning his back on the still advancing female.

Breaking into a toothy grin, Stono pointed over Carn's shoulder. "Thicket, look there," he said spiritedly.

Thicket's gaze locked on Carn. "Well, look at that," she said slyly. "Looks like you got a new friend, Corn!" She and Stono laughed like hyenas. Thicket mischievously kicked Carn in the rump, knocking him down directly at the feet of the female.

Exasperated, Carn wiped the mud from his snout. "Just wonderful," he grumbled under his breath. He slowly rose to his feet, realizing he couldn't get out of talking to this rat. He noticed she was cleaner than the rest of the swamp rats. Her chocolate coat was shiny and dense, no patches of the mange or other ailments that ran rampant through the horde.

Thicket butted in between them. She pulled the female over to the side and whispered in her ear. The two giggled wildly. She promptly grabbed the female by the wrist and yanked her over to Carn.

"Corn, this be Oleander," said Thicket, pushing the female in front of him, "my cousin."

"Hey there, Corn," said Oleander.

"Hey," he mumbled coldly. He folded his arms and stared at the ground, not wanting to give her any suggestion he was interested.

"I hear you be a snake killer," said Oleander.

"So what if I am?" he snapped.

"He be an ornery one," said Oleander to Thicket.

"They all be ornery!" said Thicket. The girls laughed madly, jumping up and down.

Carn rolled his eyes. This was a complication he did not need—not now.

Stono grunted at Thicket. "Leave 'em be, Thicket. Corn don't need help from you!"

Thicket grimaced at Stono, but surprisingly did as he asked. "Fine, then," she said curtly.

Abruptly Stono grabbed Thicket around her waist and threw her over his shoulder, his improved hygiene making him boisterous. "Put me down, ya big oaf!" she protested. Stono ignored her, carrying her off toward a willow as she banged on his back and burst into more laughter.

Carn and Oleander stood in awkward silence. Before he could speak, Oleander grabbed him brusquely by the neck. He tried to wrench away from her tight grip, but she was strong like Thicket. He knew the swamp rats were primitive, but this type of forwardness was downright shocking.

"Oleander," he barked, trying to jerk away, "let me go!"

They fell to the ground. "Quiet!" she whispered in his ear, her heavy drawl evaporating. "Do you want to get us both killed? Now listen closely. We don't have much time!"

"What?" shouted Carn in disbelief. "What did you just say?"

"Keep your voice down," she said. "I *know* you're not a swamp rat. You must meet me by the ancient willow, just after dark." The horde was beginning to observe their exchange. Using her feet, she rolled him on top of her, pretending to tussle with him in the grass.

"What ancient willow? Where?"

"It's the largest tree you'll find, just outside the front gate. You can't miss it."

Carn spun her back over. "Who are you?" he demanded.

"Did you already forget my name?" she asked with a subtle southern inflection. She laughed softly. "I'm Oleander."

"I don't understand," whispered Carn.

"It's all right," she said calmly. "We're not *all* as dim-witted as you think." Her dark eyes flashed in the sunlight. "For now, that's all you need to know. See you after nightfall, then." Abruptly she sprang up and dashed out of view, hiding herself within the ranks of the horde.

Carn lay on the ground, utterly dumbstruck.

The sun had set. The horde had settled in a heap. Carn lay nervously next to Thicket and Stono, trying to figure out how to slip away without Thicket wanting to go with him.

Carn turned on his stomach and spied the corroded gates at the edge of the plantation's gravel footpath. Like old bones, the gates hung open—skeletal creations, falling off their hinges, ruined relics of their former grandeur.

A mosquito stabbed Carn in the flank. He whipped around abruptly, flattening the insect with his fist. Blood burst from the insect's belly and onto his palm.

Thicket awoke. "Corn, what you doing?" she asked groggily. "Ain't you sleeping yet?"

"Can't sleep," he said, grabbing the opportunity. "I be eaten alive by mosquitoes—going to the pond to wash off. Maybe then the mosquitoes go and bother someone else."

"I'll go, too," she said, about to arise.

"No, no," said Carn, "you stay with Stono." He grinned shyly. "I wants to go find Oleander. She told me she may be at the pond tonight. I can't stop thinking 'bout her."

Thicket sat on her haunches, smirking mischievously. "I knew it! You likes her, too! All right then, I stays put. Go gets yourself to the pond." She tossed a clump of dirt at him. "You be looking grungy, so takes yourself a bath before you find Oleander. Now that Stono be clean, you stink worse than him!"

Carn smiled. Despite Thicket's lack of anything even mildly resembling etiquette, there was an uncomplicated sweetness about her. "I be back soon." He quickly got to his feet and trotted out of sight before Thicket had a chance to change her mind and follow.

Carn sped toward the gate, hoping no one had followed. He spotted the old willow Oleander had mentioned. It stood just outside the perimeter of the plantation, beyond the marked borders Telula had shown him—snake territory. If a snake spotted him, it would think him a swamp rat, devouring him before he'd even have a chance to explain he was on *it's* side.

The tree looked deserted. He saw no signs of Oleander or anyone. Maybe it was a ruse, and Oleander a lure sent by Billycan to lead him into a trap. Carn sniffed the air. After eleven years in the Kill Army, he was a veritable expert on the white rat's scent, an odd fusion of black mushrooms and cane molasses.

His chest heaving, Carn neared the ancient willow. It was a huge, knotted thing, wider than any tree he'd ever seen in Trillium. Its trunk looked as if it might come to life, swallowing him whole. Lumpy and puckered, its twisted exterior resembled a mass of knotted wooden mouths, poised to strike, ready to devour his flimsy rat bones.

He slipped through the corroded bars of the gate. An owl screeched. Carn leaped in fright. It seemed the hazards of the swamp were endless. How he longed for Trillium and its self-absorbed

Topsiders. Its cats and dogs, the maddening pigeons, the cars careening down the overcrowded streets—he would give anything to be faced with the enemy he knew.

"Over here," whispered a giggly voice from the other side of the tree. "Cat got your tongue?" It was Oleander. She bounced into view as if she didn't have a care in the world. Her shiny coat and pointed teeth gleamed in the moonlight.

"Keep your voice down," pleaded Carn. "Billycan could be anywhere!"

"Don't be silly. We watch him day and night. Our guards say he's stomping around the manor right now, brooding over something or other. Now, first things first. Please tell me your name is *not* Corn. Such a ridiculous name, it can't be real!"

Carn's cover was already blown, so what would it matter if he revealed his name? "I didn't have much time to think about it. My real name is Carn."

"Well now, Carn, that's much better!" she said brightly. "'Corn' is a little *too* backwoods, even for us." She giggled again.

Insulted, Carn felt his cheeks grow hot. "No one else seemed to question it."

"I'm only teasing. It was a fine choice for a name—really. I'm just happy to meet another rat like myself."

Carn crinkled his nose, peeved he had not disguised himself better. "How did you figure me out?"

"It was easy!" she said excitedly. "First off, you talk to yourself—a lot. Once, when Stono and Thicket were off eating dinner, I spotted you sitting in the grass, grumbling to yourself about Nightshade, how you missed it so—the same city Billycan speaks of. He says it belongs to him, which I've doubted from the start. Other things gave you away, too, things the horde never would have noticed. You haven't eaten your rations in two days. Even ill, a member of the horde would have gobbled them up without a second thought. And you don't walk like a swamp rat, all slack and droopy. You walk with purpose, like a soldier."

"I *was* a soldier," admitted Carn. He looked at Oleander curiously. She seemed so smart. "Why aren't you like the others? I thought all the swamp rats were a bit slow-minded—no offense, of course."

"None taken. For the most part we are exactly that—slow-minded." Oleander sighed. "The horde has existed for over a hundred years. Our lineage has plenty of dreadful qualities, which I suppose eventually overwhelmed all the good ones—aggression, bad judgment, the need to fight, not to mention an utter lack of common sense."

"But you seem as smart as me."

"I'd say smarter!" she said with a smirk. "As it turns out, every so often one of us pops out right, just like you, or Montague and Cobweb. Where you're from, I'm sure very few rats come out inferior; in my world it works the other way around."

"But who's been teaching you? How did you learn to speak—well—like me?"

"There's a small group of us. The elders of our group pass on their knowledge to the next generation. The original members of our little faction learned from the humans who built the manor. Tar, one of our forefathers, used to hide in the parlor and listen to every lesson the humans taught their children. They were a smart group, several families of scientists all living together, raising their children while doing some kind of research. The scientists left this place lifetimes ago, but since then each new generation of our kind has taught the next. Those crazy snake worshipers who bought the manor years later were all bitten by their own snakes. They didn't last too long!" She laughed.

Carn looked perplexed. "Why do you pretend to be like the others? Maybe you and your group could help the rest of the horde."

Oleander's cheery face turned dismal. "The ones who've tried were driven out. Years back, a few even got killed for it. The horde didn't understand that they were being offered help, and a couple of rats—well, they didn't mean to hurt anyone, but they did." She paused for a moment. "It's hard being different."

"What about the seconds, Cobweb and Montague? Why were they accepted into the horde?"

Oleander stared at the sleeping horde, a dark mass of limbs and fur. "I suppose it's easier to fit in as an outsider. Cobweb and Montague were only boys when they were found wandering in the swamp, starving to death. The horde would never cast off children. Not to mention that before Billycan came along, they were the only ones to keep the snakes at bay. So they were accepted—somewhat accepted, in any case."

"From the outside, they seem like nice enough fellows. Are they really aligned with Billycan? Do they know you or your group exists?"

"The elders of our group have never been sure of the gray rats, not being family and all, so they've never breathed a word. I've proposed we tell Cobweb and Montague the truth, maybe we can help each other, but they said no—both of them working for Billycan and all. The elders are rather set in their ways. I doubt they'll ever recognize Cobweb and Montague as members of the horde."

"If the horde is so set against outsiders, why would they accept Billycan?"

"Oh, he made a big show of things, saving the lives of three rats about to get pounced on by water moccasins. The horde thought he must have been sent to them, this white rat with red eyes. They believed him to be their savior. The elders knew straight off he was not what he seemed, but we were outnumbered. There was nothing we could do to keep him out."

Oleander sat at the base of the tree and leaned against its trunk. Carn sat next to her. "Your elders are right about Billycan," he said. "Let there be no doubt, he's vicious and depraved in every way, a murderer. He should be in Nightshade's prison corridor. He's set on revenge and will use your family to carry it out, leading everyone to their death if necessary."

"So Nightshade City *wasn't* taken from him as he claims. We suspected as much," said Oleander.

Carn scoffed. "The Catacombs were our original home, taken over by Billycan and a monster of a rat named Killdeer in a brutal battle known as the Bloody Coup. Eleven years later the Loyalists, good rats, freed the citizens of the Catacombs. Killdeer wound up dead and Billycan escaped like a coward, afraid to answer for his crimes. Nightshade's Chief Citizen, Juniper Belancort, was the one who headed up the cause. He is the reason we are all free today. Billycan is dead set on revenge, which is why he's planning on taking the horde to Nightshade."

"I see," said Oleander. "So you've met him. You *know* Billycan, then?"

Carn suddenly felt exhausted, as if the act of speaking had drained him completely. "Working as his aide for eleven years in the Catacombs, following each and every order he ever muttered—yes, I know him well."

In the dark hours of morning, Oleander and Carn crept back into the heart of the horde. They awoke next to Thicket and Stono, acting as if they were now together, a couple, claiming to have met at the pond during the night. Thicket could not have been happier to have Carn court her favorite cousin, and gladly welcomed Oleander into their group.

Carn's main objective was to finally get to Telula. It had been several days now, and the Council must be thinking the worst. He had to get them the news.

Oleander and her small faction had been hoping to devise a plan to get rid of Billycan. Carn thought they could join forces with the others—rats, bats, and snakes—all fighting as one.

They had just finished breakfast, a mealy muck of dried fish and tadpoles. A feeble excuse for a meal, but Carn was glad to have food of any kind. He needed to think clearly, so many new revelations were whirling about in his head. As the foursome sat in the sun, digesting their shabby rations, Montague and Cobweb approached.

"Ah," said Cobweb, looking at Thicket and Stono, "there you are. Billycan wants to see you two directly. He has devised a final plan for the attack, and you two need to learn your directives."

Stono let out an unpleasant belch. The dried fish, most likely gone bad, was not agreeing with him. "He wants us to be learning *what?*" he asked.

"Your directives," said Montague. "You know, Stono. What you're supposed to do, your orders for the attack on Nightshade."

"Oh," said Stono as another rolling burp escaped his mouth, this time with an equally disgusting scent attached.

Thicket jumped up impatiently. She grabbed Carn's paw, yanked him to his feet, and dragged him in front of Cobweb and Montague. "What 'bout him?" she asked. "Don't Billycan want to see Corn the snake killer?"

"Tomorrow, Thicket," said Cobweb. "Billycan will meet your friend tomorrow night. Our lord and leader has a special night planned for you and the rest of the horde. We've dug a pit for a lone boar spotted roaming the area. We are to have a bonfire feast tomorrow night, and then we'll go to Nightshade the following day, all with bellies full of roast boar—a reward from Billycan."

Stono clapped his paws in delighted anticipation.

"Billycan said he'd meet with Corn during the feast," said Montague. "He's certainly intrigued." He patted Carn on the shoulder approvingly. "He's very interested in meeting you, Corn." He looked over at Oleander, who deliberately clung to Carn's arm. "And Oleander as well, I see."

"Yep," said Thicket happily. "They be thick as thieves!"

"Well, then, the four of you have quite an honor in store. Billycan has requested the three of you to dine by his side during the feast. Oleander, you'll attend with Corn, then," said Cobweb.

"Come along, you two," said Montague, "Billycan is waiting."

The two seconds, along with Thicket and Stono, left for the manor. Carn exhaled anxiously. "What am I going to do?" he asked Oleander. "Billycan will kill me on sight!"

"Hush, now," whispered Oleander. "Things will be fine. We'll meet your bat friend tonight, and later I'll introduce you to my father, Mannux, Chief Elder of our group. We'll figure this out, I promise. Everything will turn out all right."

"How do you know that?" asked Carn gloomily.

"Because it can't end any other way. It just can't."

The sun had set. The horde slept comfortably in the grass. It was cool, a welcome relief from the normally sticky night air. Carn was eager to meet with Telula.

Oleander giggled in the grass. Thicket sat up and looked at her cousin. "What you laughing 'bout?" she asked. Oleander cupped a paw over Thicket's ear and whispered something. The two started cackling like old crones, and Thicket slapped her cousin's knee.

Stono frowned at them, jerked awake by their snickering. "What be wrong with you two? I'm trying to sleep. Now hush up!" he snapped grumpily.

"Aw, Stono," said Thicket, "these two want to talk in private, is all."

"They want privacy, then give it to them," he said crossly. He nodded at Carn. "Corn, go over to the cypress by the pond, no one go there but me and Thicket. That be our place."

Carn stood up and grabbed Oleander's paw, pulling her up with him. "Let's get to the pond, then," he said impatiently, worried that they would miss Telula.

Stono chuckled. "Take your time, Corn. You got the rest of your life for that courting nonsense. Other things be more important now." Stono smiled fondly at Thicket, patting her on the shoulder. She curled up next to him, wrapping her tail around his middle.

Carn studied Stono. Every time Carn thought he was just as bumbling as could be, he'd say something meaningful, utterly insightful.

"Night, you two," said Stono, watching the pair run off.

"Night," called Carn as they disappeared into the dark.

CHAPTER THREE
Dig Him Up

T HEY RACED TOWARD THE POND, but then made a wide circle so as not to be seen heading to the side of the manor. They sat against the side of the house, hidden by the pile of firewood where Carn and Telula had agreed to meet.

Carn examined the trees, looking for any sign of her. At last he spotted her, a shadowy, flapping blur against the darkening sky. She flew down onto a low branch of the nearest tree.

Carn took Oleander's paw. "Telula," he called in a whisper. "It's Carn."

Telula dived swiftly down from her perch and landed atop the firewood. She looked at him, wide-eyed. "Carn, you're alive!" she whispered happily. "We all thought—"

"I know," said Carn. "I'm sorry I worried you all, but I didn't have a choice."

"Everyone will be so relieved—" Spotting Oleander, Telula froze for a moment, distressed. "And who is this?" she asked guardedly.

"Don't be alarmed," answered Carn. "This is Oleander. She's not like the others. She's from a secret group within the horde, all smart like us."

"Pleased to meet you," Oleander said softly, staring up at the bat. "Carn speaks highly of your colony and how you've all been so obliging to his kind—well, my kind. I know you think the horde a coarse and violent sort, but they just don't know any better. They're good on the inside—truly."

Telula felt embarrassed. How harshly she'd judged the swamp rats. "If you are a friend to Carn, then you are a friend to my colony. Our rat friends are numerous. We should have known there was more to the horde than what we saw from the trees...ignorance on our part, I'm afraid."

"Oleander and her group want to be rid of Billycan, same as us," said Carn, climbing up on the logs to get closer to the bat. "Telula, you have to warn Juniper. Billycan is planning an attack on Nightshade in two days. There will be a feast tomorrow night, and then he's taking the horde to Nightshade."

"Oleander, who is the leader of your group?" asked Telula. "Who is the elder in charge?"

"That would be my father, Mannux," said Oleander.

"All right," said Telula, thinking. "I'll inform Juniper and Dresden of these new developments. My colony can get Juniper and the others into the manor, if Mannux and your group can keep Billycan occupied at the feast."

"No problem there," said Carn with a guilty cringe. "I'm... well... his guest of honor."

"Carn!" scolded Telula. "What were you thinking? *Unremarkable*, remember?"

Billycan looked out past the front gates of the manor. The moon had all but disappeared. A gluey fog had blown into the swamp, swallowing it entirely, as though heralding bad tidings. Except for the breeze whispering through the cypresses, the swamp was still—a welcoming calm. The horde slept in back, the sputtering of their snores too far away to hear.

Ears perked, Billycan watched anxiously as the light from the fire pit bounced with tall shadows. There it stood—the boar. Billycan observed from the parlor window as the mud-caked razorback scraped its great body against the ancient willow and then pushed its way through an opening in the rusted gate. The thing had been wandering for days, hopelessly separated from its clan. It had torn up large mats of earth, searching for roots, mushrooms, and insects—whatever it deemed digestible.

The boar was now perilously close to the horde. It would be only a matter of time before it sniffed them out through its muck-encrusted snout, plucking them off the ground, happily crushing them in its decaying teeth. The sooner it was killed, the better.

Billycan had commanded the horde to dig a hole, big enough for the razorback to fall into but small enough that it could not turn about or clamber its way to freedom. Once confined in the pit it would be an easy slaughter, one that Billycan looked forward to. Size was of no consequence to the white rat. A few lethal gashes to the jugular and the hog would be dead.

Billycan jumped up from the sill as the black boar neared the hole. Now inspecting the pit, it walked along its edge. "Go on, then, go on," he said eagerly. "Fall, pig, fall!"

The razorback teetered on the edge. It spotted a fleshy root growing out from the pit's wall and stuck its massive head into the hole. Kneeling down, it stretched for the root. "That's it...that's it," coaxed Billycan. "Only one more inch, boar, one tiny inch and that juicy root will be yours and *you* will be mine!"

The boar pulled delicately at the root with the tips of its teeth. The root loosened from the wall, falling toward the boar.

"No!" yelled Billycan, banging on the window with his fist. The hog grabbed the root firmly and tugged it out with ease, returning quickly to safe ground. Billycan let out a baleful shriek. His stomach had been grumbling for days, and the thought of another gummy fish dinner sickened him. He needed meat. His entire body ached for it, and he had promised the horde a grand feast on the eve of their journey to Nightshade.

Montague rushed into the parlor. Billycan kicked the window frame and glared out into the swamp.

"Sir, are you all right?" asked Montague.

Still seething, Billycan slowly turned to Montague, his eyes churning odd shades of cherry and crimson. "They'll eat anything, won't they?" he asked dryly.

"*Who* sir?"

"The boars, the boars," Billycan snapped impatiently. "They'll eat anything, yes?"

"Yes sir, they'll eat anything in sight, from weeds to weasels and everything in between."

Billycan tapped his chin, thinking. "Has the horde had any deaths lately?"

"Well," said Montague, a bit discomfited by the inquiry, "one of the old ones, Argus, he didn't wake up about two days past, died in his sleep."

Billycan's sneer shifted into a grin. "Where is the body?"

Montague hesitated. "He . . . he is buried out by the pond."

"Dig him up," ordered Billycan. "Toss his body into the hole—tonight. He will make fine fodder for the boar. We will trap the hog quickly, using the dead one as bait."

"But his family—they will protest. Sir, it's . . . it's not right," said Montague. "It's not proper. Even the horde will be troubled by such an act."

Still perched on the sill, Billycan looked coolly at Montague, who squirmed uncomfortably under his gaze. "Never again dare tell me what you deem right or proper. It is but a body, nothing more and nothing less. The horde's bellies grumble, as does mine."

"But it seems so . . . reprehensible. Even the horde buries its dead in respect. Argus helped raise Cobweb and me. He was an elder. He—"

"Silence!" barked Billycan. "Argus was a doddering fool like the rest of the horde! He was no *elder*. He was simply old, a monumental difference!" Billycan bounded down from the sill and stormed toward Montague, baring slick, yellowed fangs. He shoved Montague hard in the chest, making him stumble backward. "Need Billycan remind you, young rat, what life has in store for you if the horde fails in Nightshade? You will die or be imprisoned forever!" Billycan's piercing voice dropped to a growl, his eyes now furrowed gashes of red. "Do you expect the horde to take over an entire city on empty bellies, weak and drained? Do you wish them dead?"

"No sir," replied Montague. "You've just never made it clear *why* these rats took your city. What purpose does it serve us to destroy them, these Nightshade rats?"

"It serves *my* purpose!" shouted Billycan. "I want those self-righteous rats eradicated! I want the horde to rip them limb from miserable limb! I want them tearing through the corridors of Nightshade in an all-out killing spree! I will not be humiliated, not again!" Billycan spat white froth, stomping in a twisted circle as he lurched about the parlor floor. "If you wish to save the precious carcass of your so-called elder, then you do so at the horde's expense. They will be the ones to suffer from your selfish need for propriety. The choice is yours!"

Billycan pushed his snout into Montague's. Montague recoiled, forced to inhale the white rat's icy breath—a stench of rot and soot. Billycan seized him by the throat, digging his claws in, his voice now an eerie whisper. "Hear me now, rat. If you do not obey me, you will *not* go to Nightshade. You and Cobweb will be left here forever, belonging nowhere and to no one, orphans for all eternity." Billycan suddenly jumped back up on the sill as though nothing had happened. He looked out the window. The boar was gone. "You are dismissed."

Carn and Oleander started back toward the horde by way of the pond. The moon fought through the cumbersome fog, its light bouncing off the water, creating a pool of vaporous white.

Grabbing her arm, Carn abruptly forced Oleander to a stop. "What is it?" she asked.

He motioned across the pond. "Look there," he whispered. "Who's that by the water's edge?"

Oleander squinted, trying to make out the two shadowy figures. She suddenly pushed Carn into the grass and out of sight. "It's Montague and Cobweb." She cautiously poked her head up. "I don't think they saw us. What are they doing out here at this hour?"

Carn peered through the wet grass. "They've dug something up... there's a pile of earth by them. They're holding—something. I can't make it out. It looks dead, whatever it is."

Gasping in horror, Oleander put a paw over her mouth. She sat up in plain sight, suddenly not worried about being spotted. Shaking, she leaped up and made a mad dash for the water's edge. Carn had no idea what was going on, but was not about to leave her on her own. He raced at her heels, finally catching up to her as she approached the two seconds.

She came upon Cobweb first, shoving him forcefully to the ground. He looked at her in dazed surprise. "What are you doing?" she demanded angrily. "You fiends, you monsters, how could you?"

Carn saw why she was so enraged. They had dug up a body. The shriveled corpse lay next to the hole. He remembered the family burying the elderly rat.

"Speak!" yelled Oleander, glaring at them furiously, "I'll tell the entire horde right now if one of you doesn't say something!"

Cobweb looked at her, incredulous. "Oleander," he asked, "how are you talking like that? Why do you sound... like us?"

Oleander kicked the wet ground, spraying moist clumps of earth on Cobweb. "Because I *am* like you! We're not all so simple," she growled. "You self-righteous liars! My father told me our group could not trust you two, but I *insisted* you were good, honorable rats.

I was clearly a fool! Has Billycan changed you so much, or were you always this wicked?"

Montague's ears drooped. He dropped to his knees, almost crumpling to the ground, his voice pure misery. "All this time there have been rats like ourselves—just like us—and you've said...nothing? We've been here since we were children. Why could we not be trusted? Was it because of the way we were found, the color of our fur? Why didn't you accept us? Why?" Cobweb put his arm around his brother.

Oleander's anger suddenly changed to shame. "I'm sorry," she said feebly. "We never knew how you felt. We never thought you cared. If my father or the others had known, I know they would be ashamed. Papa says for our own safety we should never accept you into our group, but I think he's wrong." She looked down at Argus's body, withered and stiff. "That doesn't change this. What could you possibly be doing with him?"

"We were putting him back," said Montague. "I swear it's true. Billycan wanted bait for the boar. He said we'd be left here forever if we didn't dig up Argus and throw him into the hole. He said it was only a body, and we wanted to believe he was right, making this disgraceful act seem reasonable, a means to an end—a new home, away from all this."

"He wants the horde strong for the journey to Nightshade," said Cobweb. "A boar feast will take care of that. We dug up Argus, but once we saw him—his face—we could not go through with it. We knew it was wrong."

"Montague, Cobweb, you need to understand, Billycan does not keep his promises," said Carn. "He's suspicious and distrustful of even his closest allies. He'll kill you and your brother as soon as you no longer serve his purpose. He doesn't like to leave loose ends. Trust me, I know this firsthand. I'm from the same place as he."

Montague, still on the ground, stared up at Carn, his eyes wide with confusion. "You *know* Billycan?" he asked. "You're from Nightshade City and you're like us, too?"

Carn walked toward Montague. If anyone understood him, his ache and torment, it was Carn. He, too, lost his parents long ago. He, too, served Billycan. He, too, had been given empty promises of a better life. He smiled and held his paw out to Montague, who cautiously took it. Carn pulled the mystified gray to his feet.

"Yes," said Carn, "I'm very *much* like you in more ways than you know. You two can help us stop him once and for all."

"Come on," said Oleander. "I have an idea. A few days ago, I spotted a tortoise shell just on the other side of the pond. The tortoise itself was long gone, but the shell stank of decay—perfect for the pit."

With the help of Carn and Oleander, the brothers carefully buried Argus once more. Then together they threw the tortoise shell into the pit and began to hatch a plan.

CHAPTER FOUR

A Dead Boar

OLEANDER AND CARN SNUCK BACK into the horde just as the sun peeked over the horizon, turning the dark sky into a muggy orange haze. They lay next to Thicket and Stono, their hearts pounding with excitement and fear as they pretended to be asleep.

Carn was expected tonight at the feast. Cobweb and Montague said he was to be seated at Billycan's side—his guest of honor. Billycan was intrigued by this alleged snake killer. He knew that if this rat could indeed kill snakes, he could easily kill rats—strong, oversized Nightshade rats.

Oleander and Carn whispered in the grass, their voices easily masked by Stono's loud snoring. "I *cannot* be at the feast tonight," whispered Carn. "Billycan will recognize my face and scent immediately. He will kill me on sight. I was the first soldier to betray him that fateful night in the Catacombs. My words incited a riot, which aided in the fall of the High Ministry. Trust me, he will joyfully rip me limb from limb."

"You heard what Cobweb and Montague said. Their parents were healers. They know about herbs. They'll find a way to mask you properly, both your appearance and your scent." She gently reached for his paw and squeezed it. "Billycan will not unmask you. We'll figure it all out."

A grumpy Stono rolled over, giving them a bleary-eyed scowl. "What you two blathering about now?" he grunted. "I be sleeping and you two be droning in my ear like a pair of marsh bugs. Now hush up!" He rolled back over and began to snore, louder than before. Carn and Oleander covered their mouths with their paws, trying not to laugh.

Carn rolled onto his back and stared up at the brightening sky. Stono and Thicket were another problem altogether. If things did not go as planned, he'd have no way to protect them. They were good at heart, but with their primitive manner, their combative nature, they might be injured or worse.

If Carn tried to explain things to Stono and Thicket, to tell them about Billycan, the truth about who he was—*what* he was—he feared their reaction. Billycan was their knight in shining armor, an albino beacon of hope, the one who would lead them to a better life. Stono and Thicket cared for Carn now, but how would they feel about him if he spoke out against Billycan? Since the swamp rats didn't lie, how could they decide who was telling the truth? The mysterious swamp rat who appeared out of nowhere or Billycan, who fed them, protected them, claiming everything he did was for their benefit? Would Stono and Thicket turn on Carn should he reveal the truth? He could not take the chance. He could only pray to the Saints that they and the rest of the horde would be spared.

Oleander saw the fear in Carn's eyes. She felt it, too. The horde was her family. Most of them were different from her, to be sure, but that didn't matter. She loved them all.

* * *

Crouching under the derelict car in the front yard of the manor, Carn, Oleander, and her father, Mannux, watched as the horde sat idly by the pond, having a breakfast of day-old minnows and root porridge, a lumpy pulp of flavorless mush.

Mannux was an old one—old for a rat without a Trillium life span, in any case. His brown fur had lightened to fawn; his grizzled whiskers and snout were completely white. In spite of his age, he was thickly built, muscular, with brutish, oversized paws—all four faded into whitewash like his muzzle, weathered and creased from a life under the hot southern sun.

Carn watched Thicket as she tossed a minnow into the air, catching it with her teeth. "If I'm gone too long, Thicket will come searching for me."

"Not if we're past the perimeter," said Mannux in his gravelly voice. "She would never cross the plantation's border. Even Thicket's too smart for that. She will not risk getting eaten by a snake. We must go now, while the horde is busy with breakfast."

"Father, wait," said Oleander, "there is something I must tell you." She looked awkwardly at her feet. "It's about Cobweb and Montague. I'm afraid... I've broken our group's trust."

"Daughter," said Mannux, "*you* have broken no trust. You would never do such a thing. You are a loyal child and a good rat."

"But father, I—"

"You need not explain," said Mannux. "I already know. Cobweb and Montague sought me out after your meeting at the pond. If anyone has broken a trust, I fear it's been me. Those two boys... they're brokenhearted, wondering why we kept them out of our circle all these years. They were only children when they joined the horde, yet we treated them like outcasts. They've been utterly alone in our world.

48

It's unforgiveable." He curled a paw under her chin and stared into his daughter's eyes. "I should have listened to you. You are a far better judge of character than I. I'm sorry."

"Papa, don't be sorry," said Oleander. "You only wanted to protect us."

Mannux's proud face fell. "Our group, our little splinter faction of intellects, we're too smart for our own good, we are. We should have tried harder to help our clan—and those lonely boys. It's time to make up for our mistakes—my mistakes. If ever there was a time to make things right, it's now. Cobweb and Montague are going to meet us in the woods. They said we must find a black bugbane bush."

"What for?" asked Carn curiously.

"To camouflage your scent," replied Mannux. "The bush's stench could kill a black bear."

"What about my face?" Carn asked nervously. "I was at Billycan's beck and call for eleven years. He'll recognize me straightaway."

"Don't you worry," said Mannux. "Cobweb and Montague said they have just the thing for that."

Billycan climbed out of the pit, his coat splashed with the boar's blood, his claws caked thick with its flesh. He inhaled calmly, almost serenely, as his feet hit the grass. His lungs tingled as he blew out a deep breath, feeling much more like himself again.

For the moment his thoughts of the pending attack left him, replaced by visions of smoked carcass and sizzling fat. The thought of meat made all his senses prickle as he headed to the pond to wash away the blood. He dragged behind him an empty tortoise shell he'd found in the pit, licked clean by the boar. Stupid creature must have fallen in.

* * *

It was already late in the afternoon, the sun dropping, casting broad shadows through the swamp. To Carn, the day seemed to be slipping away too quickly, as if the Saints were eager to get him to Billycan's side once more.

Cobweb and Montague went on their scheduled perimeter check, secretly meeting their new allies in the woods. Their parents had taught them which plants, berries, and roots healed, which ones came with lethal consequences, and which had valuable side effects.

The black, lacy bugbane was easy to find, much out of place against the drab greens and browns of the swamp. Carn sized up the bush. "So these black leaves, they're supposed to disguise my scent?"

"Remarkably, no," said Montague. "Look up top. See those long stems of ivory flowers? Those are the culprits. You'd think the leaves, black as oil, would be responsible for such a noxious scent, but it's those little white beauties that emit the offensive odor."

Cobweb disappeared into the sprawling bush, making the black leaves dance as he headed into the center of the plant. Once inside, he went for a core stem, pulling down a long stalk of white flowers. "There, you see?" he said, holding out the bell-shaped shoot. "Beautiful to the eyes, but lethal to the nostrils. Flies actually pollinate the flowers. I suppose bees have enough sense never to go near the vile things."

Carn and Oleander sniffed the delicate blossoms. Oleander quickly covered her nose. "The smell of death!" she exclaimed. "It's positively revolting!"

"We're going to use only enough to mask Carn's scent," said Cobweb. "Granted, he won't smell good, not by *any* stretch of the word, but not as bad as these reeking blossoms."

"I don't care what I smell like," said Carn anxiously. "I just can't be recognized."

"Now we've got to find one other ingredient to complete our

ruse," said Montague. "After that, Billycan won't stand a chance of detecting you."

"What other ingredient do we need?" asked Carn.

"Elephant ear," said Montague.

"Elephant ear?"

"Yes," said Cobweb. "It's a plant."

"What does it do?"

"Well, if you're not careful, it may very well kill you."

Carn gulped.

The elephant ear did the trick. It was odd vegetation for the rugged swamp—huge, billowy leaves bordered in green, with a burst of dazzling red radiating from their centers, a tropical beauty against the commonplace bushes. As stunning as the plant was, it was equally lethal, so much so that Cobweb instructed Carn to take just one small bite, chew it up, and then quickly spit it out. Swallowing could result in his throat completely constricting, strangling him.

Within moments of chewing, Carn's snout, mouth, and tongue began to swell, rapidly distorting his features. His agreeable face warped into a globular nose, puffy gums, and an enlarged tongue that barely fit in his mouth, altering his speech into something so bumbling that Carn surmised even Stono would sound clever in comparison. "It burns," he muttered nasally.

"Sorry for that," said Montague. "You'll have to get used to it."

"Now listen closely," said Cobweb. "Montague will sit to the left of Billycan, with you on Billycan's right. I'll sit next to my brother, with an extra dose of this under my seat." He waved a leaf of the plant. "If the effects begin to wane, they'll wear off quickly, so we all must stay alert. If we don't pay attention, you'll transform from Corn back into Carn right before his eyes."

Carn began to shake. At that moment reality sank in: he would be sitting next to Billycan, able to smell him, hear his jarring voice, and feel the cold breath pushing out from his throat. "What if it doesn't work?" He began to pant. "What if he sees through my disguise?"

"Carn, you must collect yourself," said Mannux decisively. "Between your smell and that ridiculous mug, Billycan will never know who you really are. Trust me, to him you'll just be another one of us—a lowly swamp rat."

From the fringes of the plantation, the feast took on the appearance of a heathen ritual, the sizzling boar a sacrifice to the disciples' pagan gods. The lawn around the manor was lined with crooked torches, gashing the darkness like flaming bayonets.

A swamp rat with tattered owl feathers dangling from its ears thumped steadily on an otter-skin drum dragged up from the manor's cellar. Its primordial beat knitted its way through the network of cypresses, swiftly sending the other creatures of the swamp to their nests and burrows.

The horde flocked around the flaming razorback in a wide circle, barely able to contain their excitement, pushing each other playfully and giggling with childish delight. They eyed the funeral pyre hungrily, their mouths dripping with spittle, the thought of fat, fleshy pig almost too much to bear.

A young male, agitated by the boar's smoky scent, came too close to the blaze. The horde laughed dizzily as the rat's tail ignited, their teeth glinting like a pack of underworld hellhounds. The screaming rat flew to the pond, diving in rear-end first, quashing the flames that had swallowed his tail. The horde fell clumsily on each other, slap-happy with merriment.

Carn, Mannux, and Oleander appeared from the back of the

plantation. Slipping in around the side of the manor, they quickly blended with the rest of the horde. Spotting them, Thicket dashed up, abruptly stopping in her tracks. She looked at Oleander and then Carn, confused. "Where Corn be?" she demanded. "And who be this rat?"

"This *be* Corn!" replied Oleander, with a silly grin. "Dummy got stung by a bee." Mustering her best cackle, she gave Carn a good shove. "Then he done fell smack dab into a bunch a bugbane! He smell even worse than he look!"

"Ha!" screeched Thicket shrilly. "Corn, you be dimmer than Stono!" She turned and looked behind her. "Stono, come here!" Unable to look away from the cooking boar, Stono lumbered over to Thicket. "Don't mind that pig now, we be eating soon enough. Look here, Corn got bit by a bee and then wrestled with some bugbane! He be the ugliest rat I ever seen!"

Stono snorted, slapping his knee with his paw. "You smell worse than that smoking boar's dung!" he hollered. He dropped to the ground, rolling madly in the grass.

Carn reacted as he thought any swamp rat might. "It ain't funny!" he snapped nasally. "Look at my nose! Now I got to meet Billycan looking like this, and smelling worse than a dead possum! It ain't right!" He kicked the ground and shoved Oleander for laughing at him.

Mannux was impressed with Carn's performance. "Now, I be an elder," he said gruffly, "no more laughing and carrying on, you three." He wiggled a claw at Thicket, Oleander, and Stono. "It ain't right to do to Corn. Any a you three able to kill a snake? He be special to the horde." Folding his arms, he furrowed his deep-set brow and looked at everyone reproachfully.

"Sorry, Papa, you right," said Oleander.

"Yup," said Thicket, "we sorry, too. Corn, you don't look *so* bad. You smell like stinkweed, but there's no time for a bath. Billy-can's waiting."

"Yup," said Stono, "you be coming with us tomorrow!"

Carn pretended he was tickled by the news. "You mean, we *all* gonna get those Nightshade rats together?"

"Billycan be coming out any second!" said Thicket.

Thicket and Stono turned toward the gathering crowd and searched for Billycan. Carn began to wobble on his feet. Mannux put a heavy paw on his shoulder. "Steady, son," he said. "Allies are all around you. You are protected—no matter what happens."

The front door of the manor creaked opened, then closed with a heavy slam. Thicket and Stono began jumping as the horde erupted into thunderous noise. The swamp rats stomped their feet, climbing onto each other's backs, trying to catch a peek of the commanding white rat, the one who would lead them to a wonderful new life.

Carn heard a high-pitched screech far above his head. He looked at

the sky. It was Dresden calling to his colony. The bats swept in like tiny shadows, black spots against the moon, circling high over the feast— a clutch of vultures, waiting for their chance to pick at the bones.

Oleander grabbed Carn's clammy paw and held it tight. Carn's throat tightened as he beheld the White Assassin, lord of the swamp rats. Seeing that face, those eyes again, his skin turned a cold, dimpled gray. Vivid memories of Billycan crept into his head... terrifying memories.

"He's just a rat," whispered Mannux, "nothing more. You can prove that to yourself tonight once and for all. He holds no more power than you or I—as I said, just a rat."

Taking in his swarm of devoted subjects, Billycan's eyes flashed vaporous red in the firelight. His muzzle swelled into an eerily familiar leer.

Carn thought he might very well die of fright.

One by one the Council members were dropped onto the roof of the three-story manor. At one time or another the swamp rats had smashed nearly every pane of glass in the derelict mansion, making a silent entry through the round window of the attic effortless.

The Council weaved their way through the cluttered garret, which was filled with puzzling artifacts. Outlandish masks and ornate headdresses hung from the ceiling. Black velvet robes, turned gray with years of dust, lined the planked walls.

Once the attic was secure, Vincent, Victor, and Suttor immediately checked downstairs, while Ragan and Ulrich went back onto the roof, perching on opposite ends of the center gable. They sat motionless, like two stone gargoyles, observing the merriment below.

Juniper and Cole did a walk-through of the second level, making sure the manor was empty. They entered the last room on the second floor—the room where Billycan slept, which reeked of his mildewed scent. There was a musty mattress in the center of the room, covered in parchments. Juniper kept watch while Cole examined the documents.

"Juniper," whispered Cole anxiously, "you need to get in here—now!"

"What is it?"

Cole motioned toward the papers with his spear. "See for yourself."

Juniper inspected the documents. His mouth fell open in shock. They were detailed maps of Nightshade, down to the last corridor. Abruptly he thrust his spear through the papers, stabbing the mattress underneath. "Where could he have gotten these?" he demanded.

"The more important question is *who* he got them from," said Cole. "No one but the Council knows of their existence. Who would betray us?"

"We don't have time for speculation now. All the better that we are here to end this. Once he's injected with the serum, we'll find out who's working with him." Juniper grunted furiously. A traitor in Nightshade? It seemed unthinkable. "Destroy the documents," he ordered. "Rip them to shreds. I'm going down to check on the boys."

Juniper stormed out of the room and down the stairs. With every step he felt the weight of Trilok's medal, banging against his chest. Running Nightshade City was hard enough, but this? "A traitor! Why? Why now? There is nothing to gain! We have given our citizens everything they could ever need! What more could they want?" Descending the stairs, he reminded himself that *need* was a far different thing from *want*. He ran his flared claws down the length of the wall, leaving a trail of deep grooves in his wake.

CHAPTER FIVE
A Stealer of Family

BILLYCAN'S MOOD WAS HIGH. He and the horde would soon be on their way north to Trillium City—to Nightshade. The thought of his wild horde swarming through the dark tunnels of Juniper's city, flooding every hidden corridor, butchering his precious Nightshade rats made Billycan's body quake with excitement. He would once again march through the cool underground corridors beneath Trillium City. He'd be feared and respected, in command once more.

As he stood resolutely on the porch, his devotees gazed up at him, all eyes glazed with pure adoration. Billycan sniffed the night air with his crooked snout, taking in every nuance of the boar's peppery aroma. He smiled slyly at his flock of drooling zealots. He held out his lanky arms as if beholding a grand event. He shouted into the mass of firelit eyes, "Let the feast begin!" The horde went mad, cramming themselves against each other, parting down the center so their lord and master could make his way down the stairs to take his seat at the head of the feast, a white silhouette against a sea of muddled brown.

One at each side, Oleander and Mannux stood firmly next to Carn. Suddenly Carn stopped as Billycan came into full view, now only steps away. He looked taller, if that were possible. Even his yellowed teeth seemed sharper. His frame appeared meatier; thick muscle clung to his bones. Carn clutched his chest with both paws, wringing his skin into knots. His insides twisted and gurgled. He leaned on Mannux, who kept pushing him forward, though his body grew heavier with every step.

Oleander grinned blithely at Thicket and Stono, giggling as she whispered softly in Carn's ear. "Remember," she said. "Remember what Billycan put you through—what he did to your family. That is your strength. You cannot let your fear win. You cannot let *him* win." She turned to Thicket and winked demurely. She wiggled her nose in anticipation, as if this were the proudest moment of her life, on the arm of Billycan's strong new fighter, Corn the snake killer.

Overcome with delight, Thicket suddenly jumped wildly, ready to show off her new friend. "C'mon, you all be walking too slow!" she exclaimed, pushing Oleander's shoulders. Tilting her head, she smiled curiously at Carn. "Corn, why you be so quiet? Ain't you happy?" Carn, trapped in his own torment, did not acknowledge her.

"Corn!" Mannux snapped. "Answer Thicket, she be waiting on you." The old rat prodded him sharply with a strong elbow to the ribs. Mannux wouldn't allow anyone to wilt in fright. Carn jerked in response, startled out of his near catatonic daze.

He looked up into the night sky. The bats circled silently overhead. He turned his gaze to the roof of the manor. Two rats sat in the shadows on a gable, waiting—watching. He recognized Ragan and Ulrich. The Council had arrived. At that moment, Carn made his decision. Too many lives were at stake. He could not let them down.

The Saints' teachings spoke of pivotal moments in the lives of all creatures. *This* was one of those moments.

If he was marching to his death, then he would march proudly. He would not drag himself like a sopping washrag to an early grave. "Sorry, Thicket," he said with sudden energy. "I just be jumpy. You know, meeting Billycan and all."

Thicket smiled sweetly. "Aw, Corn, Billycan gonna like you fine. Me and Stono just know it."

His seconds standing behind him, Billycan lounged atop a faded cushion, facing the eyeless head of the boar. After their lord had taken his place, the rest of the horde crowded around the boar, scrambling and pushing to find a good seat close to the sizzling carcass.

Billycan watched the horde fumble to their places. He snapped two rangy digits, commanding his seconds' attention. "Where is this so-called snake killer?"

Cobweb leaned down. "He's coming, sir," he replied. "Stono and Thicket are bringing him, along with Oleander, his companion, and her father, Mannux."

"Ah, Oleander," said Billycan. "So she has chosen our esteemed snake killer as a mate?"

"Yes sir," said Cobweb. "Mannux is pleased with his daughter's choice."

"Mannux would be pleased if she chose a raccoon, the dithering old fool. It is a pity, though," said Billycan. "It seems a shame for one so pretty to unite with a swamp dullard, even if she herself is one. Of no matter. Victory is far more important than the intricacies of the horde's mating rituals. Go fetch this snake killer. Stono, I'm sure, is being his slow, cloddish self, plodding along as if he had bricks for feet. Billycan will not be made to wait any longer."

"Yes sir," said Cobweb, dashing off to find them.

"Montague," barked Billycan, glaring up at him. "What's wrong with you? You seem out of sorts."

"Sorry, sir," said Montague, trying to hide his anxiety. "I was thinking of the attack, going over our directives in my head. I want things to go perfectly."

"Well, be seated. Seeing you fidget over me from the corner of my eye makes me uneasy. Never has Billycan seen a rat so constantly racked by nerves."

Montague did as he was told, forcing himself not to wring his paws as he took his seat. He'd already drawn enough attention to himself. "Sir," said Montague, thankful to see his brother reappear from the dark, "they're here."

Billycan rose to his feet, eager to meet his newest enforcer. His arrogant expression quickly knotted into unqualified disapproval as Corn the snake killer made his entrance. The rat's face was absurd, his muzzle round and bulbous, his lips stretched like a carp's! It was almost insulting to see a pretty rat like Oleander hanging on him so.

Thicket and Stono ran up to Billycan. "Here he be!" announced Thicket proudly. "Corn, the snake killer!"

The bugbane suddenly hit Billycan's nostrils. Stepping back in disgust, he folded his arms and inspected Carn doubtfully. "So, *you're* the snake killer Thicket has been pestering me about. Is it you who kills them, or that putrid scent wafting from your hide?"

Carn stuck his chin out proudly. "I rip their jaws to pieces," he said boldly. "Then I pull them apart, right down the middle. That be how I kill the snakes."

Carn's wheezy voice and clogged nose did not help Billycan's impression of him.

"Sir," said Thicket, pushing in between them, "Corn smell bad, 'cause he fell in some bugbane and then a bee done bit him on the nose, puffing up his face."

Billycan rolled his eyes. It all made sense now. Corn no doubt looked like a typical swamp rat beneath all the swelling. "Yet another idiot Billycan must endure," he grumbled. Carn's ears perked at the remark. At least he knew his disguise was working.

"Oh, how absolutely horrid," said Billycan, feigning concern. "What an awful chain of events for our esteemed snake killer." He looked at Oleander, who hung on Carn like a new appendage. "Miss Oleander, I see you've found yourself a friend."

"Yes sir," she said, "swept me off my feet, Corn did!"

There was something about Oleander that appealed to Billycan, something different—something familiar. He chuckled at her enthusiasm. "Well, then," he purred in an oily tone, "you and your snake killer must sit at my side." He took her paw in his and patted it gently. "Would you like that, my dear?"

Despite her physical urge to recoil at his cold, bristly touch, Oleander batted her eyelashes and smiled shyly. "Yes, indeed. That would be just fine."

His hackles rising, Mannux held himself back from sinking his teeth into Billycan's white neck. Oleander turned to her father. She grabbed his arm, pulling herself free from Billycan's grip. "Papa, ain't this wonderful? We can all sit together!"

"Yup," said Mannux stiffly. "It be *wonderful* news."

"It's settled, then," said Billycan. "Let's all take our places. The horde grows restless for meat."

The feast was under way. Once Billycan and his chosen guests had been served, the horde ransacked the boar, scouring it for every string of succulent flesh and every clump of sticky fat. The rats giggled as their scrawny feet hit the coals of the dying fire. The young ones tossed them to one another, making a silly game out of who could hold the smoking embers the longest. The horde was giddy with contentment.

Despite the revolting smell, Billycan insisted Carn sit at his side. One night of the rat's stench would be well worth it, if it meant an easier takeover of Nightshade City. Billycan could mold this one into something useful. Not yet sure why, he had a sense that this rat could prove much more valuable than Stono and Thicket; something about Corn struck him.

Cobweb had arranged the seats for the feast, placing a handful of crushed elephant ear under his cushion. He leaned forward and checked on Carn, making sure the rat's snout was still fat and swollen. For now it looked as exaggerated as ever. If he needed it, all Cobweb had to do was sneak Carn a small handful while Montague distracted Billycan.

Carn nearly jumped out of his skin whenever Billycan made even the slightest gesture, reaching out for meat or scratching his ribs with his knobby knuckles. Leisurely consuming his huge portion of boar, Billycan had yet to utter a word to Carn. They ate in silence. Several times Carn noticed him tilting his head, staring strangely at him. Was it his distended muzzle, his detestable aroma, or did he recognize him, secretly seeing through his disguise?

Carn reached out for another piece of meat. Billycan suddenly grabbed him hard by the wrist. He stared Carn dead in the face.

"So," said Billycan, furrowing his brow, "how do you possess enough strength to kill a snake? You're not much bigger than the others. In fact, Stono's larger than you, and even he can't crack a snake's jaw." Flaring his nostrils, Billycan leaned in close, his liquid eyes boring through Carn's skull, waiting for an answer.

Nearly choking on his meat, Carn gulped, painfully swallowing a large clump of pork. Don't think too hard, he thought. He won't expect much. "I guess I just be stronger than most." He slowly pulled his wrist from Billycan's grasp and reached for another piece of meat, as if nothing bothered him. "I don't know why. Just lucky, I guess."

"Well," said Billycan, not surprised by the dim-witted answer, "Corn, is it?"

Carn inwardly cringed. Why did he pick such a simple name, so close to his own? What was he thinking? "Yup, Corn be my name."

"How do you catch the snakes? How do you come upon them without being attacked first?"

"Most times, I just play dead. The snakes come to eat me, thinking I'm long gone, and, well, I eat them instead!" Carn laughed foolishly, cramming more meat into his mouth.

Billycan scratched his chin. "How did you think of such a crafty trick?"

Carn relaxed slightly. Billycan seemed to be buying his masquerade. "I learned it from the possums. They play dead all the time. Just thought I'd try it one day, and it worked! I was eating snake by suppertime!"

The lord of the swamp rats smiled with delight. "Billycan is pleasantly surprised by your resourcefulness, Corn. How many snakes would you say you've killed over the years?"

"Well, back in the woods, I ate snake just 'bout every night."

Billycan's eyes brightened to a diluted pink. "Tell me," he said hungrily, "how exactly do you do it? I've always gone for their heads, chopping them clean off." Flaring his digits, Billycan thrust four razor-sharp claws in front of Carn's nose, showing him his tools of choice. "Now then, how do *you* kill them?"

"Well, sir," said Carn, slowly pulling his nose away, "it all depends, I reason." He scratched his head, as if truly thinking on the matter. "Sometimes I wait till they're right up in my face, and then I just grab them. Other times I wait till they got me in their mouths, then I use my legs and push. I push hard inside that snake's mouth until I here that *pop!*"

"What pop?" asked Billycan impatiently.

Carn's face lit up as if it were all very thrilling. "You know. That noise a jaw makes when ya break it—that loud crack. When I hear that pop, I know they be dead! Dead as dead can be!" Carn nudged Billycan chummily in the shoulder, as if he were just another rat.

A piercing cackle filled the yard as Billycan's entire body jerked with laughter. The horde suddenly froze, never having heard him laugh. Not sure what to do, Carn took Billycan's lead and joined in the hilarity with a commanding yowl, baying at the moon. Still shrieking in mad amusement, Billycan threw himself back on his cushion, clutching his ribs. The rest of the horde followed suit, howling and squealing, rolling on the ground.

Finally Billycan settled back comfortably, grinning from ear to ear. Letting out a satisfied groan, he stared up at the moon, its brightness pushing through the swamp's leaden haze. Corn's story tickled him. How truly decadent! To pop a jaw that way. He marveled that he'd never thought of it himself.

Billycan listened to his horde, still yelling and carrying on around him, a cheerful background noise. His mind shifted to Juniper, thinking what a deliciously horrible manner that would be for Nightshade's Chief Citizen to die. Billycan snorted sharply in a final fit of laughter, repeating Carn's words at the moon.

"Dead as dead can be!"

Carn leaned forward and whispered in Oleander's ear. "This is going better than I ever could have predicted. I had no idea how easy this would be."

Oleander turned to him and let out a silly laugh as though he were saying something quite charming. Eyeing his snout, she let out a muted gasp. "Your face," she hissed. "It's not swollen anymore. The toxin has worn off!"

Carn instinctively grabbed his muzzle. It was smooth, the inflammation gone. Oleander looked wide-eyed at Cobweb, and motioned to Carn.

Cobweb panicked. He reached clumsily under his cushion, all the while glancing at Billycan, still reclined on his back, staring into the night sky. Cobweb fumbled for the elephant ear. He suddenly looked as if he might vomit, his gray skin drained of all color.

"Cobweb," said Oleander, "what is it?"

"I hid it under the wrong cushion!" he whispered frantically. "It's under Thicket! I was so nervous..." He slapped his forehead with his paw. "Of all the stupid mistakes!"

"Hush," she said softly. "We'll get out of this."

Carn kept his face turned away from Billycan. His heart was beating furiously. His coolness had shifted back to terror.

Sensing trouble, Thicket got up from her seat and crouched behind Cobweb and Oleander. "What be going on with you two?" she asked, pushing between them. Cobweb looked vacantly out into the swamp, wishing its thick foliage would snatch him up and swallow him whole. "Cobweb, you look sick." She laughed. "Ate too much, huh?" She turned to Carn. "Corn, your face, it be back to its old self! You look like you again!"

Carn tried to quiet her. "Well...uh, I do be feeling better." He leaned in close, lowering his voice. "Thicket, let's hush a bit so as we don't upset Billycan. He be resting."

Feeling Carn's shaky paw, Thicket furrowed her brow. "You be so jumpy all night . . . so nervous. Billycan likes you just fine! He thinks you something special." She snickered, swatting him on the shoulder. "You worry like a scared rabbit!"

Billycan pulled back up to a sitting position. He turned to Stono and Montague, saying something about tomorrow's journey to Nightshade. Montague caught a glimpse of Carn's alarmed face. He quickly asked a series of rapid-fire questions about the assault, which Billycan was more than happy to address.

Cracking his jaw from side to side, Billycan leaned back on his elbows, looking leisurely at the horde as he spoke. "The horde will do well, Montague." He nodded at Stono. "With him and Thicket leading the way, along with our new snake killer, they'll rip those rats apart. Nightshade is ours for the taking."

"Sir," said Montague, trying to buy time, "tell me again about the Bloody Coup."

Cobweb walked stealthily behind Billycan. All he had to do was reach under Thicket's cushion unseen, snatch a handful of the crushed plant, and make his way back to Carn.

Taking a seat on Thicket's empty cushion, Cobweb feigned interest in Billycan's sermon on fighting and strategy, a history lesson of battles won.

Carn listened. His neck bristled as Billycan reminisced about the Bloody Coup, bragging how he dismantled a Loyalist booby trap, easily slipping into the Catacombs, quickly launching the historic overthrow of Trilok and the Catacombs takeover. "Yes," said Billycan, grinning, "the Loyalist rats were easily conquered."

The recollection made Carn shake, but not with fear—with fury. His stomach roiled with rage, his lungs felt as if they might burst inside his chest. It was that night in the Catacombs that Billycan had kidnapped him and destroyed his family.

"Corn," whispered Oleander, "Cobweb's got the elephant ear, no need to worry now."

"I'm not worried," said Carn sternly.

"Then what is it? You look . . . strange. Are you all right?"

"Never better," said Carn, speaking at full volume in his normal tone.

"Keep your voice down," snapped Mannux. "Are you trying to get yourself killed?"

Carn ignored him. He got to his feet, standing firmly, like a soldier, as the Kill Army majors had taught him. He scowled down at Billycan, who was still boasting about the Coup. Suddenly he said, "Were the Loyalists really overpowered so effortlessly? Is that truly how things went, High Collector—or do you prefer Commander Billycan? I was never sure."

"Covered in blood, I stole down a corridor—" Billycan stopped midsentence, his eyes wide, every hair on his body standing on end.

"Was it really that easy," asked Carn, "kidnapping me and slaughtering the entire Newcastle Clan—my clan?" Billycan did not twitch even a whisker. "Why, what could be the matter, High Collector? Is your mind racing, thinking of another quick and cowardly escape route? Not this time."

Thicket slowly approached Carn. "Corn, what's got into you? Why you be talking like that?"

"My name is not Corn," he replied, glaring steadily at Billycan. "It's Carn. I'm here for him. He is not just a killer of snakes, Thicket. He is a killer of his fellow rats."

Scratching her head, Thicket turned to Stono, who quickly joined his troubled mate. "Thicket, everything okay?"

"What's Corn talking 'bout?" asked Thicket, grabbing Stono's arm. "Why he be saying such things?"

"He tells the truth," said Oleander, dropping her thick drawl. "Billycan, our leader, is no leader at all." She called out to the horde. "He is only using us to get back to Nightshade, a city that does not belong to him as he claims. He is wicked. He killed Carn's family. He killed many families. Billycan is using you and Stono because you're strong and easy to control. Once he gets what he wants, he'll have no use for you or any of us. He'll kill us all."

"Oleander," said Thicket. "Why you talking like Cobweb and Montague?"

"I suppose because she is like Cobweb and Montague," said Mannux, putting an arm around his daughter, "as am I. We didn't want to frighten you. We are the same family that has always loved you, that will never change, but we are somehow different from the rest of the horde."

Slowly Billycan rose. He looked at Oleander, then at Mannux, not dullards at all. How did they trick him so easily? Mannux stared him down proudly. The old rat's mouth curved into an arrogant sneer.

His eyes finally turning to Carn, Billycan's face hardened, his yellow teeth bared in an ugly grimace as he stared into the eyes of the one who had served him all those years—the betrayer who had turned his army against him. Tensed in rigid indignation, his long arms quaked with wrath. One by one, each tarnished claw shot out—ready to rip out the eyes of the one who stood before him. "You!" he shrieked at Carn.

The horde was silent, gawking at Billycan and then at the strangest of happenings unfurling all around them. Oddly colored rats emerged from the manor, all brandishing razor-sharp spears. Hundreds of snakes slithered over the plantation's border, writhing around the horde from all sides, hissing wildly and flashing sharp white fangs. Screeching bats circled, closing in from above, clutching deadly spikes, ready to launch. The horde huddled close, terrified.

"Stand down, Billycan," commanded a deep voice. "Kindly back away from your former lieutenant. You are surrounded by enemies above and below." Billycan's eyes bulged. It could not be! *None* of this could be! He could hear the hissing snakes, the shrieking bats overhead, the voice of his archenemy.

Cobweb and Montague approached Billycan, one on each side. "Do what he says," said Montague. "We are with them. Your reign, Lord Billycan, is over."

The voice came from right behind him now. "You heard me, rat. Stand down!"

Relaxing his digits and popping his neck, Billycan slowly turned around and faced Juniper. He exhaled, a slight grin surfacing on his pale lips. "So... you've found me."

"Yes," said Juniper, "and with far less trouble than we imagined. The horde you've so fondly focused your attentions on shares this swamp with a bat colony, a colony originally from Trillium. Their elder is an old and dear friend of mine."

Calmly stroking his whiskers, Billycan gave Juniper a once-over. "You somehow look different than I recall," he said. "That triumphant look you typically have smeared across your weathered face has all but vanished." Stepping closer, Billycan stared fixedly at Juniper. "Yes. Something has indeed changed." He tapped his chin. "Billycan wonders what it could be."

Juniper was silent. Vincent, however, was not. "We've come to collect you, rat!" he said, lunging forward with his spear, Victor and Suttor right behind him. "It's time to pay for your crimes."

Billycan's face brightened. He laughed raucously, clearly unimpressed. He looked only at Juniper. "How very charming, the eldest son of Julius Nightshade by your side." He picked at his claws, as if the whole scene had grown rather tedious. "In fact, it appears all your merry band of miscreants is here, your filthy Loyalist friends and traitorous Kill Army soldiers." Billycan's eyes narrowed to blood-red pits. "Except for the ones I killed, of course."

"Enough!" said Juniper. "You have nowhere to run this time, and no one to protect you." He nodded at the horrified swamp rats. "Your vicious horde is no more vicious than the Kill Army you failed to control three years ago. You prey on the young and the innocent, compelling them to do your bidding, but no more!"

Suddenly there was a thunderous rustle in the trees. Hooves pounded nearby. The ground quaked. The snakes spat in fear, calling out from all sides of the plantation. "Boars!" they hissed. "Boars!"

Wicker, the snake leader, sailed through the grass. "They're coming, wild boars, they're angry! We can feel it in their gait!"

Dresden swooped in from above. "Juniper, get those rats out of here. A clan of boars is mere moments away! They surely smelled the feast! They know their kinsmen has been killed—eaten—the worst possible offense! You must go now!"

Billycan's eyes darted around, searching for an escape route. Taking his chance, he threw his body into Montague, knocking him to the ground. Hurling snakes by their necks as they tried to block him, he raced into the woods, swiftly vanishing from view.

"Telula!" called Cotton, diving into the trees. "I see him!" Telula soared to her brother.

Juniper grabbed Vincent as he ran for the woods. "No!" he shouted. "The boars will surely kill the first rat they see! They are set on vengeance."

"But he's getting away!" shouted Vincent.

"Think of Clover," Juniper said. "She's counting on your return. Billycan has already taken your family! Don't let him take away your future! Let the bats follow him now."

Telula and Cotton took to the woods, swooping in and out, weaving through the network of trees as they followed Billycan's ghost-like form through the forest.

"He's going directly toward the boars!" shouted Cotton to his sister. "What is he thinking?"

"He's thinking the others won't follow," she panted, furiously pumping her wings. "He'd rather face the wild boars than his own kind. Their punishment will be far gentler."

"But they'll kill him!" said Cotton.

"Exactly!"

His entire body heaving, Billycan raced in the direction of the boars. Anything was better than decaying in a cell, even a slow, torturous death. Death, *that* he could accept, but not captivity—never again. He came upon a pathway, a fork in the road. Perfect, he thought. A hollow tree stood before him—the boars would never find him in there. Laughing, he slipped in, huffing madly as he caught his breath.

He listened closely. The crashing hooves were only seconds away now. They'd pass him up, heading straight for the plantation, mowing down the horde, Juniper, and any other foolish creature that stood in their way. Then suddenly the hooves stopped completely. Stillness all around him, deafening silence. Billycan concentrated. His ears perked at a sound. Breathing—hard, heavy pants coming from just outside the tree.

"There," a boar grunted loudly. "In there!"

"That's him!" snarled another. "The scent from the bloody pit. Block the hole! He's mine!"

Suddenly two giant razorbacks crammed their tusked heads into the hollow, their black eyes filled with fury. They got down on their knees, allowing no room for Billycan to escape.

"Yes," snorted one, "he is here!"

"You belong to Merg now, murderer!" the other shouted at Billycan. "You are his!"

The mighty boar Merg banged his great head against the hollow tree, thrashing and pounding until his whole face bled. The wood finally burst as his sharp tusks cracked through the tree, crushing it to splinters. "You!" he hollered, blood spraying from his nose. "You are mine! You will die tonight, fiend from Hell!"

Slick from the boar's blood, Billycan tried in vain to scrabble up the inside of the tree.

"Justice is mine!" said the boar, grinning madly. "You took my brother. Now I take you!" The boar suddenly pitched forward, thrusting his entire body at the tree. He gouged Billycan with his tusk, lifting him into the air. "You are a stealer of family!"

The white rat went limp.

CHAPTER SIX
A Dark Morning

Telula and Cotton watched from above as the ancient tree plummeted to the ground, sending a tremor through the entire swamp. The boar clan galloped off into the night as speedily as they'd arrived. Their task was done.

"It's over," said Telula. "They must have finished him."

"Look," said Cotton, flying toward the base of the tree. Telula followed. "There, I see him."

The bats landed on a low-hanging branch and observed the body. Billycan lay in the mud, a tangle of twisted limbs. He was flat on his belly, a bleeding arm cocked over his neck, lying facedown on the ground. Cotton had spotted the tip of an ear, the only part of him still white.

"Poke him," said Telula. "See if he moves."

Cotton scoffed. "I'm not going near him, not a chance! What if he's alive? You heard what father and Juniper said about him."

"*Look* at him!" said Telula. "Even if he's alive, he's not going to hurt you. I doubt he can even wiggle a claw."

Cotton stood resolutely on the branch, shaking his head.

"Fine," said Telula. She flew off the branch and landed next to the wilted rat in the mud.

"Telula!" hissed Cotton. "Don't go near him! Stay there."

With that, Cotton took wing, gently landing beside Billycan. Slowly he crept next to the rat. Cotton watched him closely for any kind of movement. His body was stiff and still.

Finally he unfurled a wing, holding it so close to Billycan it nearly touched the rat's muddied snout, checking for even the smallest of breaths. Cotton waited for what felt like an awfully long time.

"Well?" whispered Telula nervously.

"Nothing . . . he's dead."

"Killed by a boar," said Juniper.

"The boar gouged him with its tusk," said Telula. "It sliced his chest and shoulder clear through and flung him over its head and into the mud—dead."

"Children, can you show me where you found him?" asked Juniper. "I need to see for myself." He looked at Vincent and Carn. "We all need to see."

"He's at the base of the hollow tree," said Cotton. "I'll take you."

"You go ahead," said Carn to Juniper. "I need to stay here." He nodded over to Thicket and Stono, both still looking utterly confused.

"Good lad," said Juniper. "We'll be back soon enough."

The Council vanished into the woods with Cotton.

Even after the snakes had departed, the horde sat stunned in a huddled, trembling mass. Oleander had her arm around Thicket. Mannux spoke to Stono, trying to explain it all. Carn approached. "Thicket, Stono," he said softly, "I'm so sorry for not telling you who I really was. I felt I had no choice. I didn't think you'd believe me if I told you what Billycan was really after, what kind of rat he really was. I was afraid of what you might do."

Finally looking up from the ground, Thicket spoke. "Seems everybody afraid of us," she said. "Oleander, Mannux, they're like you, and you're all worried we'll do you harm. I remember what happened a long time back. Those rats—the ones like you—they got hurt real bad because some of us got scared. It wasn't right, what happened to them. I always knew it . . . never said it."

Oleander rested her head on her cousin's shoulder. "It's time we all spoke up around here. No more silence." She smiled over at Cobweb and Montague, both crouching on their haunches, playing with some children who already seemed to have forgotten the horrible night. "Look," she said, gazing up at the sky. "Morning has broken."

"He's gone," said Juniper bleakly.

Cotton's whole body slumped. "I thought he was dead."

"Don't blame yourself," said Cole. "Too wounded to grab you, he probably knew if he held his breath long enough and lay still, you'd think he was dead."

"Any one of us would have reached the same conclusion," said Suttor. "How could any rat live through an attack like that—gouged by a boar?"

Thin shafts of light fought their way through the cypresses, shedding spots of pale daylight through the woods.

Inspecting the ground, Juniper touched it with his paw, sniffing.

Suddenly he sprang up. Following the ground with his eyes, he walked swiftly.

"Juniper," said Vincent, "where are you going?"

"Come along," said Juniper, "quickly now—it's a trail."

"What sort of trail?" asked Vincent.

"A trail of blood."

"This is a great deal of blood," said Cole. "I don't know how he's still alive, let alone upright."

"I don't put anything past him," said Juniper. "I suppose if I could survive his attack in the Combs"—he tapped his eye patch—"he could survive even a boar's attack. After all that's transpired, I imagine he could survive anything."

"Just like a cockroach," muttered Vincent.

They stopped at the plantation's border. The sun now high, they all could clearly see the trail of blood twisting through the grass. It led around the manor, straight to the back door.

"The manor has been his home for the last three years," said Juniper. "He's come back here to die. Ulrich and Ragan, go round up the others. Warn them what's afoot. Get Carn. You three guard the front of the manor." The twins dashed away.

Juniper spotted Cotton, hovering over their heads. "Cotton,

fetch your father. Ask him to direct the entire colony around the windows of the manor. He cannot escape this time. Cole, Vincent, Suttor, you come with me." Juniper stared at the bloody trail leading to the door. "This ends now."

Gently shutting the screen door behind them, they entered the manor. The scent of fresh blood filled the air. Suddenly there was a crash—glass breaking somewhere in the manor.

Juniper motioned to Cole and Suttor, who crept off to investigate the kitchen and dining room while he and Vincent silently entered the parlor.

The shades had been pulled. Except for a slender beam of light slicing across the Oriental rug, the room was black. Vincent halted, motioning at the broken vase scattered about the rug. He pointed to his ear. "Listen," he mouthed to Juniper. They waited in silence. Then there it was—shallow, hoarse gasps coming from under the settee, so faint they were scarcely audible. Vincent recoiled at a cold, wet feeling under his feet. Blood.

"Billycan," Juniper called out. "For your own good come out, you will surely be dead by sunset if you do not." Cole and Suttor entered the parlor. Juniper nodded to them, and they took positions around the settee. "You're surrounded. There will be no escape this time."

The breathing halted. Then "Leave me to die," came from beneath the settee. The words oozed out of Billycan's throat like air escaping from a balloon.

His voice was so feeble, Juniper knew that if he bided his time his mortal enemy would be dead. Not knowing whether Billycan was armed, he had to goad him out from under the couch before it was too late, but what could he say? What would anger Billycan enough to lure him out?

"Billycan, you must come out. There is something you need to know."

"Billycan knows all he wants or cares to know. Leave me be."

"I cannot."

A throaty snort came from under the settee. "Well, then, what is it I need to know, Chief Citizen? Please do tell." Billycan coughed out a laugh. "I'm all pins and needles."

"You need to know about your son."

The Councilmen glanced at each other, unsure how Billycan would respond. They stood in momentary silence, then laughter—loud, strident laughter—erupted from under the settee.

A stabbing pain jolted through Billycan's chest. He looked down at his gaping wound. He crawled along the floor, finally pulling himself out from under the settee. "The boy!" he growled. "You think I care about him, that my fragile heart might break at the mere mention of him? Ha! You've no doubt turned him into a sweet, sappy, pathetic excuse for a rat. He is of no use to me now. No longer *my* son! He is foul and useless!"

"He looks just like you," said Juniper calmly. "Young Julius is the spitting image of his father, down to his snow-white fur."

"*Julius?*" scoffed Billycan. "You couldn't even give him a proper name, could you?" He boiled with rage. He held his aching chest and forced himself to his feet, teeth bared. Weapons raised, everyone stepped closer. Billycan eyed Vincent. "You named him after the father of this mongrel, didn't you, with his *filthy* Nightshade blood!"

Vincent sprang forward. "Serves you right!" he sneered. "Your son is nothing like you and he knows *nothing* of you, but he's heard all the stories of his namesake. In fact, his spirit burns bright with the memory of my father, *Julius* Nightshade!"

"It's all right, Vincent," said Juniper. "Billycan, this is about you and me, not Vincent or little Julius. This is about doing the right thing. In the lab, you were bred purely for testing, given a drug that I believe made you into something you were not born to be—something wicked. I simply cannot accept that you were born as cold and pitiless as you've become. I cannot kill you—not even you." Juniper revealed the syringe, already filled with an orange solution.

Billycan laughed out loud, forcing himself not to scream in pain as more blood trickled from his wound. "You think I was born *good*? Oh, that's rich, even for you! I'll have you know, I'm quite fond of my wickedness! I savor my kills! I relish their agony, their screams for mercy, the finality of their deaths! I commanded an army! I am the White Assassin! I led the High Ministry, and now I am leader once more—a lord, a king!

"You are a king of nothing!" Juniper snarled angrily. He lunged at Billycan with the needle.

Trying to push past them, Billycan charged Cole and Suttor. Cole threw his spear to the ground, grabbing Billycan around the neck in a choke hold. A bright light flashed in Cole's eyes, blinding him. His arm became drenched in hot blood, his skin stinging in pain. Billycan was tearing at Cole's arm with a shard from the broken vase, but Cole refused to let go. He yelled furiously as Billycan slashed his flesh. "Juniper, do it now!"

Cole hurled himself backward, pulling Billycan to the ground as Juniper swiftly plunged the syringe into Billycan's neck.

Suddenly Billycan stopped clawing. He began to twist and thrash on the ground. Cole released him as Vincent and Suttor ran to Cole's aid.

A choking murmur escaped from Billycan's throat. His body shook uncontrollably. His eyes bulged as a gush of matted black muck poured from his mouth, sticking to his chest. With his last scrap of strength, he pulled himself to his feet. Wobbling, staggering, he veered toward Juniper, grabbing him by the shoulders. He looked at him strangely, as if he'd never seen him before. Billycan took hold of Juniper's face, pulling weakly at his fur with trembling paws he could no longer control. "What have you done?" he whispered. He dropped to the floor. He did not move. His body made no sound.

Bending over him, Juniper checked for a pulse. He looked up at the others. "It's over. We leave tonight."

CHAPTER SEVEN
Billy

VOICES WOKE BILLYCAN. Some he thought he recognized, but he could not put a single name or face to them. It was dark, but he knew he was in some sort of truck. He could hear its motor and smell the stinking chickens, their constant squawking jolting his brain like electric shocks. He tried to lift his head but was too weak. He grunted in agony. With every bump in the road, his whole body jerked in pain.

He was strapped to something, tied down—downright overkill, so many knots. Even if he had the strength, there'd be no escaping these ropes. His chest and shoulder throbbed. He was injured—badly—but how? He couldn't remember anything.

Billycan tried to make out the scents of his captors through those of the chickens—nothing. Whoever they were, they were happy. He could hear them chatting and laughing merrily. At times their noise even drowned out the chickens.

He turned his head toward the laughter, his eyes blurring in and out of focus. He couldn't make anyone out. A fuzzy pair of feet suddenly moved toward him, a large tail dragging behind. He quickly shut his eyes, pretending to still be asleep.

The rat stopped and stood over him, staring at him in silence. Billycan's heart raced in his chest. It couldn't be a good rat. Good rats didn't tie you up and leave you injured and bloody. That much he *did* know. He could hear another set of footsteps approach.

"He's still out cold," said the first rat.

"How he's still alive, I'll never understand," said the other. "Maybe the old ones' claims are correct after all." The rat snorted. "Maybe he *does* have magical powers."

The other rat let out a heavy sigh. "Nothing supernatural about him. I believe whatever took place in that lab, whatever drug he was given for all those years, has made him stronger than even a Trillium rat—more resilient."

"Do you really think the serum will work?"

"I suppose we'll find out soon enough."

The other rat lowered his voice. "When are you going to tell the others the truth?"

"I don't know. For now, we keep it between us."

"Agreed. The younger ones, I'm most worried about their reactions, Vincent, Victor, and Carn especially, with all they've lost."

"If I keep it to myself, they'll never be the wiser. It may save everyone a lot of pain."

"You and I have been friends for as long as I can remember, and in that time never once have you acted selfishly. You've sacrificed much of your life trying to make others' lives better. Perhaps most of the Council *would* oppose your decision to do this, but in my estimation you needed to decide—alone. You'll no longer wonder *What if?* You've a right to this, whether anyone likes it or not. There is no shame in the truth, but I leave it up to you to decide when or even *if* you reveal it."

"You are a good friend."

The second rat chuckled. "I won't disagree with you on that. We should rejoin the others."

Billycan's mind reeled. Who *were* these rats? It was maddening. He *knew* their voices. Where were they taking him? And what was this serum?

The only thing that made sense was the lab. That place... he knew it well. He drifted back to sleep, back to those days in the lab. To all the time spent in cage number 111 and the haunting smell of bleach.

"Why, that's correct," said Dorf. "You're absolutely right! Billy, I'll never understand how at your tender age you solved the equation, but you did it—wonderful stuff, just wonderful!"

The small white rat beamed through the slender window at Dorf, his teacher and friend, caged next to him. "Thank you," he said in a voice as tiny as he was. "I was practicing all night."

"I can see that. Any mother would be proud to have a son as bright as you."

Billy's face crumpled. "Do I have a mother?"

"Oh dear," said Dorf under his breath. "Well, Billy, we *all* have mothers, every creature does."

Stepping to the wire door of his cage, Billy looked out across the lab. There was a group of females caged across from him. A dark rat, the color of chestnuts, halted in her tracks as he caught her gaze. Their eyes locked. She cocked her head and looked at him curiously. "Dorf, what's a mother like?"

"Well," said Dorf, clearing his throat, "if I can be honest, most are rather lovely creatures. They care for you when you're sick or feeling sad, and they always love you, no matter what."

"No matter what?"

"Yes, mothers love you always. Most creatures have a family, a father of course, brothers and sisters, aunts and uncles and so on, but in my estimation mothers are the heart of any family. I'm sure you have a family, too, *and* a mother. You've just never met them—they don't allow that sort of thing here."

Billy had heard other rats, the ones not born in the lab, chattering from their cages about their families, how they missed them. "Dorf, can we be family?"

"Why, yes, Billy, I suppose we can. Not a family like I spoke of—not true blood relations, mind you—but a *sort* of family all the same. I care for you very much, and that's what families do. They care about each other. They love one another."

"So you love me, then?" said Billy.

Dorf smiled. "Yes, my boy. I do."

The lab technician watched as the long, lanky rat slipped through the maze. There was a lump of dried liver at the end of the unsolvable labyrinth. The test was used to establish what the rats would do when they were unable to get what they wanted. The drug, Serena, was supposed to keep them calm, coolheaded—able to control themselves.

The rat reached the end of the maze, a thick pine door lying between him and his prize of liver. He sniffed the air, so close to what he wanted! Suddenly the white rat threw his body forward, hitting the door with his shoulder and chest. The lab tech's face went slack as he watched the wood give way, cracking down the center. The rat promptly plucked the liver into his mouth, crushing it with razor-sharp teeth.

"Why, Billy, you broke the rules!" said the lab tech, laughing heartily. "You are something, aren't you, an independent thinker—a real leader. And every leader needs a special name. No more Billy, number 111—far too common for the likes of you. From now on you are Billy-*can*, because I'm beginning to think you *can* do anything!"

The technician put on his safety gloves and picked up the lively rat, which squirmed in his tight grasp. "Easy, now," said the man. "Don't worry, you've already had your shot for the day. We know how you hate those!"

The man brought the rat back to the wall of cages. He stretched up on his tiptoes, set the rat in the open cage marked number 111, and locked it.

As soon as the man's bald head disappeared from view, the white rat raced to the wire window on the side of his cage. "Did you see it, Dorf?" he called excitedly. "Did you see what I did? I broke the maze! I got the liver!"

Dorf craned his small neck to gaze up at the white rat. "Billy, how did you do it? That door is solid wood, for goodness' sake!"

"I don't know. I just knew I had to have the liver...I *had* to have it." He sighed. "Meat is so tasty."

"Yes," said Dorf, nodding toward his ceramic bowl. "It's

certainly better than the bitter kibble we're forced to eat here."

The white rat's eyes brightened. "Dorf, guess what else."

"What?"

"I've a new name!"

"A new name?" asked Dorf.

"Yes! The man says from now on I'm to be called Billy-*can*. Do you like it?"

"*Billycan*," said Dorf thoughtfully. "Yes, I do like it— very distinctive indeed. I think it suits you rather well. When I met you, you were so small, barely able to speak. Now look at you, bigger than most full-grown rats, even by Trillium standards, and you speak as well as I." He laughed. "Perhaps better."

"The man said he thinks I can do anything!"

Staring down at the broken maze on the metal table below them, Dorf nodded in agreement. "I think he may be right."

"Dorf," whispered Billycan. "Dorf, wake up, I need to ask you something."

The little rat rolled over and looked up toward the window. "What is it, Billy?" he asked groggily. "It's the middle of the night."

"I know, but it's important."

"Well, then, what is it?"

"It's about our lessons," said Billycan.

"Yes?" Dorf yawned.

"What you told me, about Trillium's great leaders, how those humans came to Trillium and took the land away from the weak, building this enormous city. They were strong, yes? They took what they wanted because they could—because they had to have it."

Dorf sat up and cocked his head. "Billy, yes, they were strong... but those were dark days for Trillium. Most of Trillium's so-called leaders were nothing more than unsavory villains—criminals and crooks. They hurt the citizens of Trillium, using their cunning and strength to take what they wanted, leaving people to starve and suffer. Why do you ask about this now?"

"Because today, at the maze, I took what *I* wanted, because I knew I could! It was so easy. It made me feel like them, like a great leader, like maybe one day I could lead a city like Trillium—a city of rats. The men who made Trillium were better than everyone else. That's *why* they could take things. That's why they won." Billycan looked at Dorf hopefully. "Do you think I could be like them someday... a great leader?"

"Billy, listen to me closely," said Dorf firmly. "You don't want to be *anything* like them."

"Yes, I do."

"I know it's hard to understand, but being a true leader has nothing to do with what you can *take* from others—"

"Why not?" asked Billycan. "Leaders become leaders by being tough and breaking rules, letting no one stand in their way."

Dorf sighed. "Oh dear, how do I explain this to you..." Dorf shifted uncomfortably. "Billy, I didn't mean—"

"Dorf, would you call me by my new name?"

Dorf lay back down. "Certainly... Billycan. I'll tell you what, let's chat about all this in the morning. I think you took my words a bit too literally. I've a lot to explain to you, but I'm simply too weary now. These shots are becoming too much to bear."

"All right," said Billycan dismally. "Good night."

"Oh, now don't be disappointed," said Dorf. "We'll talk tomorrow. I promise. Now off to sleep. Sweet dreams."

"Sweet dreams, Dorf."

As the panels of lights flickered on one by one, the lab quickly filled with the smell of coffee and sugary pastries. That meant morning. The humans had arrived.

"Dorf, are you awake?" asked Billycan through the window.

"Yes, I'm awake."

Billycan peered down at him, watching him stretch lethargically. "Why are you so much smaller than me and the other rats?"

Dorf smiled. "Believe it or not, I'm actually a normal size for a rat. I'm just small compared to you because I wasn't born in Trillium."

"Why would that make you smaller than me?"

"Well, that's the question. I don't think anyone knows why. It seems all Trillium-born creatures are slightly different from others of their kind. Rumor has it, Trillium creatures were here long before the humans arrived. Something in Trillium has permanently changed all the animals—for the better."

"Is that why I keep getting bigger?"

"I believe so, along with the shots. I've never seen even a Trillium-born rat grow as fast as you. You're already nearly as big as an adult. I noticed it with the other white rats, too— the ones born in the lab, not the adults captured from the streets. I heard the lab techs mention it. They said the drug is affecting the young ones' growth." He glanced down at his flank. "I'm far too old to grow any more; in fact lately I feel ancient. This was not how I intended to spend my old age... not in a place such as this."

"Dorf, how old *are* you?"

"Well, I'm not exactly sure, but compared to the average Trillium rat I'm almost certainly quite young. Just as Trillium rats grow larger than rats like me, they live much longer— much longer indeed. Where I was born, a rat's life is quite short, but you, Billycan, you were born here. From what I've learned, you'll live fifty, sixty years, possibly much longer." He nodded toward a pair of lab techs, both hunched over rows of test tubes. "Why, you'll live as long as they."

"Sometimes I feel like I can live forever. That nothing can stop me," said Billycan. "When I leave this place I'll become a great leader."

"Yes," said Dorf, twitching his whiskers. "Billycan, we need to address this leader talk. What I told you about being a leader...I *did* say those things, about not listening to anyone and not letting anyone stand in your way, but we should never hurt another creature in order to get what we want."

"But you told me we need to be strong to survive. The weak creatures that stand in my way are going to die soon enough. What does it matter if *I* am the one who kills them? I'd just be speeding things up."

"Billycan, wouldn't you feel bad taking the lives of other creatures—other rats?"

"But the weak don't *deserve* to live. As you said, only the strong survive. So no, I suppose I wouldn't feel bad."

"Oh dear," said Dorf. "What have I done? This is going to be harder to undo than I thought. You've got things a little muddled. What I'm trying to say is——"

Billycan suddenly hissed, hearing the lab tech's footsteps nearing his cage. "He's coming for me! I don't want the shot today, Dorf. I don't want it!"

"I know, lad. I know you don't. But right now, be like those great Trillium founders you so admire. Be brave and strong. Be fearless, a *true* leader."

"Well, hello there, Billycan," said the lab tech as he stretched to the top row of cages. "How are you, big boy?" The man unlocked the cage. "Time for your daily, but let's not cause a fuss."

Billycan uncoiled his body and stopped shivering. "Leaders are afraid of nothing," he said, stiffening his jaw. He stepped forward, refusing to flinch as the gloved hands came at him.

"You were a good boy today," said the man. "I don't know what's gotten into you, or *out* of you in your case, but you're as calm as a kitten." The lab tech hoisted Billycan up into his cage and locked the door behind him.

Quickly, Billycan scurried up to the wire window. "Dorf, are you there?" The familiar sting of bleach suddenly hit Billycan's nostrils. He looked down into Dorf's cage. It was empty, pristine, as if no rat had ever lived there. The smell of bleach always meant a rat had left the lab——forever.

"No, no, no," whimpered Billycan, "not that smell. I didn't even get to say good-bye...no."

Billycan crawled to the back of his cage and slumped in a corner, coiling his body into a circle. He noticed the same female as before, the one with the chestnut fur, looking at him from the opposite row of cages—staring. Billycan dragged himself to the door of his cage. He nodded at Dorf's cage.

Her eyes shifted toward the empty cage. Slowly, sadly, she shook her head. Billycan understood. He'd always wondered what happened to the rats that had gone missing every time he smelled bleach, hoping maybe they'd been taken to another part of the lab or maybe even set free. The female confirmed what he already knew deep down. The smell of bleach meant death. Dorf was dead.

CHAPTER EIGHT
A New Council

"**L**ook," said Victor.

Juniper and Vincent watched as Billycan opened his eyes.

Sluggishly, the white rat sat up on his cot and looked around. He turned toward the wall of bars that lined the front of his cell. Three rats, two black and one an unusual raisin shade, sat on stools, holding steel spears and staring at him. "Where am I?" he asked feebly. No one answered.

His muscles throbbing, Billycan lay back down. Who were these rats? Why was he locked up?

"Boys," said Juniper, "go for now. Leave me with him."

Billycan's ears perked. He recognized that voice. It was the same one from the truck.

"But we should stay here," said Vincent, "for your protection."

"Even Billycan cannot escape this cell," Juniper replied. "All four walls are barred. Unlocking the door is his only way to freedom. He will never escape, and he will never again be able to hurt me or any creature."

Vincent would have protested further, but something in Juniper's demeanor gave him pause. It was clear Juniper wanted them to go. He was obviously agitated. His gaze kept shifting back to Billycan as if he couldn't wait for Vincent and his brother to leave. "All right," said Vincent, "but Victor and I will be waiting for you right outside the door, and the moment we sense trouble we're coming in—no arguments."

Juniper smiled. "You'll get no arguments from me. Now off with you both."

Vincent could tell the smile was forced, but all the same he'd abide by Juniper's wishes. He turned back to the cell, glaring coldly at Billycan.

Billycan craned his neck, trying to get a good look at the black rat. He had strange eyes, green like emeralds. The rat turned abruptly and left the room, as if he couldn't stand to look at Billycan another second. The other followed, shutting the door behind him.

Leaning his spear against the wall, the older rat slowly arose from his stool and exhaled. He looked completely drained, as if he hadn't slept in days. He folded his arms and stared through the bars of the cell.

"Do you know who I am?" asked the rat.

Gradually Billycan pulled himself up, awkwardly forcing himself into a sitting position. He wanted to scream out in pain, but stayed silent, leaning his back against the bars of his cell. Billycan studied the rat's face. He wore a patch over one eye, and there was something not quite right with part of his face. "No," he answered.

"My name is Juniper. Some of your memory has been erased, at least temporarily. It's the side effects from the serum you were given—we knew this might happen."

What was in this serum? wondered Billycan. Maybe it was to help cure his wounds. "Where am I?" he asked again.

"You are in Nightshade City."

"Nightshade City," repeated Billycan, as if saying it might spark a memory. "Are we anywhere near Trillium City?"

"Yes, as a matter of fact. We are underneath it, deep underground, far away from the humans in Trillium."

"I *know* Trillium City," said Billycan, his eyes brightening slightly. "I grew up there—in a laboratory."

"I know," said Juniper. "Do you remember the swamp?"

Billycan's eyes flickered briefly. "Yes. I do." Tugging at his whiskers, he thought for a moment. "I remember it was hot and rather sticky and there were snakes, scores of them. They weren't very hospitable." He looked back at Juniper almost apologetically. "I'm afraid that's all I can recall."

"I see," said Juniper blankly. He examined Billycan's face, his eyes. Their fiery red hue seemed somehow muted.

Billycan dragged himself off the bed. Every muscle ached, but he needed to get a closer look at his jailer. The rat's manner didn't seem hostile. Billycan clutched the bars of his cage for support. "You're tall like me," said Billycan. "Why, we're nose to nose. Most rats are smaller than I."

"Yes," said Juniper evenly.

Cocking his head, Billycan peered at the rat's face. Part of it was riddled with scars, deep ones. He focused on the ragged leather patch. "What happened to your eye?"

Juniper snorted. "I suppose you don't remember that, either."

"Remember what?" asked Billycan.

Wearily rubbing the bridge of his nose, Juniper tried to decide if Billycan truly couldn't remember. Don't trust him, he thought. Maybe the serum had no effect on him after all, and this was a clever ruse—but Billycan's eyes, his stance, even his tone of voice had changed. "Never mind that for now. It will all come back to you soon enough."

"All right," said Billycan.

Reaching behind him, Juniper took a small burlap sack from his stool. "Here," he said, holding it out to Billycan. "Take it."

Billycan hesitantly reached for it. "What is it?"

"It's something to eat," said Juniper, "dried meat. You must be famished. You haven't had food in a while. We were lucky to get enough water and broth in you to keep you alive."

As he took the sack, Billycan abruptly grabbed Juniper's paw in a rigid hold. Juniper jerked backward, easily breaking free of Billycan's weakened grasp.

Juniper snarled, grabbing his spear from behind him. He should have known better! What possessed him to drop his guard even for a moment? He grabbed Billycan by his injured shoulder and thrust the spear under his chin, ready to draw blood. "Do not test me, rat! Stand back!" he growled, sneering at Billycan, teeth bared.

"I'm sorry!" said Billycan, drawing back. He grunted as his shoulder throbbed in pain. He held out his paws in a beseeching manner. "I wasn't trying to harm you, I give my word. I only wanted to shake your paw—for the food. Like you said, I'm famished. I...I only wanted to *thank* you."

Juniper threw the spear to the ground. He cursed in frustration. Exhaling, he paced the small room, trying to reclaim his temper. He eyed Billycan. His ears and tail were limp, his face showing no anger, just curiosity and confusion. An image of Vincent came to mind. At that moment, Billycan reminded him of Vincent, the day he'd first stumbled into Nightshade City—a lost, lonely boy.

Billycan looked anxiously around his cell. "Why am I here? What have I done?"

Juniper ignored the questions. "Do you remember the Catacombs?"

Twitching his whiskers, Billycan pondered the name. "The Catacombs... that's a strange name. No, I don't remember that place. Should I?"

Texi raced past the library and dining hall, nearly falling as she barreled around a turn. Her entire body trembled, she was so sure they'd catch her this time. She gasped. She could hear them gaining on her, their feet thundering through the powdery dirt. They'd been after her all morning. Her feet aching, she couldn't outrun them much longer. Finally she reached the corridor.

Swiftly she ducked into the first doorway she saw and tried to catch her breath. She gasped. They were so close now. Texi shrank into the doorway's darkest corner, hoping it would hide her gingery fur. She covered her mouth, trying not to make a sound.

Two figures tore past her. She waited a moment, then cautiously looked down the corridor. They were gone. Without a moment's hesitation she flew down the passageway and stopped at a door, banging on it, her chest heaving in panic. "Let me in!" she cried. "Please, please, let me in!"

A moment later the door opened upon the worried face of Mother Gallo. "My dear," she said, "come in, come in. What in Saints' name is going on?"

Texi ducked under Mother Gallo's arm and slipped into her quarters. "I must hide!" was all she said. Quickly she threw a quilt over herself and fell into a heap by the fireplace.

Resting her paws on her hips, Mother Gallo shook her head. "Dear, anyone can tell there is a rat quivering under that blanket."

"Not if I don't move," said Texi in a muffled voice.

Suddenly the door burst open. Mother Gallo shrieked in surprise. "Where is she?"

"Where is who?" asked Mother Gallo, trying to block the two rats' view of the lumpy quilt.

"There!" said the other, wiggling a digit at a slender tail peeking out from under the blanket. "Get her!"

The rats easily bypassed Mother Gallo and jumped on Texi. She screamed. Her attackers broke into wild laughter. Texi tried to hold the blanket over her, but Julius tickled her feet and little Nomi tugged on her tail.

"Come out, Texi!" called Julius as Nomi crawled under the blanket.

Clearly captured, Texi revealed herself.

"We always find you!" said Julius triumphantly.

"You surely do," replied Texi, tousling Julius's white fur. "You're far too quick for the likes of me!"

Mother Gallo inspected her two youngest children. Nomi, now nine months old, plopped herself on Texi's lap while Julius began making silly faces at them. Nomi giggled madly, gripping her round belly in a fit of merriment.

It had been as much a surprise to Mother Gallo as it was to Juniper when she realized she was once again expecting. Life had turned out to be a funny thing. Just three years ago she was a widow, reluctantly working for the corrupt High Ministry of the Catacombs in an effort to feed her boys and keep them out of the Kill Army's grasp. Now she was a member of the Council, married to Juniper Belancort,

Chief Citizen of Nightshade and the lost love of her life whom she'd thought dead for all those years. Now he was head of their family: her older sons—Tuk, Gage, and Hob; Nomi; and of course Julius, the little white rat found abandoned in Killdeer's compound.

Nomi took after Juniper in every sense. She had bushy, violet fur and a loud laugh that could not be ignored. Mother Gallo watched her daughter pounce on Julius, squealing in delight as he wiggled his snow-white ears, stuck out his tongue, and rolled his red eyes around in his head.

"Mother Gallo?" called a voice from the open door.

"Clover!" yelled Julius. He sprang from the floor and raced for the door. With both paws he grabbed Clover by the arm and pulled her inside.

"Well, hello there," she said.

"Hello, dear," said Mother Gallo. "Come in, come in. I'm just about to make us all some lunch, and you're just in time to rescue poor Texi."

"I see," said Clover, smiling as Julius ran back to Texi, nearly tackling her. Clover leaned in to Mother Gallo, lowering her voice. "We must talk."

"Texi, would you mind the children while Clover helps me with lunch?" asked Mother Gallo. "What is it, dear? What have you heard?" A shiver suddenly ran through her. "Have you seen him?"

"No, nor do I want to. Vincent said he's still recovering from his wounds, barely stirring. It will be days until the serum works, and everyone is already growing impatient, especially with the side effects. Virden said it may cause him to lose much of his memory—temporarily, that is. According to what we know of the serum, once his memory returns he'll gladly give up all we need to know. He'll talk quite willingly, revealing any other allies he might have who were going to help him attack Nightshade. And we can find out who gave him the city blueprints—the traitor. Juniper has called an emergency Council meeting for tonight."

Mother Gallo exhaled wearily. "I'm relieved he has finally been captured, but terrified to have him in that cell, right under my children's feet." She nodded toward Julius. "He must never find out about Billycan. Julius is our boy in every way. He's the complete opposite of Billycan. His love knows no bounds." She put her paw to her chest. "Even now, that monster still rules us. I'd sooner take my own life than allow that fiend anywhere near my boy."

Clover took Mother Gallo's paw in hers and spoke gently. "We're all eager for this to work, especially Uncle. He seems so distant, his mind someplace else."

"I've noticed," replied Mother Gallo. "Clearly something is bothering my husband. His face wears a troubled expression day and night since his return from the swamp."

"We've come so far from those ghastly days back in the Catacombs." Clover glanced over at Texi. "Look at her. It's hard to believe she was enslaved by her own brother, serving Killdeer night and day, while her horrible sisters tormented her." She smiled. "Now, though, she's happy, contented. How she dotes on the little ones as if they were her *real* family. What I'm trying to say is that this city is our family— every citizen in Nightshade. Billycan has always been a deadly threat to us, but now he's locked up. He can never hurt another soul."

"If that's true, then why do I feel as if there is more danger to come?"

Rats were gathering in the Council Chamber. Since its founding three years back, Nightshade City had become a thriving metropolis, and the Council had grown with it, from its core group of Juniper, Cole, Virden, and the twins to now include *all* the rats who had played a key role in defeating the High Ministry and those who had helped build Nightshade. Elected officials had been chosen by the citizens for their many good works throughout the city.

Someone knocked on the chamber door. Mother Gallo smiled as she opened it, knowing who it was.

With an elegant sweep of her paw, a diminutive gray rat pulled back the hood of her black cloak and entered the chamber. "Hello, my darling Maddy," she purred in her smoky accent. Born in Trillium, Elvi had fled the Catacombs during the Bloody Coup, jumping a cargo ship headed to Tosca Island. After over a decade in the desolate and perilous Toscan jungle, she found her way home, and the Nightshade rats had welcomed her with open arms.

Elvi hugged Mother Gallo. "And how are you tonight?" She smiled thoughtfully. "Happy to finally have your Juniper back safe and sound, yes?"

"Yes, indeed," replied Mother Gallo. "But Elvi, you're late *again*. Come in, dear. Juniper should be here shortly."

Elvi stepped to the side, revealing a rickety old cart with three steaming teapots on it. "Ah, yes, but I have a reason for my tardiness tonight. I come bearing gifts!"

"Your wonderful Toscan tea," said Mother Gallo, clasping her hands. "What a brilliant way to celebrate everyone's homecoming from the swamp."

"I stopped by your quarters on the way," said Elvi. "All is well. Texi already has the little ones asleep, and the boys are busy with their studies."

"My goodness," said Mother Gallo, suddenly alarmed, "I hadn't thought of Texi...the news and all. You didn't mention anything..."

"Oh, no, dearest, I would never do such a thing. That's something we should do together. It could upset Texi dreadfully. She's told me horrible stories about him. I can only imagine what she endured day in and day out."

"Yes, I don't quite know how she'll take it, knowing he's here in Nightshade. She was under her brother's and Billycan's control for so long—not to mention those wretched sisters. They were absolutely horrid to her. She's come so far from those dark days, and has been such a help to me, especially with Julius. Never have I seen a three-year-old so clever and full of life, but Texi manages to keep him in line. I don't know what I'd do without her."

"Young Julius is a clever rat, just like his father," said Elvi, weaving her arm around Mother Gallo's as they made their way to their seats at the Council table. "And don't worry about Texi. We'll break the news to her together when the time is right."

Vincent sneered in Elvi's direction.

Clover raised an eyebrow. "What was that for?" she whispered. "You're always giving her funny looks."

"I don't know," he replied. "There's just something about her. Something I don't trust. Something in her eyes. I just can't figure it out yet."

"Something in her eyes, that's what you're banking on these days? She's done absolutely nothing to earn your suspicion."

"She appeared out of nowhere, for starters, just after we ousted the High Ministry," said Vincent. "Don't you find that even the slightest bit odd? She claims to be this long-lost rat, this Elvi. How can we be sure? Everyone thought she died in the Great Flood. And she's always covered in that creepy black cloak, like she's hiding something."

Clover rolled her eyes. "Mother Gallo, Juniper, and the rest of the older Council members know and trust her. They were all childhood friends. Mother Gallo said she and Elvi were inseparable when they were girls. Instead of being so distrustful, you should be pleased that the life of a good rat was saved. And as for Elvi's cloak, that's the Toscan way. It shaded her from the brutal sun. She lived in the jungle for over a decade. Pardon her for not dressing more to your liking." Vincent tried to retort, but Clover kept on talking. "Furthermore, she's been nothing but kind to everyone since she arrived—especially Texi. It's awfully nice of her to spend so much time with her."

Vincent *was* thankful for that. Clover and Texi shared a room in Nightshade City, and before Elvi arrived he could never visit Clover without having to endure Texi's constant chattering, always tagging along behind them. It was nice to have some peace and quiet. "I guess you're right," he finally said. "I suppose after growing up in the Catacombs it's hard to trust anyone."

Clover gave him an understanding smile. "It's hard for all of us. You know, I admire Elvi. I was alone in the Catacombs, just about raising myself, but I still had help from neighbors and Uncle Juniper. Elvi was utterly alone—lost in the Toscan jungle, facing down savages and vicious beasts every day. How frightening and desolate her life must have been."

"I hadn't thought of it that way," said Vincent. "It's unbelievable to think she found her way back to us all the way from Tosca."

"The Saints were looking out for her"—Clover glanced at the other young Council members—"just as they looked out for all of us."

Clover was right about that, thought Vincent. Carn and Suttor sat across from him, still going on about their adventures in the swamp. His brother, Victor, was listening to Cole, but Vincent bet he was thinking about Petra. Since the night they'd danced together at Nightshade's naming ceremony, the two had been inseparable—well, at least when Petra's father allowed her out of the house. They were all still *alive*. They'd weathered the storm. Vincent couldn't understand why he felt another one was brewing. Something didn't sit right with him—something about Billycan's capture and Juniper's reaction since then. He just didn't know what that something was.

Juniper finally arrived. Everyone took a seat in silence as the Chief Citizen entered the chamber, shutting the door behind him. Few of the new Council members had seen him since he'd returned from the swamp. Standing at the head of the long table, he smiled broadly at the Council. "Billycan is captured!" Clapping and cheering, everyone stood up. They'd known the mission was a success, but to hear the actual words, to know Billycan was no longer hiding out there somewhere, ready to attack—it was liberating.

"We are finally free of him," said Juniper, as everyone sat down again. Thinking as he spoke, Juniper chose his words carefully. He didn't like lying. "As soon as he reveals the full extent of his plot he can rot in the prison corridor with his high majors."

A new Council member, an old rat with dreadful posture and a sagging belly that made him appear as if he'd swallowed a tangerine whole, slowly got to his feet. He looked sternly at Juniper. "What makes you think the Topsiders' serum will work on Billycan, that it will make him tell the truth? He's not human, after all. It may not have the same effect." He snorted contemptuously. "For all we know, he's not even a rat."

"Striker, from what we can tell the serum is already working.

Billycan is showing the side effects, just as the humans did—memory loss, personality changes—"

"Memory loss?" blurted Striker, cutting him off. "I was never informed that he might *lose* his memory. How is that helpful? What if he can't remember who he had working with him, leaving us open for retribution at any moment? Didn't any of you consider that?"

"Councilman Striker," said Virden, standing up, "you were indeed told of the side effects, just like every other Council member. If you think back, we all voted on this. The majority voted to proceed. And if I remember correctly, that included you. This memory loss is temporary. His memory will return—and soon. We did our research on this serum. Who do you think the human scientists tested it on before giving it to humans?"

Striker snorted. "You bring us back a half-dead rat with no memory of his deeds? I want it on the record that I think this plan was not well conceived." Council members started to murmur, many questioning whether the serum really *would* force Billycan to reveal the truth.

"So noted, Striker," replied Virden. "Perhaps you could stop yourself from nodding off at our next meeting."

Striker sputtered but quickly took his seat.

"Blowhard," muttered Vincent, glaring at the old rat.

"Can't you say anything nice about anyone today?" asked Clover. "He's very old."

Ulrich and Ragan laughed. "Vincent's quite right, and so are you," whispered Ragan, leaning in. "Striker means well, but it's true. He *is* a blowhard, and an ancient one at that!"

The whispers among the Council members grew louder. "There is no cause for alarm," said Juniper, with a decisive pound of his fist on the table. The Council quieted. "His current state is no surprise. He is a changed rat for the time being—docile, passive. Unless it's an act, which it may very well be, we'll take full advantage of his new temperament. We will discover the truth." He paused for a moment, staring at everyone with a steely expression. "There is a serious matter we need to address. We have a traitor within the Council." The whispers turned into gasps. "Someone has been helping Billycan, filtering confidential information to the swamp. We must find the culprit or culprits and punish them accordingly. There's no time to waste. Why, the traitor may at this very moment be plotting to break Billycan out of his prison cell."

"A traitor?" said Striker. "What's this?"

"In the swamp," said Juniper, "we found scores of maps and blueprints of Nightshade and its defenses, documents that Virden, Cole, and I drew up ourselves. Members of this Council are the only ones with access to those documents, which means one of us is a traitor."

Everyone stared awkwardly at one another. The new Council members could feel the weight of Cole's, Virden's, and the twins' gazes bearing down on them suspiciously.

Striker pointed an indignant claw at them. "You think it's one of us, don't you? How smug you all are. We've worked to build Nightshade, just as you have. The gall—to think one of us would betray this city for *him*, of all rats! Why would any of us do such a thing? We have everything we could possibly need."

"Striker is correct," said Elvi, nodding respectfully at Juniper. "From where the new Council members stand, I think I speak for all of us when I say none of us has anything to gain by such treachery, and none of us has anything to hide. Why would any citizen of Nightshade betray our city after everything we've toiled for—after all we've lost?"

"At this point, we are not accusing any member, old or new," said Juniper. "We only want the truth. If no one here is the guilty party, then how did Billycan come to possess the city's blueprints mapping everything out, down to this very chamber?"

Burton, a bulky brown rat, stood up. He was a key member of Nightshade Security, working tirelessly with Ragan, Ulrich, and Carn. He gazed gravely at each rat, making his way around the table. His eyes suddenly halted on the last of the new Council members, a flamboyant gray named Oberon. "Then the question remains . . . *who* would be betray us?"

Oberon momentarily struggled under Burton's withering gaze, adjusting his red robes over his ever-widening frame as he stood up. "Are you suggesting I did it?" he asked coolly. "Burton, you've always taken issue with me. Is it my fault you are not as revered in Nightshade as I am?"

"Revered?" scoffed Burton. "Why, you're a laughingstock, with your boisterous talk and exaggerations. If we didn't know better, you'd have us all believing it was you who took down the High Ministry—single-handedly, no less!" Several Council members chuckled softly at the comment, a bit tired of Oberon's tall tales. "After all, Oberon, you seemed to get along just swimmingly with Billycan and Killdeer before we overthrew them. Why, you even held an official position!"

Oberon pointed to Mother Gallo. "Juniper's own wife held an official position! We did what we had to do to stay alive in the Catacombs."

"Juniper's wife did it to feed her family," said Burton, with a scornful growl. "You did it to feed yourself."

"In my estimation, this is all about jealousy, plain and simple," said Oberon, sticking his snout in the air. "Blame the one you want to shove out of the limelight, that's how I see it!"

"The only thing keeping you in the limelight is that ridiculous red robe! Citizens can see you barreling down the corridors a mile away," snapped Burton.

"Gentlemen!" barked Juniper, pounding his fist on the table. "We've no time for such petty squabbling. It will get us nowhere. As the Council of Nightshade City we must all work as one. Our common goal is to find out who is working with Billycan before they can help him escape again—and if it's not one of us, then who?"

CHAPTER NINE

A Secret

BILLYCAN LAY ON HIS COT, shaking and writhing, his body aching, his head pounding. The pain reminded him of the blue kibble he'd been forced to eat in the lab, which had made his stomach and head hurt terribly. He closed his eyes. The rat, Juniper, had mentioned a place—the Catacombs. The name somehow seemed familiar, but how did he know it? He closed his eyes and concentrated. *The Catacombs*, he repeated as he began to doze off, *the Catacombs . . .*

The lab tech looked up at the wall of cages. "Number 111 is acting odd," he said to his colleague. "It's like his fire has gone out or something. Maybe he's sick."

"Well," said the long-necked female tech, "*he* may be slowing down, but his growth rate certainly isn't. He's a bony one, but he's the longest rat in the lab and he eats like a horse."

"I know," said the short man, "it's just that—he's usually so much livelier. Maybe he's depressed."

"Depressed?" scoffed the woman. "He's a lab rat." She shook her head. "Really, Walter, you get too attached to these animals. What did you name that one... Billycan? Such nonsense. They're subjects for our research, nothing more."

The man's face grew hot with embarrassment. "Yes, I know," he said sheepishly.

A buzzer sounded. The female tech turned back to her equipment. The man walked over to the long wall of cages that housed the males. He climbed up on a step stool and peered in at Billycan, who was curled up in the corner of his cage. "What is it, boy?" the man asked in a soft whisper. "What's got you so down?"

Billycan's fur bristled. The man was kind, different from the other humans who worked at the lab, but Billycan stayed put, coiled in the back of his cage, his face to the wall. It had been two months since Dorf had died. He felt more alone than ever before.

When the man left, Billycan turned around and sluggishly pulled himself to the front of his cage. He looked out at the lab—his home. He smelled the air, immediately crumpling his nose as the scent of unappetizing blue kibble hit it. He sniffed again, this time smelling the lab techs, reeking of coffee and doughnuts. Growing up around the humans who manned the lab, he quickly learned their favorite things to consume—coffee, doughnuts, and hamburgers. The pungent scent of the hamburgers always made his mouth water and his heart race. The short man snuck him a piece once. It tasted a bit like the dried liver the lab techs would reward him with, only far better.

"I *must* get out of here," he said angrily. He looked toward the female cages. Again the same dark female was watching him. Why was she always staring at him?

From far away, Billycan heard yelling—loud, impassioned yelling—humans. Something was wrong. Suddenly a window broke. Glass flew everywhere.

"Bless the Saints!" yelled the male tech as he shielded his face from the flying shards.

"What's happening?" cried the woman.

A silver canister landed on the floor between the walls of male and female cages. The canister hissed and shook, then abruptly exploded with dense plumes of orange smoke.

"It's those activists!" shouted the man, trying to wave away the thickening smoke. "I *knew* they were planning something! I told security they'd been snooping around!" He and the female began coughing uncontrollably.

"My eyes!" yelled the female. "They're burning!"

The male quickly took off his lab coat and covered himself and the female with it. "C'mon," he said, "this way!" Billycan watched as they clumsily escaped through a side door.

Without warning, humans dressed in black clothes and frightening masks jumped in through the broken window. They began scaling the walls of cages, setting each rat free.

It was chaos. Confused rats scurried about the lab, running this way and that. Billycan's heart thundered as the humans neared the top row of cages, his row. "Freedom!" he shouted, grabbing the wire door of his cage and shaking it.

An alarm suddenly sounded, filling the lab with an ear-piercing wail. The humans jumped off the walls of cages as quickly as they'd scaled them. "C'mon," shouted one to the others. "We have to go *now*—the police are coming!" The small band of humans jumped onto a metal table, pulling themselves out through the broken window. The last human to leave tossed something toward the lab equipment.

On the top row, Billycan was the only one left. "No!" he called frantically as the equipment exploded in flames. "Don't leave me here—please!" He threw his body against the door of his cage. "Don't leave me!"

Just then, someone called to him. "Don't worry. I'm coming. I'll get you out!"

"Who's there?"

"It's me." A rat appeared from nowhere, right in front of his nose.

"You?" said Billycan in astonishment. "You're the one who's always staring at me."

"Yes," said the female. Using her claws, she fiddled with the latch on Billycan's cage, swiftly opening it. "Ah, much easier from the outside," she said. "I could never manage to unlock it from inside my cage.

"We have to get out of here before we're recaptured. We're going to have to jump to the floor. We won't get hurt. I promise." The female grabbed Billycan by the paw. Her skin felt warm. "Can you do it?"

"I can," he said.

"All right, then. Let's go!" She pulled him from his cage

and they plunged through the smoke and landed on the floor of the lab.

"Follow me," she said.

"Why are you helping me?" he asked as they ran.

"It wouldn't be right to leave you here all alone. We all deserve our freedom," she replied.

"Well, thank you very much," said Billycan.

"This way." She nodded toward a window. Billycan watched as she leaped onto the sill. "Look here." She reached under the metal handle, easily pulling the window open at the bottom, leaving just enough room for them to wriggle under.

Billycan jumped onto the sill and poked his head outside. The cool fall air blew through his fur, making his whiskers flutter. He closed his eyes for a moment, smelling peculiar scents and hearing sounds he'd never heard before.

The female watched him thoughtfully. "That feeling is the wind," she said. "Isn't it wonderful?"

"Yes," replied Billycan, opening his eyes. He turned to her. He'd never been so close to another rat. He studied her. She had thick, wiry fur and bright yellow eyes. Not thinking, he reached out and touched her coat. It was far softer than it appeared.

She didn't flinch or recoil; instead she moved a little closer to him. "We may look different," she said, "but we're much closer than you could ever imagine." She sighed. "C'mon, then, the rat who's late may wind up with a frightful fate."

"What?"

She looked sweetly at him. "It's just a little poem. It means it's time to go."

"Go where?"

"The Catacombs, my home."

Billycan turned back to the desolate hallway. The lab was his home, but now he was saying good-bye to it forever. Would he miss it? He looked back outside and sucked in a deep breath of air. It smelled so strange. It didn't smell of coffee or doughnuts. It didn't smell of blue kibble. It didn't smell of the foamy green fluid in his daily shots. Best of all, it didn't smell of bleach. He looked at the female and smiled. She smiled back.

The pair jumped onto the fire escape and out into the cool Trillium night.

Texi couldn't stop shaking. Elvi and Clover each held one of her paws.

Clover could feel Texi's claws digging into her skin. Never had she seen her in such a state. "Texi, this is a *good* thing," she said. "Now we don't have to worry about him sneaking into Nightshade, taking his revenge." She nodded at Julius, who was playing quietly by the fire with Nomi. "I know how much you adore little Julius. Now Billycan will never be able to harm him—never. True, he's here in Nightshade, but he's locked up tight. He can't get near you."

Texi looked at Elvi desperately. "How could you keep this from me?"

"Oh, darling, I didn't want to frighten you. Please understand, we all thought it best to wait until he was captured. Then we could tell you together."

"This changes everything," said Texi. "Everything."

Elvi cocked her head, studying Texi's face. She gently patted her paw. "What does it change, darling? Tell us."

"Nothing," blurted Texi. "I'm . . . I'm just worried for Julius—for everyone. You don't know what he's really like . . . how cruel . . . how vicious."

Mother Gallo brought over a handkerchief. "We all know, dear, we do, and Julius will be just fine. He is well protected. We are *all* well protected."

Texi wrenched away from Clover and Elvi and seized the handkerchief, promptly burying her face in it. She whimpered softly, shaking. Clover looked worriedly at Mother Gallo and Elvi.

Juniper had called a secret meeting of the original Council members and those he was one hundred percent certain would never betray Nightshade.

"I knew she'd be upset," said Clover, "but Texi's reaction . . . she was so distraught. She seemed so frightened."

"Texi is fragile," said Juniper. "In some ways she was worse off than the rest of us in the Catacombs, dealing with Billycan and Killdeer day in and day out, always living in fear."

"I saw it," said Carn. "Billycan couldn't stand her . . . and those sisters. Killdeer kept them well hidden. Texi was the only one I saw much of, which was fine by me; the sisters were as unsightly as they were cruel." He cringed. "I heard them many times in the compound, shrieking like witches at her, always ordering her about and cursing her stupidity. I think she was more afraid of her sisters than of Killdeer or Billycan. They'd gang up on her. One time I saw her running from their quarters, crying. They accused her of purposely serving them cold stew, and called her an ungrateful, wicked sister." Carn paused for a moment. "So they threw the stew at her. They were absolute monsters."

"Bless the Saints," said Mother Gallo. "I had no idea it was that awful. No wonder she reacted so strongly. He brings back all those terrible memories."

"We're all here for her," said Ulrich. "She has us to lean on."

"Agreed," said Ragan, "and the best way to rally round her is to find this traitor. When whoever it is is behind bars for good, it's sure to make her—well, all of us—more at ease. Ulrich, Carn, and I have been trying to narrow down the list of suspects."

"Well, then," said Juniper, "who are they?"

"Our sixth sense about these things, our knack for picking shady characters, doesn't seem to be as effective as usual," said Ulrich. "We've questioned all the new members, and not one stands out as our culprit."

"Well, perhaps your sixth sense *is* fully intact and none of them is guilty," said Juniper. "Perhaps it's a citizen he recruited."

"It's possible, but I've a feeling it's someone we know well. Someone with easy access to the Council Chamber and all it contains."

"What about that quarrel between Burton and Oberon during the Council meeting?" asked Cole. "Could that have all been a cover, diverting our attention? Could they be working together?"

"We checked that out," said Ragan. "Turns out there is bad blood between them, dating back to when they were school chums. Story as old as time—they were after the same girl. Burton claims Oberon stole her from him. Oberon claims he was the more handsome rat—not surprising, coming from him. We checked it out with some citizens, those who've known them all their lives. It's all true. They've loathed each other ever since."

"Moreover," Ulrich added, "in the Catacombs the Kill Army majors were afraid of big Burton. Even back then, he made it clear that he had no affection for the new High Ministry *or* its majors, and no one raised even an eyebrow—too afraid he'd use that right hook of his. He's been ruled out. Oberon, on the other hand, will require further investigation."

"What about Striker?" asked Juniper. "He was quite vocal at the Council meeting."

"He's been ruled out as well," said Ragan. "He's full of hot air at the Council meetings, a true blowhard as Vincent so eloquently put it, but he has no love for the former High Collector. You see, two of his grandsons were in the Kill Army—forced in, I should say. The High Ministry proclaimed that Striker was too old to be their guardian, and with nearly all his family drowned in the Great Flood, there was no one else to look after the boys. Then, when a tunnel in the Combs collapsed, the two boys were crushed to death."

"I had no idea," said Juniper. "Striker never talks about his family."

"I knew about it," said Mother Gallo, nodding sadly. "I was called to the scene just after it happened. You see . . . it was the same tragedy that took Mr. Gallo. As you can imagine, Striker was quite broken up."

Juniper smiled faintly at this wife. "Clearly Striker is not our culprit."

"What about Elvi?" asked Vincent, careful not to look at Clover.

"Yep, we spoke with her, too," said Ulrich. "We questioned her for over an hour. None of us wanted to suspect the girl we all grew up with, but we grilled her, same as the others. She recounted her whole story. How she'd escaped the Catacombs on that boat with the others. It was pure luck that she found a boat coming back here. It was making its once-a-year run with Tosca's only export—waterchip root. In a nutshell, she'd been in Tosca so long there's no way she'd even know

Billycan, let alone be working with him. He was long gone before she ever found her way home to us."

"But how do we know she's been in Tosca all this time?" Vincent asked. "We're only going by what *she's* told us. We don't have any hard facts."

"How suspicious you are—a real detective if ever I saw one!" said Ulrich. "Are you sure you don't want to join Nightshade's security team? We could always use a fellow like you."

Vincent blushed. He could feel Clover staring at him. "I was just wondering, is all," he replied.

"And wonder you should," said Ragan. "But I think we can trust she's been in Tosca for at least a decade. Look at her skin, for one. She's our age, but the sun has wrinkled the poor girl up like a raisin. That type of damage comes from exposure over a good part of a lifetime, Vincent."

"Satisfied?" asked Clover, folding her arms in a huff. Vincent didn't answer; instead he sank down in his seat and refused to look at her.

"Now, now, dear," said Mother Gallo. "Whether we like it or not, everyone needs to be questioned. No special treatment for any of us—not Elvi, not anyone."

"My wife is once again correct," said Juniper, winking at her. "Now then, on to happier subjects. Carn, how goes it in the swamp?"

"Oleander says the snakes, for now in any case, have kept their word," said Carn. "They have not crossed the plantation borders, and have let the horde journey into the swamp for food unharmed. Dresden's colony is patrolling the area regularly. All seems well."

Vincent elbowed Carn, snickering as he did so. "And how *is* Oleander?" he asked, with a devilish spark in his eyes.

Carn ignored his friend's tone. "I don't know firsthand, but

Telula and Cotton report that she's doing just fine and sends us all her best."

"You especially, I'm sure," said Suttor, stretching over Clover and Vincent and playfully knocking Carn on the shoulder.

Carn glared crossly at them as Victor smirked and punched Carn's other shoulder.

"You're all positively juvenile!" hissed Carn, clearly aggravated. "Oleander has *no* interest in me, nor I her." Carn's skin turned red as a beet. His friends erupted in wild laughter.

"Don't be angry with them, Carn," said Juniper. "Your friends only want to see you happy." He nodded to the older Council members. "Why, you should have heard these four teasing me back when I courted Maddy."

"Yes," said Cole, chuckling, "we were unrelenting, all in the name of love—and of taunting Juniper, of course!"

"Juniper's right," said Vincent. "No matter what you say, it was clear you and Oleander cared for each other. You should have asked her to come with us."

Carn's anger evaporated. His face suddenly fell. He looked down at the table. "I wanted to," he said, "but it's too...too painful."

"Painful?" said Juniper, "I don't understand—"

"Because she's a *normal* rat! She won't live as long as we. She'll be dead before I even hit middle age." Carn hit the table with his fist. "I couldn't be with someone I'd lose just years after we started our life together." Everyone was silent. "Sometimes I hate being from Trillium."

"Carn, I apologize," said Juniper. He looked around the room. "We all do. I suppose none of us had thought of that. It's easy to forget other rats are different from us. We still don't know why the creatures of Trillium have been given so much more than others, but we're learning."

"Before all this nasty business with Billycan cropped up, we'd been doing research on the subject," said Virden. "In the early days of Trillium City, back before it was even called Trillium, there was a colony of scientists who lived here. The ground underneath their feet, the ground we now live in, is in fact the crater of an ancient volcano. What the humans call mountains are the walls of the volcano."

"Trillium City lies in the very core of it," said Cole.

"You mean we live in the center of a *volcano*?" asked Vincent.

"Dead center," said Cole.

"What was Trillium called when the scientists lived here?" asked Victor.

"Well, Cole and I did some digging Topside, a scavenger hunt so to speak, and we discovered an old journal from one of these scientists," said Virden. "It was stored in the archives of the City Museum. Cole came across it when we were searching for any information on Trillium rats—a history, perhaps. The diary reported a flammable mineral on the shores of Hellgate Sea, not far from here, with much higher quantities of this mineral here in Trillium—reportedly a result of the volcano."

"So, what was this mineral?" asked Vincent.

"Brimstone," said Juniper. "According to the diary, we lived in the core of the extinct volcano for hundreds of years. All of Trillium's creatures were entirely secluded—trapped in our own little world, untouched by the elements outside it. It wasn't until scientists discovered us that we found out we were so far advanced compared to our more worldly counterparts."

"But how did they find us way down at the bottom of a volcano?"

"They stumbled upon a small city. An aboveground city. A rat-made city."

Cole and Juniper sat just outside Billycan's cell, watching him sleep. His memory should have returned by now, but so far he still had no recollection of most of his past—or so he claimed—and he still displayed almost childlike mannerisms. It was strange.

"I don't know how much longer we can put them off," said Juniper. "I don't like lying."

"Nor do I," replied Cole. "But you know as well as I do that the news will shake everyone to the core, especially those closest to you."

"I want to tell Maddy, but the very thought of her face, her reaction . . . I don't know if I could take it. How will she ever look at me the same again? I don't know if I can tell her . . . or anyone."

"Juniper, you don't *have* to tell anyone. I will take this secret to my grave if need be."

Billycan started muttering in his sleep. Juniper approached the bars of the cell and listened. "Lenore," Billycan called out in a cracked voice. "Lenore!"

Stunned, Juniper looked wide-eyed at Cole. "Her name!" he said, his mind spinning. "Every time I'm convinced I've done the wrong thing, something pulls me in the other direction, confirming that I've made the right choice."

"It's the Saints," said Cole, "guiding you."

Juniper shook his head. "Or the devil himself."

Vincent stood in the corridor, bewildered by what he'd just overheard. He'd gone looking for Juniper, hoping to talk further about the possible list of conspirators. He thought that a few suspects Nightshade Security deemed innocent still demanded more investigation. Rather than barging in on Cole and Juniper, he stood in the corridor and waited. He couldn't help overhearing them, and what he'd heard was disturbing indeed. What was this secret they shared? What could be so dreadful that Juniper would hide it from everyone in Nightshade City, including his own wife? And *who* was Lenore?

CHAPTER TEN
Lenore

BILLYCAN'S RESTLESS NIGHTS seemed to grow longer. He wrestled with the knowledge that he must have done something very bad, or he wouldn't be here. No one would tell him anything. Juniper just kept saying in his stern and steady voice, *You'll remember in due time.* Well, he hadn't remembered much of anything other than bits of his childhood—of Lenore, whose name he was so glad to finally remember, the rat who'd unlocked his cage the night of the break-in. Perhaps she was still alive. Maybe she could help him, as she had all those years ago.

He stared at the ceiling and steadied his breathing. He thought of her face, her dark fur, her warm yellow eyes . . .

Billycan and his female rescuer bounded down the wrought-iron stairs of the fire escape. They stopped in the alley below to catch their breath.

"What is your name?" Billycan asked.

"Lenore," she replied. "I heard a lab tech call you Billycan. I like it. It's unusual. It suits you, for you seem to be quite an unusual rat."

Billycan smiled, pleased. He liked her name, too. Lenore—it sounded soft.

Just then a screaming noise erupted in the alley. Billycan jumped backward in a panic, clawing for the fire escape.

"Don't be frightened," said Lenore gently as the blare faded away. "It's all right. It's only a siren. It's from a Topsider's car."

"What's a car...and what's a Topsider?" asked Billycan, his back curved into an arch like a terrified cat.

She looked at him thoughtfully. "Come with me. I'll show you. This is something you need to learn."

He followed her to the end of the alley, just before it spilled out into the street. Wheeled metal boxes flew past them, tearing down the street. Billycan took a step back, his eyes wide, as a black truck barreled down the road, dousing the sidewalks with rainwater.

"*That* is a car," she said softly. "While roaming the streets, you must be on the lookout for them at all times. And when I say Topsiders, I'm speaking of the humans. They make their way around in these monsters with no concern for the creatures around them. We are invisible to them."

"Invisible?" said Billycan.

"Yes," answered Lenore. "And it *must* stay that way." She gave him a firm look. "They must never see you. The moment they take notice, they'll try to kill you. You must never forget that. It is their way."

"But why do they want to kill us?"

Lenore paused for a moment and shrugged. "I suppose . . . because they can."

Just as Dorf had told him, thought Billycan. Great leaders take what they want because they can. Destroy the weak, for they are useless.

"C'mon, then," said Lenore. "We've a lot of ground to cover if we want to make it to the Catacombs before dark. We'd best get to it. It's going to get much colder tonight."

"What are the Catacombs like?" asked Billycan.

"Well, it's a wonderful place, my home." She smiled at him. "Your home, too, if you'd like. The Catacombs are safe and warm and you'll meet lots of other rats, all wanting to be your friend—just like Dorf. It's deep underground, far away from the Topsiders." She gave him a serious look. "It's a *good* place, Billycan."

He considered for a moment. He glanced at her as they rounded a corner, a slight smile on his face. "I think I'd like to go there, very much."

"Then it's settled. Down this alley," said Lenore. Billycan gazed up at the building towering above them. It seemed to go on forever. "That's the Brimstone Building. The Topsiders call it the heart of Trillium City."

Billycan's blood pumped. The heart of Trillium City, he thought, as if Trillium were a massive creature, a force of nature. A surge of rage suddenly swept through him. He was angry, angry with the humans—these Topsiders—who could so easily take control of the rats, of everything. And he was angry at himself, at his own kind, for allowing it to happen. He looked back up at the building—the heart. This city would be his one day. He would be one of Trillium's great leaders—a king. He would become the heart of the city.

"C'mon, then," called Lenore again, already a few steps ahead of him, "time for your new life—your real life—to start."

They bounded down the winding alley and into the dark.

"Wake up!" shouted a voice. "You heard me, wake up. I will not be made to wait for the likes of you, *rat!*"

His mind firmly in his dream, Billycan thought he was still with Lenore. He heard the impassioned voice shouting from somewhere in the alley. Finally pulling free of sleep, he focused on the dingy bars of his cell. He saw the dark figure of a rat standing on the other side. His heart sank.

"That's it," coaxed the voice derisively. "Wake up and face me."

Slowly Billycan lifted his aching body and got to his feet. He grunted softly, his wound still painful. He homed in on the rat, immediately recognizing him. It was the green-eyed black rat—the one who had glared at him with such disgust. Cautiously he took a few steps forward. So did the black rat, leveling his gaze on Billycan.

"Who are you?" asked Billycan.

Vincent laughed. "Oh, that's amusing. Did you really think I'd fall for your little act? Do you think I'm an idiot?"

"I doubt very much you're an idiot," said Billycan. "I can't remember you, but you know me—and you hate me. I can see that. I'd like to know why." He eyes wandered nervously to the ceiling and then to his feet. "This way perhaps we can talk about things equitably. I'm quite useless, not knowing anything about you."

Vincent smiled wickedly. "Oh, you really are a talented fellow, aren't you? Your mild manner, your choice of words, *equitably* and *useless*. Why, you're perfect! Quite believable. For a split second, I almost wanted to believe you myself."

"Believe *what?*"

"That the serum has temporarily changed you—wiping out your memory, your badness. But it's all a farce, isn't it, a sick but brilliant deception? The moment you gain the slightest trust from one of us, you'll slit open his throat and make one of your famous escapes."

"I'm not pretending." Billycan looked down at his bruised body and twisted shoulder. "I do not have the strength for make-believe."

Vincent took a step closer, glowering at those red eyes. They *did* look different, as though their bulbs had gone out, turning the eerie red to a darker crimson. "Juniper and the others may think their little serum is working and you will soon reveal the truth, but I know better."

"Oh dear," said Billycan, his face falling in disappointment. "There will be no getting through to you, will there?" Vincent stayed silent, stewing with rage. "I cannot make you believe me. I've a small piece of my past right now. That's all. I've done a great wrong, or else why would I be here? Your friend Juniper, he won't tell me my crimes, but *you* can." His voice suddenly grew pleading and frantic. "Please, tell me what I've done! I want to know. I have to! Tell me—please. I beg you."

Vincent opened his mouth, ready to spew out Billycan's many crimes, but he quickly shut it. Juniper insisted they let Billycan remember on his own. Instead he asked flatly, "Who is Lenore?"

Billycan took a quick step forward, and instinctively Vincent jerked back. Billycan held up his paws. "Don't be alarmed," he said.

Vincent cringed, angry that the rat still struck panic in him. How foolish he must look. He should be braver.

"Lenore," said Billycan. "She's someone I remember. It excited me for a moment. I've been thinking about her all day."

"Who is she?" Vincent asked again.

"I don't know for certain. She rescued me...helped me out of the lab the night of the break-in. She saved me, led me to safety. She saved my life."

Maybe *she* was the conspirator, thought Vincent. A rat who would save Billycan could only be a bad one. Could this Lenore still be alive, maybe even living in Nightshade? "What do you remember of her?"

"Well, she was very kind," said Billycan, "with soft, dark fur." His neck bristled, remembering the feel of it when he touched it for the first time—so warm. "She was going to take me to her home, the Catacombs." He looked hopefully at Vincent. "Do you know that place?"

"Where is Lenore now?"

"I don't know. I was hoping she was still in the Catacombs. Maybe she could be found."

"You know quite well the Catacombs are no more—a vacant city, a ghost town. All thanks to you."

"To me?"

Billycan's ears drooped. His mouth fell open. Could he really have done such a thing, destroyed an entire city? Could Lenore have been there?

"Who are you working with?" asked Vincent. "Who gave you the blueprints we found in the swamp? Give me a name."

"I don't know," replied Billycan. He rubbed between his eyes. "I remember the swamp, being there, the snakes, the heat, but I don't remember what happened there."

"You're lying! Now give me a name!"

"Please, listen to me," said Billycan. "I don't have a name to give you. I have *nothing* for you. I wish I could help you."

"Who *do* you remember, then? Start there."

"Lenore, I remember her. My friend Dorf, from the lab, but he's long since dead." Billycan began pacing agitatedly. "There's someone else. A name keeps coming to mind, someone I *think* was a friend, but I can't seem to put a face to it."

"And what is that name?"

"Killdeer."

The Belancort household was asleep—well, for the most part. Julius and Nomi squirmed under the covers, reaching over to poke and prod each other, giggling in little bursts with each nudge.

Silently Mother Gallo got out of bed and crept over. "That's enough," she whispered, wiggling a claw at them sternly. "You'll wake your father and brothers. Now go to sleep, both of you."

"Sorry, Mama," said Julius, "we can't sleep."

Mother Gallo's vexation quickly evaporated. "All right, then. Come here, little ones," she said, taking a seat in her rocking chair. "Come sit on my lap." Julius crawled out of bed, awkwardly carrying Nomi in his arms. He hoisted her up to his mother and climbed on her lap.

One child in each arm, Mother Gallo rocked slowly, humming softly as the pair finally drifted off. She felt the most at peace when all her family was asleep around her. She kissed each child on the forehead and laughed quietly as Nomi began to snore. Just like her father, she thought. Julius moved in closer, nuzzling his mother's warm fur and wrapping his thin white tail gently around Nomi's middle.

Mother Gallo looked at her children. It was odd. She had one child who looked so much like Nightshade's mortal enemy and another so uncannily similar to her husband, Nightshade's founder and protector. It was like having Billycan and Juniper as infants.

She glanced over at Juniper, tossing and turning in his sleep. She worried for him. Something had changed. He was distracted. Billycan was captured, locked up tight. The constant weight on his shoulders should finally be lifted, yet it seemed heavier than ever. Maybe it was the serum. It had been days now, and it had still not done its job. She supposed that must be it.

Julius woke for a moment. His eyes barely open, he raised his white head and beamed blearily at his mother. She smiled back. He once again rested his head on her shoulder and tenderly squeezed his sister with his tail. Nomi giggled in her sleep. She instinctively reached for the tip of her brother's tail and tucked it under her chin. With both paws she held it tight.

Vincent tapped his foot nervously, wondering why Telula and Cotton had not yet arrived. Bats were *always* on time. It was their way. If they were late, it meant something was wrong.

As he waited, leaning against the green Dumpster™ in the alley of the Brimstone Building, he thought of something that had not crossed his mind in years—the chimneys. With still no sign of the bats, he crept underneath the Dumpster to have a look. There lay the five derelict chimneys. Juniper and Vincent had ripped their flues off three years ago when they invaded the Combs, and they were now just five holes filled with leaves and muck. It was strange to think that the Catacombs were now deserted. The once-crowded underground city, right beneath his feet, lay dark, empty, and crumbling.

It was cold and raining. Fitting, thought Vincent. Things had become strained in Nightshade. The capture of Billycan and his peculiar transformation from the serum, whether it was a lie or not, unsettled them all. Vincent still believed Billycan was lying, he *had* to be. His newfound sincerity was shockingly convincing, but after all it was

Billycan—the infamous *White Assassin*—a liar, a murderer. And who was this female, Lenore? Was she the traitor? How were Juniper and Billycan linked to this Lenore? And how convenient! The only names Billycan could recall other than Lenore's were some lab rat named Dorf and of course Killdeer—two dead rats!

Juniper was acting so peculiar. He never kept secrets. He never lied. He was the one rat everyone counted on, especially Vincent. Juniper was not only his friend, he was like his father. For a fleeting moment his heart sank. No, he thought. Juniper would never betray us. Vincent was mortified for even considering it for a second.

Everyone was on edge. Even the Council members Vincent knew to be innocent were anxious. Being interrogated was unsettling under any circumstances, and though Nightshade's Security was far different, it still must bring back memories of Killdeer's horrid high majors and their brutal methods of grilling innocent citizens.

Vincent had to find out Cole and Juniper's secret. He suspected that Lenore, whoever she was, was the key to it, but how? None of it made sense. What could be so horrible that Juniper would keep it to himself? Maybe if he revealed this secret, things would get better in Nightshade. After living eleven years under the High Ministry, Vincent knew as well as anyone that secrets and lies led only to suspicion and misery.

Looking down at the chimneys, he felt the same sinking feeling he'd had all those years ago in the Combs, but now he had so much more to lose. He still believed they should have gone to the swamp and eliminated Billycan. But Juniper had repeatedly refused Vincent's pleas to put aside their sworn oath and destroy Billycan once and for all.

"Carn, is that you?"

Vincent sighed with relief. It was Telula. He sprinted out from under the Dumpster. Telula and Cotton had landed on its lid. "It's Vincent," he announced. Carn had asked Vincent to go in his place. He couldn't bear to see the bats, who only reminded him of Oleander.

"Carn did not come," said Vincent. "Truth be told, he's...out of sorts."

"Ah, Vincent, it's good to see you," said Cotton happily.

"Yes," agreed Telula. "We've missed you. But tell us, how is Carn 'out of sorts'?"

"It's his heart, I suppose," said Vincent. "He misses, well, Oleander...quite a bit." He changed the subject. "I was growing rather worried about you two. You're never late."

"Well," said Telula, "it's funny you should mention Oleander. There's been a development."

"What sort of—" Vincent gasped, choking on his words as a brown rat stepped out from the shadows.

"Hello, Vincent," said Oleander.

"Oleander...hello. How...why are you here?" Had she heard what he'd said! How he stupidly revealed Carn's feelings for her! Carn would never forgive him.

"It's good to see you, too," she said, grinning.

"Oh, sorry, I'm just surprised to see you. *Glad* to see you, just surprised."

She had a rolled-up parchment tucked under her arm. It was starting to get wet.

"What's that?"

"We have discovered some papers in the manor attic," she answered. "Since it involves only the rats, we thought the news should be delivered by one of us. I volunteered to come." She smiled shyly. "I'm a little out of sorts myself, I suppose. I...I needed a reason to see Carn."

Vincent grinned at her. "So what did you discover?"

"It seems we, too—the horde, that is—well, we are different. Secluded in the swamp, we thought *all* rats were like us. We had no idea there was anything unusual about our kind. As it turns out, we *are* different from all other rats—except you Trillium rats. As a matter of fact, we are one and the same."

"But that's impossible," said Vincent, shaking his head cynically. "First off, your lives aren't nearly as long as ours or Dresden's colony of bats. It's impossible you're from here. Why, Trillium creatures live as long as humans. Your family, how long do they live? Maybe ten years at most?"

Oleander eyed Vincent coyly, cutting him off. "My father, Mannux... Vincent, he's *sixty-eight* years old."

Vincent stumbled backward, dumbfounded. "Why didn't you say anything? You should have told us!"

Oleander tilted her head, and her devilish smile slowly emerged. "We didn't know there was anything special about our lifespan. Besides, Nightshade, why didn't you *ask*?"

"So, has he *really* changed?" asked Oleander as they made their way down a torchlit corridor.

"He acts like a changed rat, but I don't believe it for a moment," said Vincent.

"When you saw him, how did he behave?"

"Like he didn't know anything of his past, except for dim memories of his childhood. He was agreeable, too—downright pleasant. It was jarring, to say the least; a very believable performance, but a performance all the same."

"Could this serum have changed him, at least temporarily?"

Vincent scoffed. "Trust me, he hasn't changed and never will.

He's a fiend and a murderer. It seems the older Council members are forgetting that. I feel Juniper wants to blame everything on the drugs Billycan was given in the lab—as if that were an excuse."

"Yes, but if he was *made* into a murderer because of those drugs that were being pumped into him, can he really be blamed? Would you blame, say, Victor if he had suffered the same fate and become a killer?"

"Victor could never turn into a murderer, no matter what," said Vincent flatly. "It's just not in him." He raised an eyebrow at her. "Whose side are you on, anyway?"

"Simmer down, Nightshade," she said, giving him a friendly push on the shoulder. "I'm not on anyone's side. I'm more interested in the truth. All I'm saying is, if murder is not something innate in Victor, then maybe it was never innate in Billycan, either."

Vincent didn't answer. His mind was made up.

They stopped in front of the Council Chamber. "Now, everyone's going to be shocked to see you—Carn, especially," said Vincent. He looked down at his feet, embarrassed. "Did you happen to hear what I said to Cotton and Telula, before I knew you were there?"

Oleander smiled. "I didn't hear a word."

Vincent grinned. "Thank you." Opening the chamber door, he poked his head inside. The Council was seated, waiting for Vincent to return with his report from the swamp. Everyone was chatting— everyone except Carn, who slumped glumly, a miserable lump.

"I'll be only a moment," whispered Vincent to Oleander. "Wait here." She nodded. Vincent slipped inside.

Juniper looked up from his papers. "Ah, I'm glad you're back, Vincent. You're running late. I was a bit worried."

"I've a good reason for my tardiness," said Vincent. "One you *all* need to hear." Everyone stopped chatting and looked up at him.

Mother Gallo and Elvi glanced at each other.

"Is everything all right?" asked Carn, now on the edge of his seat. "The swamp...there's no trouble, is there?"

"All's well in the swamp," said Vincent.

"Oh, good," said Carn, exhaling.

"Then what is it, lad?" asked Cole.

"What are you hiding?" asked Clover, giving him the same look his mother used to give him when he'd been mischievous.

"Why, you look like the cat who swallowed the canary," said Juniper. "Now that you've clearly grabbed the entire Council's attention, you might as well spit it out."

"Yes," barked old Striker. "Time is wasting."

"Well, it appears we are not as unique as we once thought," said Vincent. "Carn, you told me it wasn't fair how long we lived compared to other rats. How it made certain *things* impossible. You'll be happy to know you were wrong." Everyone at the table stared at each other, confused. "We were all wrong. It seems our friends in the swamp share many qualities with us. In fact, apparently they're originally from Trillium, too."

Vincent stepped back to the door and stuck his head out into the corridor. "C'mon," he whispered to Oleander, and gently pulled her into the chamber.

Clumsily Carn rose from his chair. "Oh...Oleander...you're... you're here...in Nightshade!"

The brown rat smiled her impish smile. "Yes, Corn the snake killer, I'm here."

CHAPTER ELEVEN
Violent Tendencies

PACING AGAIN, Billycan racked his brain, trying to remember something, anything. Juniper had told him it would take time for the serum to work. Why was he given this *serum* in the first place? If he'd done wrong, why didn't they just kill him? They were going to let him rot in this cell forever, weren't they... as Billycan saw it, a far crueler punishment.

He threw himself down on his cot, wincing in pain. He tried to remember the last time he had seen Lenore. Somehow it was connected to the other name he remembered... Killdeer.

It was dark. Lenore and Billycan had taken shelter from the cold under a beat-up van in a desolate alley. They quickly realized they were not alone.

"There's two," said one of the men, crouching down slightly. He motioned to his companion, signaling him to go to the other side of the van. "Stupid rats are hiding under our van, of all the dumb luck!"

"Where?" said the other man. "I don't see 'em."

"They're on your side," he said, pointing to the back of the vehicle, "behind the tire. I can see their lab tags reflecting in the beam of my flashlight. There's a dark one and an albino."

The other man made a sour face. "I hate those white ones. Evil-looking devils."

"Yeah, mean suckers, too. Bosses said we're supposed to bring back the colored ones alive and kill the albinos."

"I thought they wanted *all* those flea bags back in one piece."

"Don't you ever listen? The white ones get the ax. I heard two of the suits talking at HQ. They said the stuff they shot the albinos up with turns 'em bad—*real* bad. Makes them do stuff normal rats wouldn't do—can't do. 'Violent tendencies,' the suits said."

"Violent?"

"Deadly was another word they used."

The other man backed up a step as he spied the albino near the tire. "How deadly?"

"Like rabid dogs—and just as crazy."

"Great gig you got us, Lester. Thanks for nothing."

"Oh, can it! All *you* got to do is trap the brown one." A wicked grin materialized across his face as he cocked his shotgun. "I'll take care of the albino myself." He tossed the other man a thick pair of gloves. "Grab your cage, little brother. It's time for some fun."

"Billycan," whispered Lenore, "we have to get away from

these men." She nodded to Billycan, who followed her to the very center of the car's undercarriage, making it harder for the men to reach them.

"What should we do?" he asked.

"Whatever happens, don't let them take you. You must fight for your freedom at all costs. No matter what happens to me, just worry about yourself, all right? Don't risk getting captured or killed on my account."

"But I—"

"Understand, Billycan?" she asked firmly.

"Yes, but—"

Without warning, Lenore darted out from under the car. The man with the cage came at her, surprisingly agile given his thickset build.

"Don't let that one get away!" yelled the other. "We get three hundred a head for the live ones! Even more for the females—they're breeders!"

Billycan watched helplessly as Lenore dodged the gloved man, dashing this way and that. Finally he cornered her against a brick wall.

"C'mon, rat, playtime's over!" huffed the gloved man. "It's freezing out here!" He lunged for her, grabbing her by the scruff of her neck. "Ha! Gotcha, ya mangy rodent!"

In vain Lenore clawed at him, unable to slash through his heavy leather gloves. She snarled and hissed, writhing and twisting as she dangled from his hand.

Laughing, the gloved man cruelly swung her about as the other man went for the cage. "Not so tough now, are we?" he said. "Back to the lab with you, my little meal ticket!"

Billycan began to shake. The same feeling he'd felt as

he gazed up at the Brimstone Building swept over him, only stronger. His blood felt as if it were boiling in his veins. His head grew hot and his eyes bulged from their sockets as if they'd explode. He bolted from under the car, swiftly scaling the gloved man's leg, shoving his claws in as hard as he could and sinking his long incisors into the man's shoulder as he clung firmly to his chest.

The man screamed in agony, dropping Lenore to the ground. "Lester," he howled, "get it off me! Get it off me!"

The other man went for his gun, aiming it at Billycan as he slashed away at the gloved man's neck. "No! You'll shoot me! You've got to pull him off!"

The other man grunted, tossing the gun to the pavement. He lunged toward Billycan, trying to grab him around the middle. Billycan whipped around, lurched like a spring, and sliced the man's face from forehead to chin. The man fell to the sidewalk, wailing in agony as blood gushed from his wounds.

"Billycan!" called Lenore. "Stop! It's over!"

The gloved man covered his face, cowering against the brick wall. Billycan turned back to him, glaring at him, and backhanded the man's ear with his claws, nearly detaching it. The man shrieked in pain and terror. The sound invigorated Billycan, who panted breathlessly as he wrenched his claws free and bounded to the ground.

Chest heaving and smeared with blood, he approached Lenore. "Are you all right?" he huffed.

Her face looked pained, as if the sight of him saddened her. "I'm...I'm fine. Are *you* all right?"

Billycan looked down at his bloodied coat and claws. He

glanced over at the two men, both writhing and moaning on the ground. "I did all that—by myself?"

"Yes," Lenore said softly. "Your instincts kicked in, but don't worry. You'll learn to control it. It's just going to take some time."

Billycan shook his head. He knew whatever had taken hold of him would only grow stronger. He could still feel it inside him. The moment he'd smelled the blood, he'd wanted more. He could already feel himself aching for it. The men's terror sent him to a dark place ... and he didn't mind it. In fact, it felt like home. Maybe Lenore could manage her instincts, but he knew he could never control the power that had just come over him. "I can't stay with you," he said.

"But why not?" Lenore asked. "You must come with me. There is so much for you to learn—so much you don't know!" She sighed. "Please don't go. There is a whole city of rats who'll be more than glad to take you in, to be your family. I have so much I need to tell you—happy things—*good* things."

"There is something very wrong with me. I can feel it."

"You were just protecting me, worried those men were going to harm me. It's only natural to—"

"No," said Billycan resolutely. "I can feel it within me. It grows as we speak. I will hurt other rats. I might hurt *you*." He nodded toward the men. "You saw what I did to them. When you looked at me a few moments ago, you were frightened of me. I could tell."

"No," she said weakly. "I was not frightened *of* you. I was frightened *for* you, but those feelings—those strong urges—you *can* learn to control them. I'll help you. I'll stay with you day and night. Whatever those fiends in the lab gave you and the others, it made you this way. It's not *your* fault! Stay with me and we'll figure things out. I promise."

"Thank you for freeing me from the lab." He reached out and touched her fur. Despite the cold, it felt so warm. "If I did have a family, I'd want you to be in it."

Billycan sped off, vanishing into the night.

"Wait!" called Lenore. "Billycan, you don't understand!" She dropped to the ground in despair. "Please don't leave me. Not now...I've waited so long. There is so much you need to know...."

Steady, thought Billycan. Steady. Don't be too eager. Now! Billycan sprang across the rooftop and leaped onto the unsuspecting crow, breaking its neck with such fury that it lay dead in less than a second.

After cleaning the skeleton of all the meat, Billycan sat on the edge of the building's roof and looked down at the alley. It made him think of Lenore. It had been a month or more since he had last seen her. He hoped she'd gotten back to her city unharmed. He looked down at his matted coat, filthy and spattered with blood old and new.

Something moving in the alley caught his eye. Hanging over the edge, he peered down at the scene. Two cats were fighting. Billycan had killed several housecats since his escape from the lab. Dorf had warned him about cats—how lethal they could be—but Billycan did not agree. The ones he'd come across were lumpy and lazy, easy to overpower and kill. They didn't taste bad either.

He made his way down the fire escape. This could be interesting, he thought. He could kill them both. That would make for a bit of fun and be quite a feast. The crow had been stringy and tough. His belly ached for something meatier, fatty. As his time of freedom grew, so did his appetite. The more he ate, the hungrier he felt.

Jumping from the last rung of the fire escape, he silently hit the asphalt, sizing up the two cats. The orange tabby had cornered the other one. The tabby looked feral and frenzied, riddled with sores and emaciated. It stared at its adversary flintily in sheer hatred. Billycan glanced at the other one, a meaty gray cat with nowhere to go, trapped in the corner at the alley's dead end. Perhaps he could just let the orange kill the gray. That would simplify things, but where was the challenge in that? He grinned hungrily, slinking around a green city Dumpster.

Slowly he crept behind the orange tabby. It *can't* be, he thought, nearing the gray. It had a long, pointed snout, thick, gleaming incisors, and a hairless tail, which twisted around its ample feet like a trained snake. It was the largest rat Billycan had ever seen. Tall like him, but big-shouldered and muscled. The rat suddenly lunged toward the tabby, striking it in the face with a clenched paw. The cat jerked backward, stunned by the blow. It shook its head, blood spraying from its nose.

"Diseased, disgusting feline!" yelled the rat with an imperious air. "I'll snap your bony neck before you've a chance to touch a single hair on my head!"

The cat hissed wildly, lashing out, claws extended. Billycan reacted instinctively. He bounded at the cat, smashing it into the brick wall. Starting at its neck, he dug in with his claws, pulling downward. The cat gave a final hiss and fell to the ground—dead.

Billycan's chest heaved. Wiping spatters of blood from his eyes, he looked over at the gray rat, which stared wide-eyed at him.

The rat stayed in the corner, cautiously eyeing Billycan. It cocked its head and examined him, as if unsure what sort of creature stood before it. Finally it took a step forward. "Many thanks, my unique-looking friend. You have spared me from being that filthy feline's evening meal."

Billycan was taken aback by the gray rat's self-assurance. Every creature he'd encountered on the streets of Trillium was deathly afraid of him, fleeing at the mere sight of him. He looked down at his soiled, bloodied coat. He was quite a fiendish sight, to be sure, but this rat showed no concern.

"Allow me to introduce myself," said the rat. "My name is Killdeer, and you, my friend, look rather hungry." Billycan did not respond.

Killdeer kept his black eyes trained on Billycan's. He smiled. "Let's go find you something to eat, eh? My associates and I have more grub than we need. We take what we want." He nodded toward the Dumpster. "No garbage picking for us. You don't look the sort for picking through thrash, either— far too stately for that." He chuckled. "Let's be on our way, shall we?"

We take what we want, thought Billycan. Just like the great leaders of Trillium. He liked the sound of that very much. Killdeer was strapping and confident, the way a leader should be. He felt an immediate kinship.

"C'mon, then," said Killdeer.

Billycan looked at the dead cat, not wanting to leave the fresh meat. He salivated.

"Oh, no!" said Killdeer, seeing his ravenous eyes. "You don't want that disease-ridden thing rotting in your gut. You'll end up with worms. Come on, we'll fix you up with some real meat."

Billycan followed Killdeer out of the alley, all the while thinking maybe this rat knew of the Catacombs. He wanted to know if Lenore had gotten home all right. Maybe Killdeer knew her.

Hesitantly, Juniper entered the small antechamber that led to Billycan's cell. Perhaps today would be different. Nodding at the guard, he went inside.

Billycan's ears perked as Juniper entered. Pleased to see another face, even if it was his jailer's, he pulled himself to his feet. "Good morning," he said, approaching the bars. "It is morning, isn't it?"

"Yes, it is," replied Juniper. "You look a bit better today—healthier."

"My shoulder still throbs, especially at night, but yes, it's getting better. Perhaps you could tell me now how I got these wounds?"

At first Juniper had thought it best to keep things to himself, worried it might alter the effects of the drug, influencing what Billycan knew as the truth.

Since nothing had changed, he guessed there wasn't much sense in keeping it from him now. Perhaps it would help jar his memory. "A pack of wild boars attacked you."

Billycan took a step back. "Wild boars?"

"You killed one of their pack. Many species still believe in an eye for an eye. The boars are one of them."

"I—I don't understand how..." Billycan couldn't seem to form words. He stared confusedly at his feet. "But why would I..." His body stiffened.

For the first time Juniper saw a flash of recognition. Billycan was remembering something.

Finally Billycan looked up. "An eye for an eye," he repeated softly. "Your eye, under that patch, it's gone." He ran a nervous paw across his face. "I took it from you, didn't I?" Juniper nodded. "I have killed before, haven't I... *many* times." Juniper stayed silent. "I thought I wanted to know all of my past, but I'm afraid now." His whole body drooping, Billycan sank to the floor. He wrapped his long arms around himself and rocked on his heels.

For the first time Juniper actually felt sorry for Billycan, who truly seemed to he in pain—physically *and* mentally. Juniper wanted to distrust Billycan, as everyone else did, but he couldn't help hoping that this was no act.

CHAPTER TWELVE

Suspect

TEXI SCURRIED AROUND THE LONG TABLE, filling everyone's cup with tea. The Council had gathered, trying to make sense of the papers the swamp rats had found in the manor attic.

"My father," said Oleander, "along with Cobweb and Montague, is trying to organize everything. There are scores of papers—all about us."

Befuddled by the whole idea of it, Carn shook his head. "The swamp rats are from Trillium? I don't understand any of this."

"Remember how I told you about the scientists who used to live in the manor with their families? As it turns out, they were from Trillium. When they arrived in the swamp, they had cages of Trillium rats with them."

Juniper rubbed the bridge of his snout wearily. "What are the odds, then, of Billycan ending up there? Could he have known? So many questions we don't have time to answer right now—not until we know Nightshade is secure. Speaking of that, until we've found the traitor, we've posted round-the-clock guards outside Billycan's cell, just in case this traitor is planning to help Billycan escape."

Vincent glanced over at Elvi. She shifted awkwardly, as though the conversation bothered her. Texi suddenly popped up before him, refilling his teacup. Vincent jolted. The little rat was always coming out of nowhere at Council meetings, passing out tea and biscuits at the most inopportune moments. "Thanks, Texi," he said, not wanting to be rude.

She smiled sweetly at him. "You're welcome," she whispered.

"Wait," he whispered back before she could slip away. If Texi wasn't taking care of children or doling out tea to the Council, she was usually with Elvi. "What's wrong with Elvi today? She looks upset."

"I'm not sure." Texi glanced at her. "She seemed out of sorts earlier. Mentioned something about a day of reckoning, how it would soon be coming to Nightshade... Wonder what she meant?" Texi hurried off before Vincent could ask her anything else.

A day of reckoning—what could that mean? "Elvi," said Vincent across the table, "I'm just curious. As a newer member of the Council, what do you make of it?"

Surprised, Elvi looked up. Everyone stared at her. "What do I make of what?"

"Why, of Billycan going to the swamp and finding the swamp rats, who just happen to be like us, from Trillium. What do you make of it?"

Clover gave Vincent a look. His tone was clearly suspicious, not curious.

"Well...", said Elvi, "I think there is possibly something to it. Who's to say? He's been missing for three years. He could have learned about the swamp rats from anyone. Perhaps rats no one here knows." She looked directly at Vincent. "Or perhaps from someone you'd never suspect, someone who has always appeared honorable and brave." She gave a barely noticeable smile. "Perhaps someone . . . like you."

Vincent sat huddled at a table in Bostwick Hall with the rest of the young Council members and Oleander. They looked furtively around the hall, eyeing everyone as they finished their dinners.

"Who do you think it could be?" whispered Oleander to the others.

"We've no clue," said Clover.

"Nearly all the Council members have been questioned," said Vincent. "No one has even a hint of scandal." He eyed Clover. "Except Elvi."

"Oh, not that again!" she said. "You're talking about the Council meeting, aren't you? She had every right to turn the tables on you—putting her on the spot like that. It was obvious you were trying to catch her off guard, hoping she'd say the wrong thing, something that would out her as the traitor."

"Besides," added Carn, "Elvi's been cleared by Ragan and Ulrich, and they have a knack for that sort of thing."

"Well, maybe their knack is off-kilter for once—maybe she's just a brilliant liar," said Vincent.

"Oh, hush!" snapped Clover.

"What sort of *knack*?" asked Oleander.

"You know, a sixth sense—they can sniff out the bad apples," said Carn. "They run Security with me, and we've never had a wink of trouble. When we interviewed the Kill Army majors after we defeated Killdeer, we found that many of them were innocent. They didn't hurt anyone while they served in the army. They were uncorrupted by Killdeer and Billycan, simply doing their jobs as I was, all trying to stay alive. Because of that they've remained free, and not one of them has caused any problem in Nightshade, not in three years. Ulrich and Ragan have questioned them again, in case one of them is the traitor, but none showed even a trace of deception."

Vincent leaned in, his voice lowered to a whisper. "Do any of you know of a rat named Lenore?" He looked at Clover. "Has Juniper ever mentioned her to you?"

"No," said Clover, thinking back. "Why?"

Vincent hesitated, thinking maybe he shouldn't share the information, but then he recalled that feeling he had back in the alley, waiting for the bats. No more secrets and lies, he thought. "I was looking for Juniper and wound up at Billycan's cell. I was about to enter when I heard Cole and Juniper talking. There is something they're hiding from us, some dark secret we are not to know. I could hear Billycan muttering in his sleep. He started calling out that name—Lenore. Juniper was upset over it. I could tell by his voice. She's someone important, I just don't know how."

Cocking his head, Victor turned to his brother. "Maybe she's someone from his past, but what of it? Perhaps you're making too much of this." He smiled. "Just like the big fuss you're making over Elvi."

"No," said Vincent firmly, "this is different." He looked down at his plate of untouched chicken pie. "I spoke to Billycan."

The entire table's eyes widened. No one said a word.

Suttor broke the silence. "Nightshade, are you crazy? We are under strict orders to stay far away from him unless Juniper or Cole authorizes it."

"Exactly!" said Vincent. "Why are they keeping everyone away from Billycan? What don't they want us to know? I had to investigate." He shook his head. "After what I overheard, I *had* to see Billycan for myself."

"But how did you get in undetected?" asked Victor.

"He was still so weak. The guard had not yet been posted. I knew I had to do it soon—and alone—without any of you trying to stop me."

Clover shook her head, disappointed in Vincent's brashness.

"Were you scared?" asked Victor.

"More like terrified," admitted Vincent. "Even behind bars, wounded, and changed by the serum, or at least acting that way, he made my heart race like a rabbit's."

"All right, Nightshade," said Carn, growing impatient, "what was he like? What did he say?"

Vincent related the encounter.

"You're sure Juniper knows her?" asked Suttor.

"I've no doubt."

"Why don't you just ask him about it?" asked Oleander.

"I've thought of that, too. I'm torn. I want to say something, but Juniper is probably just trying to protect everyone as he always has. I want to know, but I don't want to offend him. I've never known him to react like that—ever. If you could have heard his voice...he was shaken."

Suttor's eyes scanned the room. He looked at every face. "Juniper saved my brothers and me from the Catacombs. I just can't believe... I mean, you don't think..."

"Don't even say it," warned Clover. "Uncle would never betray a soul, and shame on you for thinking it, even for a second." She studied her friends' faces. They all looked down, unable to meet her eye. "You can't be serious. Uncle would never—"

"We must *not* rule him out," said Vincent. "As Elvi said back at the Council meeting, it could be the rat we least suspect—someone who's always appeared honorable and brave. I may not like her, but the way Juniper has been acting—how he's been lying—she made an excellent point."

"You're becoming obsessed with this," said Clover. "Accusing Elvi I can understand, but Juniper—after all he's done for you?" She looked around the table. "For all of you."

"No one's accusing Juniper," said Victor. "And I'm the first one to agree that my brother is becoming a bit of a conspiracy theorist. But if the evidence suggests there's a chance, then we must investigate it."

Vincent squeezed Clover's paw. "We just need to clear Juniper once and for all. Why is he acting so suspicious? For my own peace of mind, I need to know. We all do."

Suttor nodded in agreement. "Vincent's right. Juniper is not giving us much of a choice."

"If Juniper, Cole, or anyone else on the Council is going to hide things from us, then we'll have to find out the answers on our own," said Carn. "If we work together, perhaps *we* can uncover the traitor." He looked at Clover. "I don't believe for a second that Juniper's involved, but we must check him out, and the sooner the better. Then we can all move on." Carn looked around the table. No one protested the idea. "So then, are we all agreed?"

Everyone nodded.

Julius held Nomi by her front paws and hoisted her into the air with his hind feet. As she swayed back and forth she giggled hysterically. Julius was making silly faces.

Juniper and Mother Gallo had just returned from the Council meeting. "What's going on in here?" demanded Juniper sternly. "Why, you're loud enough to wake the Saints! We can hear you children all the way down the corridor."

"You're not *really* mad, Papa!" said Julius.

"Oh, I'm not, eh?" He growled, crossing his eyes and jutting out his jaw in an exaggerated scowl. Nomi screamed with laughter as her father scooped her up in one arm and plucked Julius up in the other. Opening his mouth, he snarled at them as if he might take a bite.

"Papa, you're pretending!" shouted Julius. Nomi squealed blissfully as her father spun them in a circle.

"You found me out!" Juniper smiled contentedly. It was in these moments that he stopped worrying about Nightshade and quietly reveled in his children's happiness. Nomi pulled softly at Juniper's scruffy hair while Julius grabbed his face and giggled. Both beamed at their father.

Mother Gallo went to the table and patted her oldest son, Tuk, on the head. His snout was stuck in a schoolbook. "How goes the studying, dear?"

"Fine, I suppose," answered Tuk. "I haven't been able to get much done, though."

"Were the children bothering you?" Mother Gallo sighed. "I told them to keep quiet while you studied. I should have had Hob and Gage stay back to help. The library could have waited."

"Julius and Nomi didn't bother me," answered Tuk. "It was Texi. She stopped by and didn't seem to want to leave. She read them stories and played games with them. It was so noisy I couldn't concentrate."

"How was Texi? We've been worried about her." Mother Gallo lowered her voice to a whisper. "I'm afraid the whole Billycan matter may just be too much for the poor dear."

"Now that you mention it, she did act a bit peculiar," said Tuk.

"How so?" asked Juniper.

"Well, she was whispering to Julius over by the fireplace, and then she asked if she could take him for a walk—in fact, she insisted on it. I said you wouldn't approve. She kept pressing me, but finally relented after I told her under no circumstances was I to let the children leave our quarters." He smiled at his mother. "I can't risk you getting cross with me, or you'll never extend my curfew."

Mother Gallo smiled at her son. "You did the right thing, Tuk. It is certainly too late for the little ones to be out for a stroll."

"Julius," said Juniper, "did you talk with Texi tonight?"

"Yes," said Julius. "She told me she was very sad."

"She did? Did she tell you why she was so sad?"

"She said she needed to make things right or she'd never be forgiven. A rat was very mad at her for what she'd done."

"Oh," said Juniper, glancing at his wife, "that *is* very sad. Did she say *who* this mad rat was? Did she mention a name?"

Julius nodded. "Yes, it was a funny name."

"And what was that funny name?"

"Killdeer."

Crouched in a ball on the floor of his cell, his head buried in his arms, Billycan remembered—remembered Killdeer who had taken him under his wing, showing him how the criminal set operated in Trillium City.

Billycan took to crime as easily as one breathes air, never regretting one merciless act. Always in his mind was Dorf's teaching, *Only the strong shall survive.* Billycan's loyalty, cunning, and love of the kill made him priceless to Killdeer.

Feeling the cell's cold floor under his feet, he remembered distinct moments from his past—terrible moments. Bad things, dreadful things, were coming back to him. . . .

"No, no, no!" Billycan barked at Lithgo. "You're being too soft. If the dock rats won't give us what we want, then simply exterminate them!" He leaped from his stool, kicking it across the room. "If we want to be taken seriously, we must show brute force from the onset—not an ounce of indecision."

Lithgo, Schnauss, and Foiber all eyed Killdeer, waiting for him to say something. He stayed seated in his chair, deadly silent.

With paws clasped tightly behind his back, Billycan marched around Lithgo in a crooked circle. "The early leaders of Trillium did not mollycoddle the populace. They did not give them peace offerings and warm blankets. They gave them nothing, took everything. The dock rats are foolhardy if they think I'll accept their insolence, their defiance."

"Billycan is right," said Killdeer. "They were given the opportunity decades ago to go underground. Trilok offered them sanctuary in his precious Catacombs. They unwisely refused, too stubborn to leave their beloved docks and plentiful food supply. Now I want that food, and I shall have it. The dock rats will get what they deserve."

"Yes," said Billycan. "If they do not hand over their operations peacefully, then they will be eliminated."

Lithgo had had enough. "No," he said decisively. "If we slaughter them all, who will do the work? I'll tell you who— us! The whole point of this was diplomacy—a gentle bending of wills—to allow *them* to labor, while we reap the benefits." He stepped close to Billycan, who glared at him unflinchingly. "*You* are not one of us. You never have been. Killdeer took you in only because you did him a favor. We taught you the ways of our kind at *his* request." Lithgo's chest started to heave as years of resentment spilled out. He motioned to the mob of rats behind him. "None of us wants you here!" Billy-can stayed silent. "Look at you, with your snow-white fur and eyes like blood. You don't belong and never will. There is something *off* about you—something inherently foul. Never have I seen a rat so eager to kill, so full of bloodlust."

Billycan gave Lithgo a grin, a grin that slowly broadened into a menacing sneer of pointed yellow fangs. Billycan's eyes narrowed, their shade shifting from a composed red to a fury of sizzling orange. "Finished?" he asked snidely.

Taking a step back, Lithgo stuttered, "Y-yes."

"Good," replied Billycan, clasping his paws theatrically, as if delighted by the answer. "Now then, I believe it is my turn to speak—unless of course anyone has something to add?" He turned in a circle, eyeing the entire throng. Except for Killdeer, everyone shifted uneasily. "Let me be clear right now so there will be no further need to speculate about *my* motives." He turned back to Lithgo. "You're quite right. I am...oh dear, what was the term you used?" Billycan abruptly lurched forward, thrusting his snout nose to nose with Lithgo's. He snapped two digits. "Ah, yes, *inherently foul*, that's it. I learned that about myself some time ago. And now, thanks to my dear friend Killdeer, I've come to realize that my skills are needed—greatly needed. He has taught me that I should not fight who I am, but *embrace* it! So that is exactly what I've done. That being said, Killdeer has made me an offer, and, you'll be delighted to hear, I've accepted."

"What *sort* of...offer?" asked Lithgo.

"Dear Lithgo, we are ready," said Billycan, "finally ready to invade the Catacombs, and *I* will lead the way."

Finally Killdeer got up from his chair. "Yes, gentlemen, it's time to take back our home. The home Trilok banished us from. Old fool should have killed us when he had the chance. We will once and for all destroy High Minister Trilok, along with his wretched group of advisers. With Billycan at the helm, we cannot fail." He stood next to Billycan, who kept his paw firmly latched to Lithgo's neck. "Billycan is no longer just another one of you." Killdeer glared angrily at Lithgo. Lithgo gulped. Killdeer turned to the rest of the rats. "Henceforth, you will address Billycan as Commander. Commander Billycan reports to me, and each and every one of you reports to him. You are now an army, *his* army. Is that clear?"

Silence filled the room.

Billycan wrenched Lithgo close to him and whispered in his ear, "Major Lithgo, you are *my* major now. Do not ever address me in such a manner again—do you understand me?" He could feel Lithgo's hackles rise under his grasp. "For if you do, not only will you die, but you will die in such a prolonged and, dare I say, *ghastly* manner that you will be utterly mad by the time I finally finish you off. I will quite literally skin you alive bit by bit, until there is no skin left. You will beg for death."

Juniper sat on his stool and watched Billycan in silence, thinking. He thought of the secret and what it was doing to him. And what it would undoubtedly do to his family, his friends, the Council—all of Nightshade. Everything trickles down, as they say, one poor decision leading to another.

More than ever he wished his brother Barcus were alive. Barcus always seemed to know the answers to life's sticky problems, giving sound advice, but in this situation Barcus might well have been equally confounded. Juniper felt as though everything was tumbling down around him. Lost in reflection, he didn't notice Billycan staring at him from his cot.

"Juniper," Billycan called out groggily, "are you all right?"

Juniper looked up. "Oh," he said, getting to his feet, "yes, I'm fine." He folded his arms and leaned against the bars of the cell. "I was thinking about you, actually. I've been coming down here for days now, hoping you'd remember something of the swamp, because I so badly need you to remember whom you were working with. But I've neglected to ask about you. How you're *doing*. What you're feeling. And you may think my asking is a ploy to win your favor, to get you to talk, but I do care about you, what happens to you . . . what *happened* to you."

Billycan cocked his head and stared at Juniper, perplexed. "But why? After all I've done, why would you care anything about me, other than the day I'm to be executed? I don't remember it all—not yet—but I do remember many, many things, horrifying things that I did. Worst of all, I remember liking it." He pulled himself to his feet. A sudden chill sent a shudder through his body. His stomach churned and his hackles rose. He looked at Juniper as though he'd been slapped hard across the muzzle. His voice grew angry. "I don't want you to care about me! I don't want anyone to *ever* care about me! What I've done cannot be forgiven, nor should it be. There will be no pity for me, only loathing and disgust at what I've become—a wicked, wicked creature."

"What if I told you you are not solely responsible for being that wicked creature you describe?" Billycan stayed silent. "What if I told you that in that laboratory you once called home a dangerous drug was pumped into you by humans? This drug, supposed to make you calm and content, had the opposite effect. It made you violent, sadistic. It was manufactured out of greed, and the humans knew full well its vile effects."

"I don't believe you," replied Billycan flatly. "You're just saying this to get answers out of me—clever of you, just what I would do in your place."

"I speak the truth. That is exactly what happened, and there is a chance at redemption. Everyone has that chance, even you."

Billycan shook his head. "Every time I look at you, all I see is that night in the Catacombs when I attacked you, ripping that eye from your skull. I can't think of anything else! I wished you dead. I remember hearing you growl in pain. I reveled in every moment of it." His shoulders slumped. He fell back down on his cot. "Whatever this serum is, its effects will wear off eventually. I will turn back into the soulless killer I was. I know it. I *feel* it. I hope you get your answers before that happens."

Two cups of tea between them, Juniper sat across from Elvi in the Council Chamber, his expression one of utter astonishment. "I don't understand why you'd ask me this. Elvi, it makes no sense."

"I know it's a strange request," said Elvi, "but one I thought was quite vital. You said the serum you gave Billycan *is* working. He *is* starting to remember things—many things—but slowly. Maybe I can help hasten his memories along. Perhaps your presence is impeding him, keeping his memory from moving forward."

"I'm sorry to say, I think you'd only be wasting your time."

"Since I returned I've heard nothing but unsettling, grisly stories from all of you about Billycan," said Elvi. "Maybe that fear—that history you all hold with him—is preventing him from giving you answers. He may not remember details quite yet, but perhaps his subconscious knows he should not talk to you. If he's as cunning as everyone says he is, even with the drug maybe he's found a way to hold back."

"You do make sense," Juniper agreed. "He did mention that he can't stop thinking about the night of the Bloody Coup, when he attacked me in the Catacombs... perhaps you're right. Maybe it *is* preventing him from remembering more." He pushed away his tea and smiled. "And you do have a way about you—that Toscan charm."

Suddenly Elvi's paws trembled.

"Elvi, what is it?"

"Juniper, all those years ago, when I was hustled onto that boat to Tosca, I was terrified. I had no idea what horrors lay in store for me in the vast Toscan jungle. My greatest fears were realized. Not only are Toscan creatures savage, they are wicked, too. They kill because they are born to it. They *like* it. But I'm strong. I used my wits—and my wiles—to deal with those cunning creatures, to talk to them. I'm quick and I'm clever. I can cajole Billycan, worm the truth from him, bend his will just as I did with the brutish Toscans."

"But—"

"You *have* to let me do this," she pleaded. "Don't you understand, Juniper? I want to help. Now I have a chance to truly contribute—to give back to the Saints for taking care of me in Tosca, and to give back to you. You and the others welcomed me with open arms." Tears welled in her eyes. "Please. You *must* let me do this."

Juniper considered. It was natural that Elvi needed to feel she was helping. She seemed to care about everyone in Nightshade, always there with kind words, always compassionate. She doted on poor Texi. She was a dear friend to his wife. She was a caretaker—someone who wanted only to help. "All right, Elvi," Juniper finally agreed.

Elvi wiped her eyes. "Thank you. I know I can help."

"Tomorrow, then."

CHAPTER THIRTEEN
Appalling Tea

ULRICH HAD ALWAYS had a soft spot for Texi. Some thought she was slow, simple, a dim, damaged dullard. He'd never believed that. There was nothing *dim* about her. He reasoned Texi's heart was merely so pure and generous she couldn't fathom others being cruel and calculating. She was a benevolent soul who was lucky enough to live in her own special world.

With that in mind, he and his brother made their way to her and Clover's quarters, hoping to ease Texi's mind about Billycan and decipher her strange words to little Julius. They had to question her regardless, so the timing made good sense. Talk of Killdeer, dead for three years now, troubled them greatly. Perhaps Texi had become overwrought from Billycan's return. Her grip on reality might just be slipping.

"You must be gentle with her," Ulrich urged his brother as they walked toward her door.

"Your fondness for her clouds your judgment," said Ragan. "We discussed this at Council. No one gets special treatment—no one." He patted his brother on the back. "You've always told me she's special. I understand that. We just need to check everything out—just to be safe."

"I know," agreed Ulrich. "It's just that in all my days working security with you, I've never interrogated anyone as altruistic and innocent as she."

"You've no need to convince me. We're only covering the bases. After all, she is Killdeer's sister. She must have some loyalty to his memory, no matter how evil he was. And what have we always told each other?"

Ulrich sighed. "Trust no one."

"Exactly," replied Ragan. "Besides, I think you like her so much because she's the only one in all of Nightshade who admires that stubby excuse for a tail."

Looking back at his nub of a tail, Ulrich frowned. "What are you talking about?" He wiggled it back and forth. "My tail is beautiful!"

Ragan laughed. "That it is, brother. That it is." He knocked on the door. Clover opened it. "Hello, dear, we're here to check on Texi, see how she's managing."

Ulrich and Ragan had a charming way about them, which made them good at interrogation. "Your timing is perfect," Clover said. "We're just about to have some tea."

Ulrich and Ragan tried to hide their grimaces. Clover made appalling tea, and Texi's didn't go down much better.

"I see your faces!" Clover said. "You're both awful. But neither Texi nor I made the tea, Elvi did."

"Oh, thank the Saints," said Ragan, putting a paw over his heart.

"Why, you're terrible, Ragan!" said Clover, laughing, "I admit it. My tea *is* dreadful."

"Sorry, dear," said Ulrich. "As you know, we're quite particular about our tea. Our mother spoiled us with her currant spice. I must admit, though, I've grown quite partial to Elvi's. Here again, is she? Elvi's certainly fond of you."

"And I her, but truth be told she's here for Texi—they have a special friendship. She's taken Texi under her wing."

"It must be hard for Texi," said Ulrich, "She had a large family in the Combs, and now they're all gone. I for one would be glad to get rid of a family like that—but Texi has such a forgiving nature. I'm sure in a way she misses them."

Ragan and Ulrich sat with the three ladies in Clover and Texi's small parlor. They knew they needed to get down to business, but the setting was so pleasant—the company, the roaring fire, and Elvi's perfect tea.

"Texi," Ulrich finally started, in his most delicate manner, "Ragan and I have come here to speak to you about, well, Billycan—and Killdeer." Texi stayed quiet. "We heard from little Julius what you said to him—about your brother. And I know there must have been a good reason behind it, but what did you mean? Something about Killdeer never forgiving you if you don't make things right? After all, he's been dead three years. And we're curious about what you said about Billycan's capture—that 'this changes everything.' Could you tell us what you meant by that? Please, it's important."

Texi looked around her. The twins, Clover, and Elvi all stared at her hopefully, yet at the same time with troubled expressions. She gulped, promising herself she would not cry, and stared into her cup of tea. "Oh, I tried so hard not to pile my troubles on dear little Julius, but when I see his smiling face, I know things will be all right—that I'm doing the right thing."

"What do you mean, 'the right thing'?" asked Ulrich.

"I'd worked myself into such a dither over Billycan, and Julius seemed the perfect companion. He's like real family to me, and I suppose I only want to do what's best for him. I was so upset last night. I just knew I needed to see Julius and I'd feel happier again. He reminds me why I'm here—my purpose. I suppose I sounded ridiculous, didn't I?"

"Not ridiculous," said Elvi, "simply troubled, which happens to all of us at some time or another."

"Elvi's right," said Clover. "Back in the Catacombs, there were many times when I felt anxious."

"Dearest, what is going on in that head of yours? Please tell us," said Elvi. "We only want to help." She took Texi's paw and patted it gently. Cocking her head, Elvi smiled sweetly at her. Her big black eyes looked sympathetic, but something about Elvi's unflinching gaze suddenly unnerved Ulrich. He nudged his brother, who nodded.

Texi took a long sip of tea and let out a tired sigh. "Growing up in the compound, I was taught that family stays loyal to family, no matter what. It was drummed into our heads. Killdeer insisted that if my sisters and I weren't loyal to him in every way, we might very well lose our lives. That's the way my brother was. When he was killed, I was relieved. I finally had freedom. It's just . . . as time wore on I started feeling, well, guilty—disloyal. And when I learned of Billycan's capture, in some way I felt . . . sad. Now everything is over. Once and for all, the High Ministry, my brother, Billycan—all of it—is gone forever. My brother was not good to me—or my sisters—but he was *still* my brother. He was my family." She shook her head, confused by her emotions. "Does that make any sense?"

"And your sisters," said Elvi, "are you sure they're all gone—missing Topside as you told me?" Texi nodded. "Even though they weren't the best sisters, still you must long for them sometimes."

Texi stared solemnly into her tea.

"I've never had much of a family," said Clover. "As you know, my parents and brothers died when I was little. All I've ever had was Juniper, whom I rarely saw. I suppose what I'm trying to say is I know how you feel. If someone had offered me a family, even one such as yours, I can't say I wouldn't have accepted. Being alone was very hard back then, and I think you're feeling that same aloneness now. I hope you know you're not."

"Texi, you and I are very much alike," said Elvi. "I, too, know what it's like to have had a family and lost it. After I returned to Trillium, to Nightshade, my sorrow slowly faded. For now, this place—all of you—are my family." She put an arm around Texi. "You are a sister to me. Never forget that."

Ulrich smiled. "You see, Texi, you've family all around you. There's nothing to be sad about, and you've no need for forgiveness from anyone."

Texi smiled weakly. "Sometimes it's hard to make heads or tails of your own thoughts. I feel so mixed up lately, as if I'm walking in a dream." She gazed fondly at Elvi and Clover. "Luckily I have you two."

"Oh, dearest, you'll *always* have me," said Elvi. She hugged Texi, who seemed to squirm a little in her grasp, as though the hug was too tight.

It was early morning in Nightshade, still dark Topside. Oleander and Clover crept down a corridor near the Council Chamber.

Oleander had been staying with Texi and Clover but was unable to sleep. Being a southern rat, she was used to warm evenings, dewy grass, and her family all around her. Sleeping underground in such tight quarters, so cold this time of year, had made a good night's sleep difficult. On top of that, she could only marvel at the sounds coming from Texi. As small as Texi was, her snoring rivaled Stono's.

Still mulling over Vincent's story, his bizarre conversation with Billycan, and Juniper's secret involving this Lenore, Clover was restless as well. She didn't understand why her uncle would keep a secret from her. He'd always been honest with her, never treating her like a child, so why now? What could be so awful that he couldn't tell *her*, after all they'd been through? Maybe Vincent *was* acting overly suspicious, but still, Juniper was acting strange—mysterious, even.

Wide awake, the two girls decided to search for answers together. Clover patted the Council Chamber key she wore around her neck. "All the original maps and blueprints have been taken, Uncle and the others verified that, but maybe the traitor left behind a clue."

"Good idea," said Oleander.

Turning the corner to the Council Chamber, they suddenly stopped at the sound of quick footsteps just ahead of them. The tails of a red cloak whipped around a turn. "I think that was Oberon," whispered Clover.

"I remember him from the Council meeting—hard to forget that bright red cloak."

"What would he be doing here at this hour, and why did he bolt when he heard us? C'mon."

Trying to stay quiet, they stole along the corridor after Oberon, just missing the red tails of his cloak as he barreled around another corner. Before they knew it they'd reached the city square. Out of breath, they stopped running.

Already the square was filling with early risers and peddlers.

A small band of fiddlers was playing. Smells of tea, coffee, and fresh biscuits filled the air, along with many voices of Nightshade rats. Despite his vivid cloak, Oberon had melted into the crowd, gone.

Oleander, senses heightened, gaped at the expansive square, with its high ceiling and cobblestone floor, every sound echoing around her. Taking it all in, she suddenly felt very alone and very ill at ease. "What *is* this place?" she asked.

"This is our city square," Clover replied, "where everyone gathers for all sorts of things. Every city has one, even the human cities. It must seem very different from the swamp."

Oleander nodded silently. "Wait," she said suddenly, pointing at a pushcart, "over there. Isn't that Elvi talking to Oberon?"

"You're right," said Clover. "Elvi!"

Elvi spotted her and waved. Without even a nod in their direction, Oberon rushed out of sight, losing himself in the crowd. "Coming, darling," called Elvi as she took a small sack from the peddler's cart. She strolled over and smiled at the girls. "What are you two doing up so early? I thought the young liked to sleep the morning away."

"Between everything that's going on *and* Texi's snoring, neither of us could catch a wink," said Clover. "Elvi, wasn't that Oberon you were just talking to?"

"Yes, he was in a horrible rush," said Elvi evenly. "He didn't even have the good manners to say good-bye." She changed the subject. "Speaking of Texi's snoring, one afternoon she fell asleep in my quarters. I thought all of Nightshade would collapse from the noise!" She pulled down the hood of her cloak. "I was just buying some herbs." She held up a small burlap sack. "The earlier I come, the better pick I get—seems my tea has become a Council favorite."

Oleander studied Elvi's face. Elvi wasn't any older than Mother Gallo, but the sun had taken quite a toll on her skin, giving her wrinkles before her time. Strangely, it comforted her. Mannux had the same wrinkles, as did many of the grown swamp rats. Elvi had that distinctive Toscan accent, clearly marking her as being from someplace else—just like her. Oleander looked wide-eyed around the square again, unconvinced she could ever feel at home in such a hectic place.

Suddenly Clover thought of something. "Elvi, when you lived in the Catacombs, did you ever hear of someone called Lenore?"

"Lenore, Lenore," said Elvi, tapping her chin. "Such a pretty name, but no, I don't remember anyone called that. Why don't you ask Juniper or some of the other old guard? They all lived in the Combs far longer than I."

Clover looked guiltily at her feet. "Well...I was hoping you wouldn't mind if we kept this confidential."

"Oh, I see," replied Elvi, "our little secret."

"Would you mind?" Clover wanted to kick herself. Vincent still wasn't sure of Elvi's loyalties. Even though she didn't think Elvi could possibly be the traitor, she shouldn't be offering up information, either. "I just... I overheard the name by accident," she stammered. "Down by Billycan's cell."

"Your secret is safe with me," said Elvi. "I understand about young curiosity. Luckily for you, curiosity killed the cat and not the rat!" She laughed, but suddenly her demeanor changed. She became quite stern. "All the same, Clover, I must say I'm rather disappointed in you. Other than Cole and Juniper, you know everyone is forbidden to go near Billycan's cell. Whatever would make you do such a reckless thing after all you've been through with that wicked beast?"

"I... I..."

"It was *my* fault," blurted Oleander. "Clover was just protecting me. I wanted to see him for myself. I needed to see him locked up with my own eyes."

Elvi patted Oleander's shoulder. "You're a good rat, aren't you?" She nodded to Clover. "One who looks after her friends. We all owe you a debt of gratitude. Without you, Billycan would never have been captured. Nightshade would have been invaded. Many lives would have been lost, and power could have shifted back to the dark ways." She smiled at both girls. "Well, my darlings, I must be off. I have a meeting with your uncle, and I don't want to keep the Chief Citizen waiting, now, do I? And Oleander, why don't you stop by my quarters during lunch today?" She held up her sack of herbs. "I have fresh muffins, and I'll make us some tea. I'll tell you all about Tosca and you can tell me about the swamp."

"That would be nice," said Oleander. "Talking about home will do me good."

"Please give Uncle my best," said Clover.

Abruptly, Elvi's face drained of color. Her smile suddenly seemed forced. "Of course, dear, I will."

"Did you see that?" whispered Oleander as Elvi left.

"Yes, she looked worried."

"Wait," said Oleander, "look there." She pointed on the ground near the tea cart. A rolled-up parchment lay between two cobbles.

"Oberon must have dropped it," said Clover, staring at the parchment as they walked into Bostwick Hall. "It has the Council seal."

"What about Elvi?" asked Oleander. "She acted so odd when she left."

"I don't know anymore. All I know is I wish we'd never found this," said Clover, eying the parchment, her face a mask of misery. "That'll teach me to go sticking my nose into things."

"You have a right to know the truth," said Oleander. "My father and I learned the hard way that hiding the truth and ignoring things can lead to tragedy. You may not like what you've found, but now you can address it."

"But why would my uncle do such a thing—behind everyone's back, no less?" said Clover, pointing to the scroll. Her shoulders drooped. "Vincent was right."

They spotted Vincent and Carn waiting in line for breakfast. Clover anxiously motioned them over to a small table tucked away in a corner of Bostwick Hall.

"What is it?" asked Vincent as he and Carn set down their plates. "I was waiting in line for Lali's griddle cakes. She only serves them once a week."

"And today she has buttercream," added Carn. "This had better be good." He smiled at Oleander. She smiled back, but she looked troubled.

"You two look as though you've seen a ghost," said Vincent.

Clover whispered so softly that Vincent and Carn had to lean in close as she spoke. "We were by the Council Chamber this morning. Someone heard us coming and took off down the corridor. It was Oberon." She revealed the parchment, setting it before the boys. "We think he dropped this in the city square. It has the Council seal."

"Well, what is it?" asked Vincent. "And why do you both look so upset?"

"Because," said Clover, her voice starting to tremble, "Uncle lied to us. He lied to all of us. You were right."

"What?" said Carn, unrolling the parchment.

Carn and Vincent started reading. Their jaws dropped and their ears sagged.

Pushing away his plate, Vincent felt the key around his neck, the key to his and Victor's quarters that Juniper had given them years ago. "I don't believe this. I wasn't crazy to have suspected him. I knew he was hiding something. I thought—I *hoped*—it would be something inconsequential, something personal...but never this. How could he betray us like this—for Billycan?"

CHAPTER FOURTEEN
The Parchment

"T HERE HE IS," said Suttor, "over there."

By now all of the young Council members had wandered in to breakfast and been told about Juniper's secret.

They watched in silence as Oberon took his plate of food and strode through Bostwick Hall, proud as a peacock.

"He's as garish as that obnoxious red cloak," whispered Clover.

"How did he ever get elected to the Council?" asked Oleander.

"He's exceedingly bright," said Vincent, "that much I'll give him. He's brilliant with numbers and measurements, and with Nightshade growing so big, Virden needed help and said Oberon was the rat for the job. The library, the city square, they were engineered by Oberon."

"He engineered his election as well," added Victor. "By the time he was done gloating to the citizens about all his good works in Nightshade, you'd have thought he single-handedly built the place. Needless to say, he won by a landslide. He's as clever as a country cat."

"Which makes him as dangerous as one," said Carn, "especially when he has everyone's trust."

Picking up the parchment Clover and Oleander had shown them, Vincent nudged his brother. "C'mon, then."

Oberon had chosen the center seat at the center table in Bostwick Hall, surrounded by families known throughout Nightshade—families that would reelect him. He fawned and smooth-talked all the while, constantly praising Cole's wife, Lali, now Nightshade's head cook, calling her food a national treasure. Given his ever-growing waistline, Vincent was sure that was one thing Oberon was honest about.

The Nightshade brothers stood behind him for a moment, listening to his shameless flattery. "Oh, I do say, Lali's sausages are as good as or better than anything I ever had when I lived in that Topsider's gourmet restaurant. I told you all about that, didn't I? Why, Lali's a master chef.... What? You say you've gained weight, Missus Nelson? Why, you're as fit as a fiddle—still turning heads as a great-grandmother!"

Vincent cringed. Then he leaned down, tapped Oberon on the shoulder with the scroll, and grinned broadly.

Looking up from his meal, Oberon gave him a greasy smile. "Well, as I live and breathe, the famous Nightshade brothers, fighters for freedom and equality among all rats—the heroes of our time!"

The others smiled admiringly at them. Vincent nodded, but quickly turned to business. "Oberon, there is something my brother and I need to talk you about." He tapped him again on the shoulder, this time making sure he saw the scroll. "A Council matter, if you please."

Oberon's eyes widened. He dropped his fork to his plate, biting his lower lip, clearly panicked. "Oh...I see...," he said uneasily. He noticed all his supporters staring at him. Quickly his bravado returned. "A Council matter? Of course, I've always got time for *that*, young Nightshade." Trying not to look nervous, which succeeded only in making him look more nervous, Oberon awkwardly stood up, knocking the table with his belly in the process. "I'll be back momentarily. Duty calls, dear friends."

Glaring at him, Vincent motioned to the table where the other young Council members were seated. "This way, Councilman." Hesitantly, Oberon obeyed.

"I did *not* have prior knowledge of this, I swear," said Oberon, pushing the parchment away as if it were diseased. "I'm innocent. You must believe me."

Victor and Suttor sat on either side of him while Carn, Vincent, and the girls scowled at him from across the table.

"Then why did you run when you heard Oleander and me coming?" demanded Clover.

"I didn't know who it was. I only knew I had to get out of there, and fast. I was just leaving the Council Chamber. I heard footsteps coming and I was worried it was Juniper. He's been spending so much time going over the resident logs, anything and everything, to determine who the traitor might be. I reasoned it *must* be him, up and at it early once more. I didn't want him to see me. I was worried he'd guess what I was up to. The moment I heard footsteps I knew I had to run." He looked down guiltily at his belly. "At my size, there are few rats I could outrun without a good head start."

"Why were you looking for this? How did you know it even existed?" asked Vincent.

"I didn't know for certain. It was Cole and Juniper—their actions, their words. It was very suspicious. Those two are open books. It was easy to tell they were hiding something. That day before Council when everyone was gathering, Juniper was talking about the serum to Cole—its effects—and suddenly Cole shot him a look. I wouldn't have thought twice about it, but I *know* that look. I receive it from my wife quite often—a look that plainly means 'Shut up before you ruin everything.' When they saw me coming, Juniper said softly, 'It's safely in Brimstone.' Cole nodded, and the conversation quickly ended. I didn't think much of it at first, until I realized what Juniper meant."

"What did he mean? How did that lead you to this?" asked Carn.

"The Council has a map of Brimstone."

"Brimstone?" asked Victor.

"Yes, it's Trillium City's original name from the old days. The map was taken from Killdeer's War Room. We kept it because it shows the location of the old city museum. New maps do not. Rumor has it that early city documents are still kept in the old museum, an endless archive of history—perhaps *our* history—but we needed to worry about our future before delving into the past. In other words, Nightshade had to be built. So the map was stored in a closet with stacks of other old documents, piled randomly on a shelf, waiting for someone to organize them—a perfect hiding place, for who would want to go through mounds of dusty old papers? Long story short, I knew Juniper and Cole were keeping something from the rest of us. I remembered how they were so furtive when they mentioned Brimstone that day, so I went looking for whatever was 'safely in Brimstone.' I was determined to find out what it was before anyone else. Sure enough, that document lay hidden inside the folds of the Brimstone map. I thought I could use it to give me a leg up in the upcoming

Council election. If the Chief Citizen and Deputy Chief Citizen were keeping secrets from us and I was the one to publicly expose them, well, perhaps I'd be elected to a more important position. Maybe one day I'd be Chief Citizen."

"Perish the thought," muttered Carn.

Vincent shook his head. "So you had no idea what information the parchment contained before you stole it?"

"That's right," said Oberon. "And when I realized how scandalous it turned out to be, I decided to confront Juniper and Cole myself. This information could change everything for me, but even I have my limits. Think what you wish, but I don't want Billycan to be the reason I win an election. He's tainted—vile as a plague. That will never change."

"Well, Councilman, on that we can agree."

"Elvi, should you need him, the guard is just down the corridor. And the moment you feel uncomfortable, fearful in any way, or if something simply doesn't feel right, *please* leave immediately." Juniper took Elvi's paw. "I realize you want to do this, but you will not disappoint me if you've changed your mind. In fact, now that I've thought things through, perhaps this was not a good idea. I know your intentions are good, but—"

"No, Juniper. I'm going to do this," said Elvi confidently. She was so small she had to crane her neck to smile up at him. "Facing Billycan will be no different from what once was my daily life in Tosca. I talked my way out of many a tangle back there. Billycan is smart and cunning, you've all said so time and time again, but so am I. And I really do think I may learn valuable information. Sugar does catch more flies than vinegar. Maybe it works on rats, too."

"I'm so sorry for what you went through on that island. How

you survived, I'll never know. Sheer will, I suppose." He patted her paw. "Now Elvi, I promised Maddy I'd be back for a late breakfast with the children, but I think I should wait here for you instead. She'll understand."

"Please, Juniper, go be with your family. You've spent little time with them since your return."

"All right." Juniper unlocked the outer door to Billycan's cell. "Here," he said, taking the key from around his neck. "This unlocks the outer door, along with the door to his cell, so guard it well. Be sure to lock up tight when you leave. You can return this tonight at Council." He gave her one last look, his expression a mix of admiration and unease.

Elvi slipped inside.

Except for a small candle, the cell was dark. Elvi's heart began to race as the scent of the white rat hit her nostrils. She wasn't quite sure if it was fear or just nerves, but it was hard to concentrate.

Suddenly something moved in the back of the cell. She saw two long, white feet descend to the ground as a darkened figure arose from the bed.

"Juniper?" said a voice. "Is that you?"

Frozen in place, Elvi could not answer.

The white rat approached. "Oh," he said, taken aback by the sight of her. He cocked his head curiously and stared fixedly at her. "Who are you?"

"I—I'm Elvi."

Smiling politely, Billycan moved closer. He held the bars. "That's a pretty name," he said. "Elvi, if you please, there's a torch over there. Juniper keeps matches near it." He pointed to the door. "Would you mind?"

"Ah—y-yes," stammered Elvi, backing up toward the torch affixed to the wall. Shakily she picked up a match and lit it. The room filled with dim light and shadows, highlighting Billycan's elongated features.

She expected to see a monster, fierce eyes of shifting reds and a maniacal grin of yellowed teeth. Instead she beheld a creature very different from what she'd imagined. The demented leer was instead a calm and hopeful smile, and his eyes had a gentle quality about them—almost kind.

"That's better," he said, stepping back so that he could take a look at her. "You're a rather small thing, aren't you? A friend of mine, someone I knew back when I was little, was small like you."

Regaining her confidence, she regarded Billycan's wounds. She spoke softly. "What happened to you?"

"I was gouged by a wild boar, of all things. Can you imagine? Juniper says it's a wonder I'm alive."

"Indeed," said Elvi. "From what I've heard, no one's too surprised you're still alive. In fact, many think you have supernatural powers."

Taking a step closer, Billycan chuckled. "Powers, me?" He looked around the cell. "If I had any sort of powers I wouldn't be in here, would I?" He changed the subject. "Your voice . . . it's unusual. Where are you from?"

"I'm from very far away. A place called Tosca. Have you heard of it?"

Shaking his head, Billycan sighed. "No. It does not sound familiar. But you . . ." He leaned toward her, sticking his snout through a gap between the bars. "I . . . I know you." He cocked his head. "I have no idea how I know you, but your face is familiar."

"I doubt very much you know me," replied Elvi evenly. "Look at me again, closely. Concentrate on my face."

Billycan stared into her eyes. They were a beautiful black, sloped like diamonds. He bowed his head, busying himself with his claws, clearly uncomfortable with her gaze. "Maybe I'm wrong. In my head, one face seems to blend into the next. I'm not quite sure of anything."

Pulling a stool up to the bars, Elvi took a seat before him.

"Aren't you afraid of me?" asked Billycan. If he wanted to, he could reach out and grab her at any moment.

"From what I've been told, there is no longer a reason to fear you, but I've an inkling you know far better than others. So you tell me. *Should* I fear you? I hope that's not the case."

"It seems there was a time in my life when there was some good in me." He smiled. "Or perhaps I simply hadn't become my true self. I'm not sure who I am right now, or even who I need to be."

Elvi tapped her head. "You have knowledge. I think deep inside, you know who you are—you just need to remember. It's all locked away under layers of memories. If you concentrate, you can remember everything." She lowered her voice to a whisper. "Close your eyes and think back, Billycan. Unmask your identity. Go back to the swamp. Start there. Why were you there? With whom were you working?"

Billycan closed his eyes, going over the parts he *had* remembered. Three years in the swamp, he thought. It had all been so easy…the escape, the night Killdeer died…the beginning of his plan to attack Nightshade and claim it for his own…the trips back to Trillium to meet his informant, to collect the stolen blueprints and maps that showed him every inch of Nightshade City.

"Billycan, do you remember who helped you? Please, tell me if you know anything at all." She spoke urgently. "I must know. It could change everything."

Grasping the bars tightly, Billycan opened his eyes. He remembered! Everything flooded back, not just bits and pieces. There was no longer any doubt in his mind. He knew the conspirator. He knew all about little Julius. And with his memories, his spirit reawakened. He needed to act. If he wanted something, he'd have to take it by force. Once again Dorf was right, and this time the stakes were higher than ever.

His chest heaving, Billycan was transformed, no longer the pitiful excuse for a rat he'd been since Juniper injected him with the serum. He knew what he had to do. His body began to shake as his eyes narrowed, their calm hue shifting to red slashes. He homed in on the little gray rat before him. He *did* know her!

Elvi saw recognition dawn on Billycan, and then a look she'd seen many times. It was the look Toscan creatures had given her seconds before they attacked. She had come prepared, though. Used to danger, she always came prepared.

Swiftly jumping from her stool, Elvi backed away from him. She reached for the dagger hidden in her cloak and doused the light.

The entire Belancort clan sat at the table having a late breakfast of Juniper's famous bitonberry porridge. It was not famous because it was delicious, but because it was the one dish Juniper could create without burning down the Belancort quarters.

"Eat up, now," said Mother Gallo to Julius as she wiped porridge form Nomi's whiskers and nose. Nomi sneezed in response. "If you want to be big and strong like your brothers and father, you must *eat*."

Julius pushed his porridge around with his spoon, a gloomy expression on his face. "I'm just not hungry, Mother," he said.

"Not hungry," said Juniper. "But you're *always* hungry. What's the matter?"

"Why hasn't Texi come by?" asked Julius, staring into his bowl. "Doesn't she like us anymore?"

"It *is* always more fun when she's here," added Hob.

Juniper and Mother Gallo looked around the table at the boys. Even Tuk, the oldest, seemed glum.

"So you're all a bit lonely without your Texi, are you?" asked Juniper. "Hob's right. It *is* a little lackluster without her cheery face round here, isn't it?" They all nodded.

"Is this about the other night?" asked Tuk. "Is she upset with me because I wouldn't let her take Julius for a walk?"

"Oh, no, dear," said Mother Gallo. "She's just been a little out of sorts lately, but she's doing much better now."

"Is she mad at *me*?" asked Julius. He'd seen Texi nearly every day of his life. Even a few days without her felt like weeks.

Mother Gallo leaned toward her youngest son. "My dear, Texi could never be mad at you. She loves you very much. How about this. Papa is meeting with some of the Council later today, and I was going to stop by and visit with Lali, but what if instead I drop Nomi off to play with Lali and her boys and you and I go to the library? Gage and Hob need to run off to their lessons, but Tuk has some extra time before his first lecture. He can tell Texi, and maybe if she's not too busy she can meet us there." She smiled at the others. "You and I can spend the whole day with her, and then tonight we can all have supper together. Tuk, would you mind asking her, darling?"

"No, old Professor Brummell's always tardy for first bell anyway," said Tuk.

"I'm sure Texi will be happy to join us," Mother Gallo told Julius. "And you know, it's Fairytale Day at the library. Longtooth will be reading one of her favorite stories to a group of children just your age. I'm sure she'd love to have you and Texi there, too. Now, does that sound nice to you?"

Julius smiled bashfully into his porridge and nodded.

"Good," said Mother Gallo. "It's all settled, then."

CHAPTER FIFTEEN
A Well-Timed Visit

OLEANDER HESITATED BEFORE ELVI'S DOOR.

Knocking softly, she called from the corridor, "Elvi, it's Oleander. May I come in? I thought I'd take you up on your invitation." The door creaked partially open, and she peeked in. "Elvi?"

A muted light flickered from the back of the room. Oleander went inside. "Elvi," she called again. Much of the furniture was draped in exotic textiles, fiery reds and brilliant blues, all half in shadow, only a dim candle lighting the room. Outlandish masks and foreign symbols hung from the walls and ceiling, things from Tosca. Oleander looked around nervously, the bizarre décor making her uneasy. It reminded her of the horrible things the humans had left in the manor's attic, back in the swamp.

Something shook above her head, a harsh flapping of wings. Oleander gasped, nearly jumping from her skin. She snatched the candle off the table and held it up to the darkness. A cage hung from the ceiling. A blue moth stared at her from inside. Moths were sweet creatures. "Why, hello, there," said Oleander. She laughed softly, embarrassed by her reaction. "I'm afraid we scared the life out of each other, didn't we, my pretty friend?"

The blue moth kept its eyes trained on her, cautiously moving forward on its perch. "It's all right," said Oleander soothingly. "I would never hurt you. You remind me of the dragonflies in the swamp, beautiful and quite charming. I wish you could talk. Maybe you could tell me where your mistress went."

"Why, she's right here," said a voice from the door.

"Oh!" blurted Oleander, spinning around. The moth flapped agitatedly. "Elvi, there you are. Your door was ajar. I hope you don't mind—"

"Not at all, darling. Not at all," said Elvi welcomingly. "I hope I didn't frighten you. I was just returning from a visit with Juniper. Please, have a seat while I light a fire and muster up some tea—always so very cold in Trillium. How I long for Tosca's warmth, as I'm sure you do for the swamp's." Elvi lit a match. The blue moth jumped about his cage, eager to get at the flame. "I see you've met Mol, my little companion."

"Yes," said Oleander, looking up at the moth as she took her seat. "He's fascinating."

"He's as foolish as he is stunning," laughed Elvi. "I must keep him locked up so he won't fly into the fireplace, silly creature. Mol nearly singed his wings off the last time I let him flutter about." As the fire started to blaze, Elvi took a seat across from Oleander. "Now then, I'm so glad you came to see me. It will be good for us to talk. We're quite alike, you and I."

"I feel the same way. Even just talking about the warm climate makes me feel closer to home."

"It's funny," said Elvi. "When I first arrived in Tosca I loathed the hot sun, the sticky air. It was enough to make me sick! And now I miss it so. I'm sure you'll be returning to the swamp soon enough, but are you homesick, darling?"

"I've never been away from my family. It's been harder than I thought it would be, especially with everything that the horde went through with Billycan. They trusted him and he broke their hearts. It was hard for them to understand—still is."

"Trust is a hard thing to come by, it seems. In Tosca I could trust no one but myself. To survive I had to be hard, cruel. It was the only way to get by in such a lethal place." The teapot whistled.

"Elvi, if you don't mind my asking, how did all the adult rats die on the boat? It must have been so awful for you. You said you were around my age."

Elvi sighed wearily as she poured them each a cup of tea. "It was ghastly—a scene I will never forget. I felt guilty about it for years, being the sole survivor. I was not feeling well that day—seasick. The constant churning and swaying of the boat, my innards couldn't take it. Someone had found a can of fish that had rolled under a shelf in the small pantry of the boat's galley. One of the males had managed to open the can with a screwdriver, poking a hole and prying the lid off. Everyone rejoiced, so happy for food after three days with nothing, but they were only celebrating their demise. They quickly fell deathly ill."

"The fish had gone bad," said Oleander.

"Precisely," said Elvi. "They were poisoned."

"And you were too unwell to eat."

"Yes, my weak stomach saved my life."

"How helpless and alone you must have felt."

"And in a way, alone ever since. The Toscan rats are not like us. They are primitive, uncultured."

"How did you survive? How did you get them to accept you?"

Elvi smiled. "Let's just say I became very good at pretending to be someone else." She gazed up at Mol, still captivated by the flames. "When those rats hustled me onto the boat bound for Tosca, I was terrified. I was being taken away from everything I knew. It was as though my whole childhood was erased and my new life—a most unkind existence—had begun. I shall never forgive those rats who took me," she said bitterly.

"But Elvi, I thought the rats who took you on the boat were only trying to rescue you from the flood. Clover said they were kind citizens who kept you from drowning."

"I could have taken care of myself. I know those rats meant no harm, but they should have left me alone. I learned long ago, from someone I once admired, that in order to survive, to get what you want, *you* must take it. No one else will do it for you." She smiled weakly. "I suppose I'm trying to say that had they not taken me, I would have survived on my own. I would never have had to leave Trillium."

"I understand how you must have felt. My father can be overprotective at times. He needs to know that having grown up in the swamp, with all its dangers, I can take care of myself. Even with Carn and the others around me, he didn't want me to come here. He's still worried about Billycan."

"I'm quite sure you won't need to worry about him any longer."

"Well, I'm glad for that." Oleander took another sip of tea, glad for the warmth it offered. "A flood, poisoned rats, and surviving in the jungle—what a life you've led. You must have learned so much."

Setting down her tea, Elvi hid her paws in the sleeves of her cloak and curled her feet up under her on the chair. "Yes, I've learned plenty in my day. By the way, how are you enjoying your tea, dear?" Elvi sat contentedly, a gentle smile on her face. "It's a very special recipe. You're the first one to try it in several years."

"It's delicious," said Oleander. The room went out of focus for a moment, and she suddenly felt very hot. She shook her head, unsure of what was happening. "What do you call thi…th…" Oleander tried to keep talking, but the only sound to leave her mouth was a sickly gasp. She felt dizzy, and coughed. Her head abruptly fell back, hitting the chair. Her whole body went slack. Mol hopped fretfully on his perch as her teacup dropped from her paw and burst into pieces on the floor.

"Oh, darling," said Elvi coolly. "Are you all right? What do I call *this*? Is that what you were trying to spit out? Well, here one would call the flower sweet pea, quite a nice, friendly ring to it, no? In Tosca we call it something entirely different—devil's seed. Much more appropriate."

Oleander panted. Blood rushed to her head, the sound flooding her ears as she realized Elvi had poisoned her. Why?

"Now, now, you must not panic." Elvi stood up and dumped her cup of untouched tea back into the pot. "You see, living so long in the jungle, I learned a thing or two about poisons. I learned what different herbs can do. Which ones heal"—she grinned at the broken teacup—"and which ones harm. It's quite a science. I practiced on the creatures of Tosca for years." She laughed. "They called me a sorceress—silly beasts. Some flowers and herbs cause instant death, while others make you linger on for days in abject agony; and then there are others that leave you paralyzed, unable to move even the tip of your tail."

Able to move only her eyes, Oleander looked toward the door. Under the gap she could see the shadows of feet walking by. If only they knew she was trapped. If only she could move or scream. If only she could yell out that Elvi was the traitor!

Elvi grabbed Oleander's chin and squeezed it hard. "You all should have left well enough alone back in the swamp," she said angrily. Then, her voice syrupy sweet once more, she said, "I have an errand to run now. Why don't you stay here and wait for me?"

Her cheeks wet with tears, Oleander closed her eyes. She thought of Mannux. He'd feel responsible for letting her come to Nightshade. And poor Thicket and Stono, how they'd mourn her. She thought of Carn and what might have been.

"Hush!" hissed Elvi, glaring up at Mol as he flapped in his cage. "You with your constant flailing, always interrupting my every thought!" Mol hushed.

Elvi got up from her chair and patted Oleander's head. "Such a pretty rat," she purred, and as her cloak moved, Oleander spotted a silver dagger strapped to Elvi's leg.

Oleander's lungs felt like they were on fire and her heart raced as if it might burst. Her eyelids fluttered and her head fell to her chest. She let out one last little groan.

"Poor little dear," said Elvi, pushing Oleander's head back against the chair. She went to the mirror. Her sloping black eyes blinked back at her. She threw the black hood of her cloak over her head. She smiled at her reflection, and her face grew dark. "Don't worry. You won't remember a thing."

The outer door to Billycan's shadowy cell softly closed. He jumped to his feet. He knew what was coming.

"Where are you, little one?" asked Billycan in the dark. "I knew you'd be back. Business to take care of, I suspect—rats like us always have business to attend to. I can hear you breathing on the other side of the bars. I can smell you. Come out, come out, wherever you are. I have no time for your games today. You like games, don't you? You always did—always will." A laugh came from the other side of the bars. "How clever you are. You've fooled everyone. But for how long, my dear? It's only a matter of time now before they figure you out. They've been too wrapped up in me, but that's about to come to an end."

The laugh broke out again, but this time from the back wall of Billycan's cell. He whipped around. "Show yourself, my dear," he said. "Billycan deserves to see the face of his attacker."

Suddenly the rat came at him. Elvi wailed and screamed as she slashed at him with the knife. Billycan easily dodged her. Even after all this time he knew how she fought, how she wielded a knife.

"You will not ruin my plans!" she wailed as she took another swipe. "I've waited too long for this moment!"

Lunging forward, Billycan grabbed her by the neck, slamming her against the wall. "Nor will you ruin mine!" She pushed against his chest with her feet and dug her claws into his wounded shoulder. He howled in pain, dropping her. "Ah, I see you've learned a few tricks in Tosca. How very sly of you!"

"Don't you dare mention Tosca," she said, panting in the shadows. "You have no idea of the horror I suffered!"

Billycan laughed riotously. "Suffered? Really, now, you expect me to believe that? Do you take me for bighearted Juniper, so easily swayed by your kind acts and gentle nature?" He sighed. "You really are something, aren't you?"

Her breathing quickening, Elvi moved in. "Don't you dare laugh at me. No *one* laughs at me!"

Billycan's voice dropped to a conspiratorial whisper. "Then let's get on with it, Elvi... or do you prefer your real name?"

With that, Elvi screeched wildly. She ran at him with the dagger. Instinctively Billycan dodged right, remembering that was the side she always came at first. Suddenly a stabbing pain jolted through him. He gagged. His chest burned as she pulled the dagger from it. He reached for her, grabbing at her cloak.

Elvi stood proudly before him as his body crumpled to the floor. "What a pity," she whispered. "You left me no choice, Billycan." She produced a match, striking it on a bar of the cell. With one paw she reached for Billycan's chin and held it up to the light.

Clutching his chest, Billycan looked at her. He smiled weakly. "Ah, but you see, you always have a choice." He coughed, swallowing a mouthful of blood. "You chose yourself."

His head dropped to the ground.

Elvi rose to her feet. "I will *always* choose myself."

CHAPTER SIXTEEN
Born on Hallowtide

EXCEPT FOR LONGTOOTH READING ALOUD and the restless shuffle of little rats waiting to hear what happened next, the library, even though it was brimming with children, was quiet. Mother Gallo and Julius sat on the floor in the very back of the children's section, scarcely able to see Longtooth's gnarled ears.

The former High Cook was now a caregiver to little ones and Head Librarian at the Nightshade Library. Fall was upon them and Pennies-or-Pranking would soon begin Topside, so she decided to read her favorite Hallowtide tale. She rocked steadily in her chair, grinning at the children as she read about a coven of wicked witches, cackling with every word. "I'll get you, you unruly brats! Just you wait!" she shouted.

Mother Gallo whispered in Julius's ear. "Sweetheart, why don't I get you some juice and cookies? Maybe I can find Texi somewhere in the crowd." Julius nodded silently, not wanting to miss a word of Longtooth's story.

Mother Gallo rose to her feet. She turned and smiled at her son, so content, then headed past rows of books and off to the lobby, where juice and cookies had been set out for the afternoon guests.

Julius's neck bristled. Someone gently brushed his shoulder with a claw, sending goose bumps down his spine.

He turned to look, and gasped.

Juniper sat in the Council Chamber with only the original members, the four rats who'd seen him through thick and thin and everything in between. He had finally told them he'd been hiding the truth from them. He could stand it no longer.

Virden shook his head, incredulous. "But *why* didn't you tell us? You know you can trust us. We've all been together since we were children." Ragan and Ulrich nodded in agreement.

"I didn't want to hide anything. I didn't know how you'd react. I haven't even told Maddy yet. I don't know if she'll ever be able to look at me the same again."

"Well, you don't give us too much credit, now, do you?"

"You're right and I'm sorry, but please understand, it had nothing to do with trust. I trust you all with my life and that of my family. It was something I had to come to terms with in my own time. It took all I had within me to reveal the truth to Cole. He was with me just days after we received the report from Dresden about Billycan's whereabouts. The timing of the news—coming so soon after Cole and I had learned about the serum—seemed as though it was brought to us by the Saints."

"How did you learn about the serum?" asked Ragan.

"One night Cole and I were Topside in a rundown building inside City Hall. We'd been hunting for food. It was storming hard and we'd snuck in for shelter. There was a small television on at the front desk, left on by a guard, I suppose. I wouldn't have given it a second thought, but it was a news report about Prince Laboratories."

"And . . . ," said Ulrich impatiently.

"The reporter said that Prince had lost a class-action lawsuit, forcing it to dole out millions of dollars to the victims of the Serena scandal."

"But what does that matter?"

"Well, not only did Prince have to pay the victims, but it would have to provide each victim with a dose of the remedy—a new drug called Cortexa, formulated to reverse the psychotic and violent effects of Serena."

"In other words," said Cole, "a cure for Billycan—provided, of course, he wasn't simply born bad."

"Yes, a cure. Serena is the drug they were testing on Billycan. It was supposed to help the humans battle depression, but instead it turned them into heartless killers, exactly like Billycan! Cortexa was originally formulated at Prince as a truth serum—something the humans' military could use against its enemies—but then they discovered Cortexa did much more than that. It reversed Serena's violent effects. I thought if we could acquire the remedy, this Cortexa, we could *stop* Billycan once and for all. Not only could we find out if he had anyone working with him, but we could change him—*cure* him—at the same time holding true to our sacred oath to never kill another rat. Nightshade would be secure once and for all."

The others sat in silence for a moment. Finally Ragan said, "Do you think the serum is working? Has he truly changed?"

"Everything about him is different—his mannerisms, his eyes, his voice—he doesn't even talk like himself anymore. Remember that vexing way he used to speak, always referring to himself as if he were talking about someone else, Billycan this and Billycan that? It's gone! It's as though the white rat we knew and hated has vanished."

"How can you be so sure?" asked Ulrich. "He could be feigning all of it, every action forced and purposeful."

"It's true. He could be that same evil creature—born bad, as Cole put it—but I just don't think it's possible, not seeing him now."

"But Juniper, I worry your judgment may be clouded," said Cole. "You *want* to believe." The others nodded in agreement.

"What about the young ones?" asked Virden. "How are they to handle this? Vincent, Victor, Carn—he took their families away, assassinated them. How are they to cope with such news?"

"I've been thinking about that since all of this began. Many times I've thought it best they never know."

There was a sudden pounding at the door. The fist slammed the door so vehemently Juniper thought it might split the timber. "Who the devil—"

The door suddenly swung open, nearly ripped from its hinges. Vincent, followed by all the young Council members, stormed into the chamber.

Everyone stood up.

"Vincent!" barked Juniper furiously. "What's the meaning of this?"

Enraged, Vincent threw the parchment on the table right in front of Juniper. "What's the meaning of *this*?" he demanded.

Juniper's gaze locked on Vincent's. He was clearly angry, but his eyes were filled with pain. "How could you lie to us all this time? You've been trying to *cure* him? What's to cure, Juniper? He's evil, wicked. He killed my family! Carn's family—right in front of his eyes, no less! What did you think this would accomplish? Tell me! You owe me." He looked back at his friends. "You owe us *all!*"

Juniper stayed silent.

"Uncle," said Clover in a trembling voice, "make us understand . . . *please*."

Studying all the young, broken faces before him, Juniper finally spoke. "I will be forever sorry for my decision on this matter, but I feared just such a reaction. Even three years free from the grasp of Killdeer's High Ministry, your wounds are still raw. With that in mind, I made the reasonable choice."

Vincent clenched his jaw and stood rigidly before Juniper. "Or perhaps you were afraid that had you put this brilliant plan to a vote at Council—as you should have—you would have lost! I implored you to eliminate Billycan. That was the *reasonable* choice! I don't care about our oath never to kill another. This is different, far different—he's a monster! Death is what he deserves! Why do you care so much about him? Even if your precious cure—this Cortexa—works and he starts acting like a normal rat, he'll only want his son back. He'll try to take Julius from you! And what if this cure is temporary? What if it doesn't last? What then?"

"Vincent, whatever happens with Billycan, he *will* have to answer for his crimes. He will not lay a claw on Julius, or anyone else for that matter. Now, I realize how disturbing this must be, but—"

Vincent cut him off. "But what, Juniper? But your need to uphold your silly oath outweighs the value of our lives? Or is Billycan just more important to you now? You put Carn in great danger—a rat who has been nothing but loyal to you and every member of this Council. He could have been killed by the horde—or by Billycan himself! You were just lucky that things turned out the way they did! Had something happened to him, had the horde or Billycan ripped him to shreds, his blood would have been on your claws alone!"

"Vincent!" roared Juniper. "Need I remind you, that oath was one we all took willingly, including you, young rat!"

"It doesn't matter anymore! You put Carn in peril for selfish reasons!" barked Vincent defiantly. "We could have captured Billy-can and imprisoned him for life along with his Kill Army majors. If he was killed in the attempt, so be it! Those are the risks of war. But no, we had to take him alive. I see now that was because you wanted to cure him! You act as though you care more for Billycan—the White Assassin himself—than any of us! What about my father? What about Julius Nightshade, your son's namesake—this city's name-sake? Billycan killed him—*your* friend! Do you no longer care about my father? Is he nothing to you now?"

Juniper seethed with anger, every word making him more incensed. "Why, you impudent little—"

"And what of your brother, Barcus?" continued Vincent. "Don't you have any respect for his memory? Barcus may be dead, but he's still your brother—your own flesh and blood!"

Juniper growled, looking balefully up at the ceiling. He grabbed the sides of his head, yanking at his hair in frustration. "Vincent," he snarled, "Billycan *is* my flesh and blood! He *is* my brother!"

Everyone gasped, then silence filled the room.

Juniper exhaled heavily, relieved to finally say the words out loud. The younger rats all glanced worriedly at each other. Cole stood next to Juniper and set a paw on his shoulder.

Vincent cocked his head and spoke softly. "Juniper, what are you saying? How can Billycan possibly be your brother?" He took a step closer. "Are you sure you're feeling all right? It's been a rough road, these past few weeks. The strain can plays tricks on the mind."

"Don't give me that look," said Juniper, shaking his head at Vin-cent and the rest of young Council members, who looked back at him as though he were out of his mind. "I'm not crazy. Billycan, the High Collector, the White Assassin—*whatever* you wish to call him—he *is* my brother. My half brother."

Cole cleared his throat. "Juniper's mother was briefly captured by a Topside lab. The lab personnel bred her with one of the albinos. Billycan was the result of that union. The rest of her litter were not strong enough to survive the toxic injections. She escaped the lab during a break-in and returned to the Combs alone. She married and had her children, Barcus and then Juniper. She died without ever finding out what happened to her first son."

"And for that I'm glad," said Juniper. "To know what he'd become...she'd only have blamed herself."

"How long have you known this?" asked Victor.

"I figured it out shortly after we defeated the High Ministry."

"Lenore," said Clover, making the connection. "She's the one that Billycan mentioned. Lenore was your mother?"

"Yes," said Juniper, "your grandmother, whom you never had the pleasure of meeting." He gave her a stern look. "I'm not even going to ask how you got that information. I don't think I'd like the answer, now, would I?" He gave her a small smile. "You would have liked her."

"Papa always called her Mama Nori," said Clover.

"Yes, that's what everyone called her around the Combs. Nori was short for Lenore."

"Juniper," said Vincent, "even if all this is true, how does it change anything? Brother or not, he tried to murder you. He's twisted and depraved. You're disfigured, missing an eye, because of him—your *brother*."

"It changes nothing," said Juniper. "He *is* my brother. I must help him or die trying, no matter what the cost to me. It would go against everything in me to leave my brother forever thinking he's some monster he was not born to be. If there's a chance to bring him back to us, with a heart, a soul, I *will* do it. I must. But hear me now: brother or not, he will have to answer for every ounce of suffering he has brought upon us."

196

Juniper took Victor by the shoulders, steering him face-to-face with Vincent. "If Victor, *your* brother, changed for the worse—better yet, if something beyond his control changed him for the worse, turning him into a fiend like Billycan—could you kill him for his sins?"

Vincent looked down at the ground, ashamed. "No," he said softly, "I could never do that. It's just hard to imagine Billycan being anything but..." Vincent couldn't finish his thought, still flummoxed at the idea of it all.

"Uncle, if Billycan really was altered by those drugs, made violent and malicious like the Topsiders were, then what's a fair punishment for his crimes? How can we hold him responsible?" Clover shook her head, just as confused as Vincent.

Vincent sat down next to Juniper. "But after all he's done, how can we not?"

Juniper slumped wearily into his chair. "Billycan is the cause of many tragedies in our world, the demise of many families, pain that will never go away. I pride our city on hope, the hope of staying *above* the fray. To kill only when crucial to our own survival, to help rats in need. That's what Nightshade City is based upon—how we came about. Vincent, I suppose you're right in some ways; maybe I do take our oath too far. I just wonder... I don't think creatures are born evil. That answer is simply too easy. I do believe, though, in the possibility of redemption."

Carn furrowed his brow, still skeptical of the earlier declaration. "Juniper, I don't wish to argue your claim, but I'd be foolish if I didn't ask how you came to learn he was your brother. How can you be so sure it's true? Where is your *evidence*?"

"That's a fair question," said Juniper, "Shortly after we brought Clover to Nightshade, she gave me a few things she thought Barcus would have wanted me to have, among them a metal tag. It belonged to our mother from her time in the lab. On the front of the tag was etched the number 111 and the word 'mother.' On the back of the tag it read 'Prince Laboratories' and the date, October 31.

"On her deathbed, long before Kildeer came into power, my mother had told me about her time in the lab, letting me know the ugly truth of what happened there but never revealing that any of her litter had survived. She was a bit incoherent at the end, in and out of consciousness, but she kept mumbling about a white rat in the lab, whose cage was right across from hers—number 111. She said she'd looked at that rat every day, watching him grow from a fragile infant into the oversized rat he became, but never being close enough to speak a word to him. She kept saying, 'My son, my son.' She said, 'He's lost Topside. You must find him!'"

"That still doesn't mean he's your brother," said Vincent. "You said it yourself—your mother was very ill, confused. If she was losing her grip on reality, she could have been talking about any number of rats—even you or Barcus. Back in the Combs, when Victor and I lost our guardian, Missus Cromwell, she was like that. All her thoughts were jumbled, Juniper. She had everything mixed up. Maybe that's what happened to your mother."

"My boy, I've wished many times for that to be the case, but facts ring louder than mere wishes. When Billycan attacked me all those years ago—you all know the story—I grabbed hold of that bony alabaster throat, trying to squeeze the life out of it. In the process I ripped off his lab tag, still attached to his neck. I kept it all this time, a sort of souvenir—something to keep me going after the attack, signifying who the citizens of the Catacombs were up against and why it was so important that Billycan be defeated."

"It's true," said Cole. "When we pulled Juniper from the scene, bloody mess that he was, he insisted we take the tag."

"I still have it, a grim reminder of how lucky I was to still be alive, disfigured or not. Billycan's tag, number 111, with the word 'offspring' etched along the bottom. On the other side, 'Prince Laboratories, October 31.' My mother's and Billycan's tags are identical—mother and offspring, both numbered 111, both dated October 31. Without a shred of doubt, Billycan is my brother—born on Hallowtide, no less."

Stunned, Clover suddenly looked at Juniper. "This means Billycan is my...uncle."

Smiling weakly, Juniper nodded. "It also means little Julius is really a blood member of our family." He leaned his head back, resting it on the chair, and looked up at the ceiling. "There was one night, back in the Combs, when I thought I'd lost you forever, that I would be the sole survivor of the Belancort Clan. Now I have a daughter, a brother, and a nephew—and of course I have you."

Clover took a seat at the table. "I don't know how to feel about this, Uncle." She shook her head. "Billycan...family?"

Juniper rested a paw on Clover's. "In the months I've been carrying this information, I've asked myself over and over—how can any of this be? How could the Saints do this to us, after all we've been through? But then it occurred to me, it is not for us to ask why. They have their reasons. Perhaps we'll learn them in the future."

"Perhaps," said Clover, "but what about now?"

"Now we—"

"Juniper!" screamed a voice from down the corridor. "Juniper, he's *gone!*"

"Maddy?" called Juniper, leaping up from his chair.

Clutching Nomi in her arms, Mother Gallo and Lali raced into the chamber. "Juniper, he's gone!" she shouted once more.

"Who's gone?"

"Julius," she said, choking out his name. "He's vanished! We've looked everywhere. He went missing during Longtooth's reading at the library—we've been looking ever since! All the children and parents helped us search. He's nowhere to be found!"

"We searched high and low," said Lali. "We scoured the library, Texi's quarters, your quarters, the city square, everywhere."

"All right," said Juniper, trying to keep his composure. "We'll break into groups. Lali, please take Maddy and Nomi back to our quarters. He may have just wandered off for a while. You know how he is, always wanting to explore. He probably lost track of time. He could be sitting at home as we speak, wondering where *we* are. Cole, Virden, you come with me, we'll search Nightshade Passage. Ragan and Ulrich, you take Bostwick Hall." He ran an uneasy paw down his face. He looked at the younger rats. "Vincent, you and the others search everywhere else—any place you can think of. Pound on every door, call his name down every corridor. Enlist everyone in sight to aid in the search."

"Wait," said Carn. "Where is Oleander?" With all the excitement, he'd only just realized she hadn't arrived yet. "She was supposed to meet us here. Juniper, she knew why we were coming to see you—about the Cortexa. She should have been here."

"She left to have tea with Elvi," said Clover, "to talk about their homelands, but she said she'd be gone only a short while. Maybe Julius is there! You know how close Texi and Elvi are! Maybe Julius thought Texi would be there."

Sighing with relief, Mother Gallo put her paw over her heart. "Oh, Clover, I didn't even think of that!"

"Okay, then," said Juniper. "Children, start the search there. Meet us back at Nightshade Passage in exactly one hour's time—or the moment you find them."

Oleander awoke to a soft tapping on her cheek. "Oleander? Oleander, dear, it's time to wake up. It seems you fell asleep while I was telling you about Tosca." Elvi chuckled. "I must say, I thought I was a better storyteller than that!"

"Oleander woke with a jolt. "What?" she said. "I—I fell asleep?"

"Why, yes, dear. You've been asleep for a few minutes. Are you sure you're all right? I was just telling you how I landed in Tosca, and you nodded off. Don't you remember?" Oleander shook her head. "You looked so peaceful. I let you rest while I made some more tea. Perhaps you're under the weather." Elvi set a paw on Oleander's forehead. "After I came here from Tosca, I found myself sick often. I think the climate change is what did it. And you, coming from that hot, humid swamp. It only makes sense that you could have taken ill from Nightshade's drafty corridors."

Slowly, Oleander lifted her head. Everything felt fuzzy. "Now that you mention it, I really don't feel like myself." She looked around the room. "Are you sure it was only for a few minutes? It feels much longer."

"Some of my deepest sleeps happen when I've been out for only a few moments. I wake up in such an awful haze. It seems like I've been asleep for hours."

"Yes, that's exactly how it feels." Oleander rubbed her brow. "Maybe I'm just exhausted from the journey from the swamp—not to mention Texi's snoring. I woke up so early this morning, but still, even tired, I never sleep during the day." She smiled. "How rude you must think me. I was so interested in your story, too. I don't know what came over me. I feel so silly."

"You've nothing to feel silly for, darling, as long as you're all right."

Oleander stood and stretched. Her muscles were sore and her head ached. Elvi was right. She *must* be getting sick. She looked at the fire, still blazing, the same as when Elvi set it earlier. Surely if she'd been asleep longer than a few minutes, the fire would have died down. Everything seemed so foggy. She could barely remember their conversation . . . something about the rats taking Elvi onto the boat, that was all she recalled. She supposed it didn't matter. She and Elvi could talk another time. Besides, she should leave—they were going to confront Juniper about the document they'd found. "Elvi, I really should go. I'm supposed to meet Clover back at her quarters."

"But we've barely had a chance to talk. I want to hear about the swamp and your family."

"I know, but I made a promise to be—"

"Elvi," called Vincent, banging on the door. "We're looking for Julius. He's gone missing from the library. We thought maybe he'd come to see you."

Oleander and Elvi looked at each other. Elvi raced for the door. "Vincent," she said, wrenching it open. "He hasn't been here. I have no idea where the poor dear could be."

"We've been here since lunchtime," said Oleander. "Where else might he have gone?"

"We don't know," said Carn, entering the room with the others. "No sign of him anywhere."

"Oh dear," said Elvi, shaking her head.

"What is it?" asked Clover.

"It's just that . . . Clover, when I told you I was going to meet your uncle earlier, it was a white lie. I was going to see Billycan. I thought I could help get the truth out of him."

"What of it?" asked Carn.

"Billycan remembers Julius. He told me no matter what, he would soon reclaim his son."

"Billycan," growled Vincent. "We need to see him—now! Maybe whoever the traitor is took Julius."

"I have the key to his cell," said Elvi, feeling around her neck. "Juniper gave it to me." Suddenly she gasped, her eyes widening. "It cannot be!"

"What can't be?" asked Vincent.

"The key . . . it's gone!"

The guard lay facedown on the ground, just outside the door to Billycan's cell. Vincent tried to rouse him, but he would not stir.

"He's out cold," said Vincent. "Someone knocked him out from behind. He's got a sizable bump on the back of his head. He didn't know what was coming."

"His breathing is strong," said Elvi, leaning over him. "Victor, go find Virden. He can help him. Then bring the others here." Victor nodded and took off at a gallop, disappearing down the corridor.

"Elvi, please stay here and watch over him," said Vincent, nodding at the guard. He picked up the fallen guard's spear and approached the heavy wooden door leading to Billycan's cell. Armed with only their claws, Suttor and Carn followed.

Carn turned to Oleander. "Stay here with Elvi and Clover," he said. "I don't want you getting hurt."

"Boys," said Clover, rolling her eyes. "They'll never learn." She raised her eyebrow at Carn. "We're going too. You can't stop us."

"You forget, *Corn*, I'm just as strong as you," said Oleander. "Maybe stronger."

"Suit yourselves," said Carn with a scowl. "Maddening sort, you two are."

"Take it from me," said Vincent, "they only get worse." With that, Vincent kicked open the door.

They stormed the cell at full force, Vincent's spear poised to strike, the others with claws at the ready. They halted dead in their tracks. The barred door hung wide open, blood smears everywhere, Billycan's cot strewn with trails of murky crimson.

Elvi came in behind them. She covered her mouth and gasped.

The cell was vacant.

"Bless the Saints!" said Suttor. "What happened in here? Where's Billycan?"

"Where's Julius?" asked Vincent grimly.

CHAPTER SEVENTEEN
A Clutch of Crows

HOLDING HIS HAND SNUGLY, Texi steered Julius down corridor after pitch-black corridor with nothing more than a small candle to guide them. They scuttled around fallen beams and heaping piles of powdery earth that had dropped from the crumbling ceilings of the Catacombs. Texi burned away scores of cobwebs with the candle's flame.

"It's dark, Texi, and cold," said Julius uneasily. "I don't like this place."

"Don't be frightened, Julius," said Texi, putting an arm around him. "Everything will be all right. I promise."

"But where are we going?" asked Julius.

"We're going to see the aunties."

"The aunties? I don't think I have any aunties."

"Well, they're not *really* your aunties, but they said you should think of them that way. Besides, it's easier to remember my sisters that way. There are ten of them, after all."

"Why?"

Texi stopped walking. She knelt down in front of Julius and held him by the shoulders. "The aunties are friends of your father."

Julius felt relieved hearing that. "They know Papa?"

"No...not your papa, not Juniper, your other father. You've never met him. His name is Billycan."

Julius quieted, thinking. He shuddered as he heard something skitter in the walls behind him. Finally he said, "Texi, isn't that the bad rat—the one that everyone talks about?" His voice dropped to a whisper. "The only albino left in all of Trillium."

Texi cocked her head. "Julius, you're an albino, too. Didn't you know that?" Julius shook his head. "Why do you think you're so special, with snow-white fur and eyes red like fresh apples? Why, you're like no other rat in Trillium—*except* Billycan." She smiled. "And Billycan would never be mean to you. I was promised. My sisters told me a boy should know his father, that it would be cruel of me to keep you from him. I couldn't do that to you. Does that make sense?" Julius nodded. "You know what else? Billycan looks just like *you.*"

Julius gasped. "Like *me?*"

"Yes, stark white fur, red eyes."

Julius's mind whirled with possibilities. He'd never known another white rat. He always felt alone in that way, never quite fitting in. He got funny looks sometimes from the other children, even from some of the grown-ups. He knew it was because he was different—strange. "Can I meet him now?"

"Right now, it's time to meet the aunties. They are very excited to see you. They haven't seen you since you were a baby. They've been waiting three years for this day."

Texi stood up and continued down the corridor with Julius. She stopped before two heavy wooden doors. "Now, the aunties are

a bit...different. They may act a little unusual, but don't let it scare you, all right? They won't hurt you." She sighed. "Deep down, they mean well. Now then, are you ready to meet them?"

Texi swallowed hard and then knocked three times on the door. It opened just a crack. Julius heard giggling and snorting coming from inside.

"It's all right," said Texi. "I promise." She whispered under her breath, "They promised."

They entered Killdeer's shadowy compound.

His feet now damp with blood, Juniper inspected the cell. "All I can smell is Billycan. There's no way to tell whose blood this is. Being here all this time, his scent has masked everything." Juniper turned in a circle, taking in the horror of the scene. "Maddy mustn't see this. It will destroy her," he said gravely. "Elvi, how could you have lost the key?"

"I don't know," said Elvi hopelessly. "I pulled up a stool to the cell and spoke to Billycan. At first he was very quiet, acting as though he did not want to talk to a stranger. I kept having to lean in—just so I could hear him—but not so close that he could have grabbed the key. Then again, the cell was rather dark. I was going to light the torch, but he asked me not to. He said the light hurt his eyes." Her lower lip began to quiver. "Oh, Juniper, I'm so sorry."

"It's not your fault," said Juniper. "It's mine. I should never have allowed you to see him. He's sly. I'm sure he knew all along what he was doing, easily clipping the key from your neck with his claws without you feeling a thing."

"Even so . . . I should have known better." Elvi covered her face.

"Looking around this cell," said Cole, "there's little evidence that Billycan has changed. Whose blood is this—Billycan's, or perhaps the traitor's, who must have knocked out the guard and opened the outer door? Maybe Billycan attacked him, thinking him a liability now. Whether this blood is Billycan's or not, he's vanished yet again, loose in Nightshade."

"We'll find him," said Clover, putting her arm around Elvi. She looked at Juniper. "Uncle, did anyone find Texi? I know it's a slim chance, but maybe Julius is with her. You know how those two are— they're practically inseparable."

Gasping, Elvi put a paw over her heart. "Texi!" she said. "I completely forget to tell you, Juniper."

"Tell me what?"

"I was a bit nervous going to see Billycan. It completely slipped my mind, not seeming that important at the time, but Texi . . . what she said. Now it seems so significant."

"What did she say?" asked Cole.

"Elvi, tell us," said Juniper impatiently.

"Just this morning, on my way back from the city square, I stopped by her quarters to check on her. She acted odd. Nothing she said made much sense to me. It was about her sisters—and Julius."

"What about them?" asked Juniper.

"She said, 'My sisters were right all along. I am a wicked girl, keeping Julius from them.'"

"Why would she mention her sisters? She hasn't had contact with them since we defeated the High Ministry. They escaped Topside and no one's seen them since."

"That's what I thought, too. When I asked her about it she quickly changed the subject. Said that Mother Gallo had asked her to meet her and Julius at the library, and she rushed off without even a good-bye. It was very strange."

"Maddy said she never made it to the library," said Juniper.

"Uncle, you know how upset Texi was after Billycan was captured, how she went on about Killdeer and those sisters, how she felt guilty for not being loyal." Clover looked at Vincent. "What if..."

Vincent shook his head. "Of all the theories I had, all my suspicions, she never crossed my mind. Texi the traitor? Could it be possible?"

"Bless the Saints," said Juniper. His face fell in sheer disbelief. "She had access to everything! She's the only one other than the Council who could have given Billycan the city blueprints." He slumped down on a stool. "I gave her full run of the place. Never in a million years would I have thought that she would betray us... that she would take my son. Why would she do such a thing?"

"We don't have time to speculate," said Cole. "We need to think clearly. Texi may be a victim, not a traitor. We don't know for sure. Could Texi's sisters still be alive? Is it possible that they're hiding somewhere Topside? What do we know about them that could help us?"

"They were ignorant, for one," said Carn. "Killdeer kept them that way on purpose, in order to keep them under his thumb. I can't imagine they'd have survived Topside. They don't know the first thing about taking care of themselves. Texi took care of their every need."

"They were entitled," said Clover, "just like Killdeer. Texi told me they made her call them all princesses, and they always refused to help with chores round the compound, no matter how much work was piled onto Texi. They told her chores were beneath them."

"Well, if you were one of Killdeer's sisters," said Cole, "unintelligent, selfish, and scared of Topsiders, where would you go?"

Juniper touched the scarred skin under his patch, feeling the roughened edges where his eye had once been, now just rutted skin and bone. "I'd go home," he said soberly. "I'd go to the Catacombs."

Julius recoiled. Backing into Texi, he hid himself in her fur. "Bitsy, please, you're scaring him," said Texi. "Julius, these ladies are the aunties, they would never hurt you." She smiled at her sister. "Now would you, Bitsy?"

Bitsy unfurled her hunched back and removed the hood of her soiled cloak, revealing a gnarled grin of rotten teeth. "No, sister dear, never, never," she hissed. She curled down toward Julius, pulling at his white fur. "What lovely white fur you have. Why, I only want to see you, lad, our little crown prince. You were only a tasty morsel when I saw you last. Let me see how big you've grown. Come out, come out, little lamb. Don't you want to meet Auntie Bitsy?"

His heart pounding in his chest, Julius squeezed his eyes shut, wishing all of the aunties would disappear forever. They were disturbing. They didn't act like normal rats, all ten of them shrouded in deathly black like witches, all ugly, with cackling voices and scary, hungry smiles, like the ones in the fairy tale Longtooth had just read in the library.

Bitsy pulled on Julius's ear. "I've got you now, little lamb," she said in a singsong voice. "Come out, come out. There's no escaping your eldest auntie." Julius felt Bitsy's cold digits tug at his ear. It wasn't a friendly tug, either. It hurt. He knew he was in trouble. He hoped his parents would find him soon.

With Julius refusing to turn around, Bitsy finally relented and scuttled off to join the other sisters, all sitting at a long table in the shadowy compound, half giggling and half bickering, five on each side.

Texi bent down and put an arm around Julius's middle. "I know you're afraid," she whispered, "but you've nothing to fret about. The aunties only want the best for you, and would never hurt a hair on your little head." She gave a worried glance toward the table and then back to Julius. "My sisters all promised me they'd be good."

"Why aren't they like you?" asked Julius. He looked down at his paws and sniffled. "They don't seem very nice."

"Because I'm not smart like them," Texi replied. "They said I was born dull, simpleminded." She smiled. "Not clever like you. That's why I didn't understand how important it was that you meet your father, Billycan. They explained to me that if I helped him and let him meet you, one day I'd make up for all my mistakes, for being a bad sister." She crumpled her nose. "It doesn't feel like I'm doing the right thing, but I thought about it…and maybe if I do the opposite of what feels right, then I *will* be doing the right thing. Understand?"

"I'm not sure," said Julius.

"Me either," said Texi. "My sisters say my brain works funny, so I thought if I switched things around maybe it would work right. And maybe they'll finally forgive me for being bad."

"You're not bad," said Julius softly.

As she hugged Julius tight, Texi's eyes welled with tears. She looked over at her sisters as they called her and Julius to the dinner table. For once their voices weren't cross, they were calm—and they were smiling instead of scowling. Bitsy had even patted Texi's head when she and Julius came in. Bitsy had never done that before. Tonight her sisters weren't screaming at her. They weren't calling her names and ordering her about. For the first time, they were being nice...in their way. Then why did everything feel so wrong?

Juniper, accompanied by Cole, Ragan, and Ulrich, gathered with the others in Nightshade Passage. Virden stayed behind with the fallen guard. Although he was not yet conscious, Virden said the rat's breathing seemed to be growing stronger as the minutes ticked by—a good sign.

The Chief Citizen stared down the desolate corridor that led to the Catacombs, now blocked off by a bolted door of heavy timber. He held a wrought-iron key in his paw, the only key that could unlock the door—a key that had never been used since it was forged.

The younger rats readied their spears as the older rats readied themselves. Stepping back in time was not an easy thing.

"Juniper," said Oleander, "why don't you tell the rest of the Council and the citizens what's happening? Surely they'll want to help find Julius and capture Billycan and Texi."

"My dear, your suggestion is a good one, yet I'm afraid it would result in chaos. The very mention of Billycan's name sends many of our citizens into a panic. I worry many could get hurt."

"Many believe Billycan possesses some sort of supernatural hold," said Carn, "something in his eyes that can bend any rat to his will—all hogwash, if you ask me."

Clover's gaze drifted down the corridor. Her face suddenly went pale.

"Are you all right?" asked Juniper. "I know you're old enough to make your own decisions. You've made that *quite* clear to me. But it's all right for you to stay behind. In fact, I'd much rather you did."

"Uncle, at your asking, I stayed behind three years ago. I know you worry for me, but my mind is made up." She glanced at Vincent, who knew there was no use arguing over the matter. Clover would not be told what to do, not even by him. "I have to do this."

"Then what is it?" asked Vincent. "For a moment you looked as though you'd seen a ghost."

"I suppose I had," replied Clover. "I was remembering those dreadful days in the Catacombs—that Chosen One business with Killdeer. Billycan came to my quarters one night, scared me something awful. When he fixed those shifting red eyes on me, that withering gaze froze me in my tracks, as if my feet were fastened to the ground. I could not shake his stare. I could not breathe. It was as if he had a stranglehold around my heart. I know it sounds silly, but I felt, well, completely under his control—spellbound."

"That was nothing more than simple terror," stated Carn firmly. "I spent eleven years with that rat. There is nothing magical about him. It's high time we put the legend to rest."

"Agreed," said Vincent, smiling reassuringly at Clover.

"Juniper, we're ready," said Victor.

Mother Gallo had been pacing in a circle, wringing her paws. "Good, then we must go, now," she said anxiously.

"Maddy, please," said Juniper, "I want you to stay here." He turned to Elvi. "Elvi, I know you want to see this through, but please stay here with my wife. You're her dearest friend."

"Of course," said Elvi, putting an arm around Mother Gallo. "You mustn't go to the Catacombs, Maddy, dear. It is no place for a worried mother."

"You don't understand!" cried Mother Gallo. "He's my son. What must be happening to him..." She ran to Juniper and buried her face in his fur.

"The Saints only know what awaits us in there," Juniper told her gently, "and if something happens to me you must stay safe so you can take care of the family and—"

"Don't talk like that!" she blurted, unable to hold back her tears. "You must never, *never* talk like that again. Do you understand me?"

"Yes," said Juniper, smiling softly at her, "I do." He hugged her tight. "We'll be home soon, I promise you."

"I'll hold you to that promise," she whispered.

"No servants for three long years," hissed one of the aunties as she plopped the ladle back into the cauldron of murky stew. "Entirely absurd that we should have to serve ourselves, positively degrading, it is."

Summoning up her oiliest of smiles, Bitsy suddenly turned to Texi, who sat with Julius on her lap at the head of the table. "Youngest sister, dear, when he returns, will you once again serve us? Will we trudge and toil no longer?" Twisting her neck, she cocked her head at an uncomfortable angle and batted her eyes. "It always made us happy, the way you took such good care of us. We miss it. We miss you."

"You do?" asked Texi.

"Why, of course," cooed another sister.

"Such a prized baby sister," added another.

"Yes, our precious Texi, it's so good to have you home," said Bitsy, grinning ghoulishly. "And when, sister dear, will he be arriving?"

Clearing her throat, Texi shifted uneasily in her chair. "There is something you all need to know. You must understand, there was nothing I could do." Sitting on her lap, Julius could feel Texi's heart beat faster.

All ten sisters leaned toward the head of the table like a pack of shrouded wolves, their eyes glinting in the candlelight. "What is it, sister dear?" asked Bitsy.

"Yes, yes," clucked Persephone, just months older than Texi, though she looked ancient and haggard. "Do share, dearest sister. When will he arrive?"

"Tell us," croaked another as she choked down a scrap of dried fish.

Julius shrank back against Texi as the aunties gazed at him hungrily. Texi grabbed him firmly around his waist. "He will not be joining us—ever," she said flatly.

The aunties began to whisper and growl. "What?" Bitsy barked. "What do you mean, he *won't* be joining us?" She jumped up from the table, knocking her chair to the ground. "How are we to reclaim our power without him? What has happened? He was supposed to invade Nightshade, killing anyone who mattered. What has gone wrong? Tell us!"

"He was captured in the swamp!" cried Texi. "There was nothing I could do—nothing!"

Persephone banged a skeletal fist on the table. "What did you do, Texi?" she demanded. "This is your fault, brainless girl—always the blundering fool! Did you give him up to your precious Nightshade rats? Did you betray us yet again? You wicked, wicked girl!"

The aunties began to bicker among themselves, cursing and spitting. One sprang up and smashed her goblet against the wall, coating it with blackish wine. Terrified, Julius hid his face against Texi, who shrank back in her chair, clutching the little boy tight.

A sister shrieked balefully. Frothing at the mouth, she lunged forward from her seat, clawing at Julius as Texi tried to cover him with her arms. "Leave him alone!" she cried.

"Boneheaded, stupid girl!" roared Bitsy, aiming her bowl at Texi's head.

"Dumb little troll!"

"Treacherous imp!"

"Silence!" roared a voice from the shadows. "Silence right now or I swear on everything you hold dear I will kill each and every one of you, slashing your throats without a moment's hesitation!" Everyone gasped, then fell deathly silent. "Now take your seats and keep your mouths shut."

Clutching Julius, Texi jumped up and was backing away from the table, heading toward the door.

Picking up a candle from a pedestal, Billycan held it up to his face, creating black shadows under his eyes. "Not so fast, little one." Texi froze in her tracks, squeezing Julius tighter with every step Billycan made. "You wouldn't deprive me of my only offspring, now, would you?"

Julius held Texi's shoulder and leaned forward, captivated. He tried to catch a glimpse; the rat's fur was stark white, *exactly* like his. Even in the darkness he could see the vivid red eyes. He was startled, petrified, and—joyful. Was this rat *really* his father, this rat who looked exactly like him?

"My word," said Billycan in a stunned whisper. "Let me have a look at you."

Before Texi could stop him, Julius jumped to the ground, his curiosity greater than his fear. He took a bold step toward the large rat, mesmerized.

Dropping to one knee, Billycan held the candle up to his son. Goose bumps traveled up his back and arms as he inspected his boy. They stared at each other in silence. Finally Billycan said, "I never imagined I'd see you again." He swallowed stiffly. It felt as though there were stones in his throat. "You are a handsome chap now, aren't you? How old are you, then?"

"I'm nearly four," said Julius in a small but proud voice.

Billycan smiled. "Nearly four. Amazing." He gave Julius a stern look. "Good with your studies, I trust?"

Julius was not afraid. The aunties no longer worried him. Something about this rat made him feel protected. "My teacher says I'm the smartest in my class."

"I'm quite sure she's right," said Billycan softly. "When I was little, I was smart like that, too."

Julius looked at Billycan's chest. The right side ran thick with dried blood. "What happened to you?" he asked, concerned. "How did you get hurt?"

Looking up at the table of sisters, Billycan rose to his feet. "I'm all right, little one." He held out a spidery paw to Julius, who instinctively took hold of it. They walked over to the table. "In fact, I'm better than all right," he said. "My mind has never been sharper. Things have never been clearer. Everything I need to do, the reason I'm here, has finally come to me." He patted his bloodied coat. "I only needed to be reminded how lucky I am to be alive."

"Are you really my father?"

Without warning, Billycan swept Julius off his feet, hoisting him up on his arm just as Juniper always had. Julius gasped, now nose to nose with the great white rat. Billycan whispered in his ear. "Julius, listen closely. I *am* your father, and everything you feel at this moment, looking at me as though I'm a looking glass, is true. We are very much alike, with good reason. You see, child, *you* have saved me, giving me back my certainty—I now know who I am. I know *what* I am. I owe all of that to you."

Leaning his head back, Julius studied his father's face. "To me?" he asked.

Smiling, Billycan tousled the fur on Julius's head. "Why yes, my boy. You see, I never had a father. No one ever looked after me. I never knew what it meant to have a family, but now that's all changed. Never forget, from now on, everything I do, good *or* bad, I do for you."

"All the years of planning, the child, the swamp," said Bitsy, "digging you that secret tunnel to Nightshade. I thought everything was a waste when Texi told us of your capture. I thought we had lost our great commander forever. I *knew* you would not let us down. I knew you were only waiting to emerge victorious once more!"

Smiling broadly, Billycan nodded at all the sisters. "Yes, I will take power once more."

Persephone rubbed her paws together eagerly. "Do tell us, High Commander, *how* did you escape Nightshade? Did you bite through anyone's neck?"

The sisters grew agitated.

"Did you rip off any limbs, pull off any skin?"

"Did you cut any throats with a rusty knife, a shard of glass?"

"Did you carve out any eyes?" The sisters laughed with diabolical glee at that.

All of a sudden Julius reached out and took Billycan by the chin, turning his face toward him. Julius looked hard at Billycan. He inspected the thick, black scar running down his muzzle. "You have a scar," he said. "My papa has scars, too. He wears a patch. He's missing an eye."

"I know," said Billycan. "This scar—your papa gave it to me."

"But why...," asked Julius, wrinkling his forehead. "Why would Papa do that?"

"For the same reason I took his eye. We both thought we were right—for very different reasons."

"Do you hate him?"

"Don't fuss about that right now," said Billycan. "All that can wait." He looked at Texi. "Texi, come. Explain to Julius why you brought him here tonight."

"Julius," said Texi, "you're here to claim what is rightly yours. My sisters told me I needed to do what was right for you. They made me realize it was wrong to keep you from your father."

"But what about Mama and Papa, won't they miss me? Won't they be sad I'm gone?" Julius was puzzled. Texi had always been good to him, and she would never hurt him. He was sure of that. He looked up at Billycan and focused on his eyes. There was something there, something more than just a mirror image of his own. This rat *was* his father. "What is going to happen now?"

"Well," said Billycan, "it's high time we got to know each other as father and son, don't you agree?"

"I suppose," said Julius, "but if *you're* my father, what will happen to Papa?"

"You needn't worry your head about him," replied Billycan. "Sometimes our greatest enemies are the ones we hold most dear." He glanced over at the sisters with a calculating grin. "Juniper used your love to keep you close to him—a son that was not his to have. He kept you from me, your father. What kind of rat would do that to someone he loved? Don't you think that was a horrid thing to do?"

"Yes, absolutely ghastly!" screeched Bitsy from the table.

All the sisters called out in agreement.

"Utterly appalling!"

"Hopelessly disgusting!"

"Cowardly and desperate!"

Silently Julius nodded at his father, his eyes beginning to tear.

"Oh, you mustn't feel that way," said Billycan in a compassionate tone. "You've nothing to be sad for, son. A whole new life—your real life—awaits you." He wrapped both arms around Julius and patted his back. He whispered in his ear, "There, there, Julius. Father's here, and I'm sure your papa will be here soon—any moment now."

They made their way to Killdeer's den in silence, weaving around mounds of parched earth and the many fallen timbers that once held up the endless maze of the Catacombs.

Cole suddenly jolted backward, nearly knocking Ragan over, as a rather sizable spider skittered along the wall past his head.

"It's only a funnel weaver, old man, perfectly harmless," whispered Ragan, steadying Cole by the shoulders. "Nothing for you to worry about."

"Speak for yourself," muttered Cole. "It's bad enough being back in this place. Why does it have to be crawling with spiders and beetles?"

"Quit being so squeamish," whispered Ulrich. "You faced down the High Ministry majors and Billycan himself, yet you're afraid of a lone spider."

"Quiet down," said Juniper. "Empty corridors carry sound a long way."

The others knew better than to talk, but the Catacombs, once their home, had become a bleak warren of crumbling tunnels and mixed memories. Talking kept their minds off the past.

As they rounded a corner, Juniper patted his niece on the shoulder. Nearing the halfway point of the corridor, the two stopped in front of a rickety door to what was once the bustling home of Clover and the Belancort clan, now just a gloomy hollow.

Clover stared at the door's number, 73, still there, glowing a vaporous white. Softly she pushed the door open with her spear. Her parents' bed, their belongings, were all still there, everything a cindery black from the fire Billycan had set the night of her escape.

She'd tried never to think about that night again, but why not, she wondered now as she gazed at the decades-old carving of Duchess Nomi still deep within the wall, carved by her mother. That was the night Clover met Vincent, the rat who only days later would rid the world of the High Minister. It seemed to be the night that launched everything that had become Nightshade—a victory woven of desperation and determination.

Juniper rested a paw on her shoulder. "I'm all right," she whispered. "Let's go."

Except for Bitsy, all the aunties had finally shuffled off to bed. They insisted Texi go with them to rub their scaly feet, just as she'd done in the old days, but Billycan ordered her to stay and watch after Julius. They relented, convinced that they would once again be royalty, princesses in the new monarchy led by Billycan.

The thought made him laugh—*princesses!* They were as revolting as a clutch of quibbling old crows. Princesses, indeed.

He and Bitsy sat at the long table, talking about the future, while Texi cleaned up some of the mess the sisters had made. Julius, who had clung to his father throughout the entire meal, had fallen asleep on his chest.

"So, Bitsy," said Billycan, "as Killdeer's eldest sister, you shall be granted a title of great importance under my rule. High Mistress, Countess, what shall it be?"

"I prefer High Duchess," croaked Bitsy, batting her eyes at Billycan. "I like the sound of that."

"Yes...," said Billycan, trying not to show his disgust, "whatever you like."

She looked over at Texi, busy cleaning. She sneered. "Moronic little dunce, she'll be my chambermaid."

"Hush!" he suddenly hissed. "I hear something." Eyes wide, Bitsy bolted upright in her chair as Billycan stood up, holding Julius, still fast asleep. "Stay there." He nodded to Texi, who quietly stepped away from the table. He motioned to the darkest corner of the room. "Hide."

Billycan left the throne room and stole down a narrow corridor to the War Room. Maps and blueprints still clung to the walls, and rows of vacant chairs sat waiting for the majors of the High Ministry to return once again and reclaim their seats.

"Julius," whispered Billycan. "Julius, you must wake up." Bleary-eyed, Julius looked up at him. "Son, you must listen to me. We haven't much time. I need you to stay here. No matter what transpires, you must stay here and stay quiet. Do you understand me?"

Julius lifted his head. "What's happening?" he asked.

"Pay attention, now. You mustn't leave this room no matter what you hear—screaming, fighting, things falling to the ground—you *must* stay put. Your life depends upon it. Am I understood?" Julius nodded. "Good." Billycan snatched a large map from the wall. "Over there in that corner, that's where we'll hide you, under this," he said, his voice somewhat strained.

Now fully awake, Julius sat up in Billycan's arms. His small chest felt damp. Julius looked down at his coat, smeared with fresh blood— his father's blood. "You're *bleeding*," he said. He wrinkled up his face. "Will you be all right?"

"Yes," whispered Billycan. He smiled. "I'll be fine, just fine. It seems I have a knack for pulling through moments like this."

"Who hurt you?"

"Don't you worry about that. I'm sure the rat is long gone by now."

"I'm afraid," said Julius. "Don't leave me here."

"Fathers always defend their children at all costs," replied Billycan. He winced as a jolt of pain tore through his chest. "So you have nothing to be afraid of. It may not feel like it, but you are well protected here. I will see to that, and I will come for you soon, I promise. Now it's time for you to be brave. You must be a great leader now, afraid of nothing." He carried Julius over to the corner. "Your directive is to sit very still and stay covered, young soldier. Do you think you can manage that for me?"

"Yes," said Julius.

Billycan smiled. He embraced his son and kissed him on the forehead, then set him down, covering him with the large map. He grabbed some chairs and set them in the corner in front of Julius as if someone had carelessly left them there years ago. "Now then, stay still and stay quiet, my boy. I'll be back for you." He leaned in and whispered, "I thought I'd lost you forever. I'm so proud to have you for a son." Giving one last look to make sure Julius was fully concealed, Billycan left the War Room, gently shutting the door behind him.

The little rat crouched nervously under the musty map, thinking about what Billycan had told him. He must be a great leader now—afraid of nothing—and for whatever the reason, Julius wasn't afraid. Worried, yes, but no longer afraid.

Billycan raced back to the throne room. Bitsy sat stiffly in her chair. "Where is the boy?" she asked anxiously.

"I hid him," replied Billycan, "safe from harm."

"I've been listening," said Bitsy in a panic. "I hear them. I think I even smell them. How did they know we were here? What are we going to do?" She searched the room for Texi. "Where is that little monster I'm forced to call a sister? I bet she gave us away—once a traitor, always a traitor!"

"You and your sisters need to leave now. I will handle Juniper and his Council."

"No!" said Bitsy. "I finally have a chance to be revered, an esteemed High Duchess. I will fight to get what I deserve!"

"Juniper is out for blood," said Billycan. "We've taken his son. You stay any longer, trust me—you *will* get what you deserve!"

"The boy belongs with us!" barked Bitsy. "Juniper stole him from my sisters and me—a spineless kidnapper!"

"Juniper stole nothing from you! You left my boy starving in the Combs to save your own hides! You and your witless sisters promised me long ago that if anything ever happened to me you'd take care of him. You left him behind—my son!" hollered Billycan. "Had Julius not been found, he would be dead. Juniper is the *only* reason the boy still lives!"

Bitsy scoffed. "He has turned your son into a soft, sentimental excuse for a rat! He has ruined him. Juniper is the cause of my suffering. He brought down the High Ministry, forced me into three years of wretchedness. And now it's his time to die!"

The door to the compound suddenly burst open. Spears at the ready, the Nightshade rats rushed in, forming a half-circle around Bitsy and Billycan.

"Where's Julius?" barked Vincent.

"You!" screeched Bitsy. "Son of Julius Nightshade, killer of my only brother, you will join your father in the grave!" She charged Vincent, swiping at his face with her jagged claws.

Vincent howled in pain, his cheek cut deeply. No matter how much he wanted to strike back with full force, he swore he'd uphold his oath, as all the Council members had that night. No one would die by their claws unless absolutely necessary. Instead of running her clean through, Vincent knocked her backward with the side of his spear. Suttor and Carn came at her, but she dodged them, swiftly maneuvering out of their reach.

Lurching forward, Billycan grabbed for Bitsy, trying to pull her from the fray. Juniper and Cole pushed him back, with one spear aimed at his head, the other his heart.

"Where is my son?" growled Juniper.

Billycan held his paws up, trying to back down the corridor to the War Room.

"Stay put!" shouted Cole. "No more of your clever escapes. Juniper asked you a question. Where is Julius, *rat*?"

"You don't understand," said Billycan.

"I understand everything!" snarled Juniper, gnashing his teeth. "You are a liar and a killer—*nothing* has changed. Why are you covered in blood?" Juniper began to shake, fearful of the answer he might receive. "Whose blood is that?"

"It's—"

Before Billycan could answer, the rest of the sisters tore from their room, hissing like hellcats and wielding knives and razor blades. One even clutched Billycan's infamous billy club in her bony fist, swinging it around her head, banging on the rafters, shrieking and wailing like a demented ghoul. As the armed sisters charged, Billycan withdrew into the shadows.

All shrouded in grimy black cloaks, the sisters looked like the ghost of Batiste, rumored to haunt the Catacombs, materialized ten times over, ready to finally reclaim his stolen sweets. Eager for blood, they grunted and laughed, gruesome smiles on their faces as they approached the opposing rats, sizing them up.

"Who are they?" whispered Oleander to Clover.

"The dead High Minister's sisters," said Clover, "ignorant, hateful things. Carn says they'll cut your throat out just for a giggle."

Bitsy grinned deviously. "Let's play a little game, shall we, sisters?" The others howled wildly in approval, clapping their paws, as they followed Bitsy to the long table. "What Nightshade rat can we hit first?" She grabbed a clay mug from the table and hurled it at Cole, clipping him hard on the shoulder.

"Shrew!" muttered Cole, pulling bloodied chunks of pottery from his fur.

The sisters snickered as they continued their game, throwing anything and everything on the table at the Nightshade rats. Ragan got hit in the head by a soup ladle. Another sister threw a cleaver at Ulrich, just missing his backside. His eyes widened when he saw how close it had landed, relieved that he'd already been missing his tail.

"That's enough!" shouted Carn. "Remember me?" He glared at Bitsy as Suttor and Victor came up behind him.

"How could I forget?" said Bitsy in a shrill, mocking tone.

"Billycan's groveling servant boy—Carn! Don't worry, boy, you will be his servant once more."

Carn snatched a plate from the ground and flung it toward Bitsy at full speed, hitting her square in the incisors. She grabbed her face, screaming in agony as blood spurted from her mouth and nose, a front tooth now dangling from her gums.

"Ingrate!" hissed Persephone. "After all Billycan and my brother did for you, hitting a relation of the High Minister—a lady, no less."

"There are no *ladies* before me," snapped Carn, "only a slithering pack of witches! Now, where's Julius?"

"Cheeky one, isn't he, sisters?" sneered Persephone. "Tricky, tricky servant boy. Perhaps we should teach him some manners."

"Oh, yes," said another, "quite disrespectful. Ungrateful slave."

"Thinks he's the cat's meow," said another, and her sisters cackled madly.

Vincent, Oleander, and Clover stood ready for battle behind Victor, Suttor, and Carn, the long table between them and the sisters.

Persephone leaped onto the table. "Here's Juniper's precious boy," she shouted, "what's left of him!" She kicked over the heavy cauldron of stew, drenching the ground with a slick, greasy muck. "He was delicious!"

"That's enough," growled Oleander. "You wouldn't last one day where I come from. My cousin Thicket could take out the pack of you!" She bounded onto the table and charged Persephone, tackling her with such force that she propelled them both to the ground. Landing atop the other sisters in a mountain of claws and tails, Persephone moaned in pain. The others began tearing at Oleander, ripping at her skin with claws and blades.

"Oleander!" yelled Carn. The young Council members jumped

on the sisters, pulling them off Oleander, hitting, clawing, biting, whatever it took to get them under control.

Clover grabbed one of the sisters, breaking her brittle wrist against a table leg, forcing her to drop her dagger as she screamed, "Little brat!" Clover tossed the dagger to Oleander, who scrambled to her feet and whipped around in a circle, slicing the air, trying to keep the sisters at bay.

Using his tail as a whip, Victor snapped Persephone in the paw, flinging her dagger across the room only seconds before she could plunge it into Vincent's spine.

"You horrid, horrid boy!" she screamed, holding her throbbing paw.

Carn knocked a sister down with a hard elbow just as she charged him with a razor blade. Another came at him from behind, about to propel her knife into his neck. He heard a loud crash and turned in time to see the sister fall to the ground, unconscious, surrounded by large chunks of stoneware from the pot Oleander used to had thump her over the head.

"Oleander," exclaimed Carn, "you saved my life!"

"I told you I'm as strong as you!"

Juniper, Cole, and the twins rushed through the chambers of the compound. Billycan and Julius were nowhere to be found.

They came upon another door, and Juniper pushed it open with his spear. The rats entered an egg-shaped chamber.

"Empty like the rest," said Ragan.

"Juniper, they're gone," said Cole.

"The War Room," said Juniper, gazing at the tattered maps. Just then, something rustled in a corner. Juniper put a claw to his mouth. He slowly moved toward the sound, noticing the large map crumpled in the corner. He motioned to the others, who followed behind him, spears ready to plunge.

"We are armed," he called out. "You'd best come out now. If you do not comply, we will be forced to attack."

As he drew nearer, Juniper realized no grown rat could be hiding under that map. It was far too small. His heart raced. It could be a shrew. It could be a beetle. It could be his son.

The creature did not move. Juniper nodded to Cole, who suddenly lunged forward, knocking the wooden chairs out of their path, hurling them across the room.

A panicky gasp came from under the map. "Julius?" said Juniper anxiously. He reached down and snatched up the map. "Julius?" The creature jumped up, swinging a dagger, grazing Juniper's lip.

"Stay away from us!" screamed Texi. She had her eyes closed tight, blindly swinging the knife around the room. "I won't let you hurt him!"

Ragan and Ulrich came up from behind, ready to strike, but Juniper quickly held up his paw. "Stop!" he commanded, spitting out blood. "It's Texi."

Texi clutched Julius around his middle. "Stay back! Don't hurt us! Leave Julius alone! You can't have him. He belongs in Nightshade, and I will *never* allow you to hurt him!"

"Papa!" blurted Julius.

Shaking, Texi finally opened her eyes, which darted between Juniper and the others, stricken with fear.

"It's all right, Texi. It's Juniper," he said softly. Dropping his spear, he held up his paws, giving as warm a smile as he could manage. "Texi, put down the knife. Julius will be just fine." He spoke evenly. "It's all over now. We've always kept you safe, and we always will."

Throwing the knife to the ground, Texi dropped to her

knees, holding Julius. She rocked back and forth. "I thought you were Billycan!" she cried. "I'm so sorry, Juniper. I thought I was doing the right thing for Julius. I wasn't trying to hurt him. My sisters *promised* to be good. They said no boy should be kept from his father, and the Saints would punish me if I didn't help Billycan find a way into Nightshade and reunite him with Julius. I should never have believed them. I'm so sorry." She looked at Julius. "I would never, ever hurt you."

Sitting up in her arms, Julius held her face in his small paws. "It's all right. You're not bad. And I knew Papa would come for us."

Slowly Juniper knelt down and took Julius from Texi, hugging him close. "Thank the Saints!" he whispered. "You're alive." He checked his son over. "Julius, you're covered in blood! Where are you hurt?

"I'm not hurt, Papa. It's not my blood." Juniper struggled to keep his composure. "Papa, I'm fine."

Juniper smiled. "I thought I'd lost you forever."

"That's what Father said, too."

"Father?"

"Yes, he hid me in the corner. He said he thought he'd lost me forever, too." Julius looked down at his chest. His ears drooped. "This is his blood. He's hurt badly."

"You mean the white rat?"

Julius nodded.

Screams and shrieks emerged from the throne room, loud thuds as bodies were hurled about, followed by wails echoing through the corridors of the compound.

Clutching Julius, Juniper snatched up his spear and ran from the War Room. Cole grabbed Texi by the hand, while Ragan and Ulrich followed.

They entered Killdeer's throne room, now deathly silent. The candles had been snuffed out—all but one. Juniper took it from its stand and held it out to the darkness. "Bless the Saints," he muttered as he took in the scene.

The sisters' bodies lay on the ground in awkward, broken arrangements, their black cloaks now death shrouds.

A sound like thunder suddenly pierced the walls of the compound, and the room shook.

"What was that?" asked Cole as dust sprinkled their heads.

Before anyone could respond, the sound rumbled again and then again from the west end of the Combs. Bits of earth fell from the ceiling, and the walls began to tremble.

"We've got to get out of here!" said Juniper. "These walls can only take so much."

Juniper searched the room for others. "Clover!" he called out. "Vincent, Carn? Where are you?"

They raced down the corridors calling for the others. Clover appeared from around a corner. "Uncle!" she shouted.

"Clover, are you all right?"

"I'm fine," she replied, rushing toward him.

"What happened here?"

"Uncle, it was Billycan." She panted, shaking her head in disbelief. "He saved us. He saved all of us."

"Where is everyone now?"

"One of the sisters struck Vincent hard in the back, and he dropped his spear. While we were fending off the others, she chased after him with a knife! Everyone is searching for him." Her voice trembled with desperation. "Uncle, Vincent is unarmed. We can't find him!"

Large clumps of earth rained from the ceiling. The walls were breaking apart, the rumbling almost drowning out their voices. "Listen to me," said Juniper. "Vincent can take care of himself. Take Julius, Texi, and the others, and go back to Nightshade—now! The twins will go with you."

"Uncle, I can't leave Vincent. I won't!"

"Clover, I will find him or, I swear, I'll die trying. Leave now! The Catacombs are going to cave in!"

"But—"

"Go!" roared Juniper, handing her Julius. "Gather everyone and run as fast as you can! I will find him!" With Julius in her arms, Clover ran off with Texi, both trying to cover Julius's head as they rushed down the corridor. Ulrich and Ragan raced close behind, using their spears to try to keep the falling earth from striking Julius and the girls, shouting to the others as they vanished down a corridor.

"Cole, you are Deputy Chief Citizen. It is your responsibility to run things in my place."

Cole stood firm. "I'm not leaving you here."

Shoving him in the shoulder, Juniper glared at him. "Go now, Cole! You owe it to the Council, to all that we've worked for. You owe it to every rat in Nightshade."

Growling into the air, Cole slammed the end of his spear against the wall. He knew Juniper was right. "You'd *better* come back alive!" He muttered something under his breath and raced out of the compound.

"Vincent!" called Juniper, running in the opposite direction. "Vincent!" A support beam fell in front of him. He jumped over it and kept running, sizable clumps of falling earth now battering him.

He came to the compound's storeroom—the very room where

Julius had been found as an infant, half dead from starvation. Bitsy lay motionless on the floor, a knife protruding from her chest.

There was Billycan, throwing his body against Killdeer's immense silver throne. Vincent lay lifeless on the ground next to him, his leg trapped beneath the throne, blood trickling from his temple.

Juniper stared at the scene, not sure what to do.

Billycan leaned against the throne, his chest heaving wildly, trying to catch his breath. He finally looked up and spotted Juniper. "Well," he said, panting heavily, "why are you just standing there? Come help me!"

Juniper shook his head like a dog, trying to unclog his tangled thoughts. He dashed over and positioned himself next to Billycan. Billycan nodded and they began pushing in unison, grunting and clenching their teeth as they struggled against the weight of the throne.

"He's alive," huffed Billycan. "Bitsy threw... her dagger at him, hit him in the temple... he fell... grabbed the throne for support, but... the vibrations, the tremors... it toppled down on him."

More earth poured from the ceiling, rocks and pebbles pelting their eyes. "We've got to get out of here *now!*" said Juniper.

"I knew this place would crumble one day," grunted Billycan as they gave another push. "C'mon, then, on three... one—two—three!" They looked at each other and pushed with all their might. Finally, with a synchronized groan from both, the silver throne moved. Billycan held it up while Juniper grabbed Vincent, pulling his leg free just before Billycan's hold gave way. The throne came down with a fury, smashing to the ground in an explosion of dust and debris.

Rumbling thunder enveloped them. Anything still standing in the storeroom crashed to the ground. Juniper and Billycan each grabbed Vincent under an arm. "Quickly!" yelled Juniper.

They made their way out of the storeroom only seconds before the room imploded, an avalanche of rubble traveling fast at their heels as each corridor collapsed behind them. They raced through the Catacombs in the dark, years of memories guiding them.

Finally they reached the long tunnel back to Nightshade. They stopped for a moment, their lungs and limbs burning. "Take him," huffed Billycan. "You need to get him to safety." The tunnel shook again. "You must leave *now*."

"Come with us," said Juniper. "This entire place is disintegrating. Look at you—you're bleeding! You'll die if you turn back. You'll never find a way out."

"I *always* find a way out," Billycan replied calmly.

"But what about Julius? What will I tell him?"

"Julius is *your* son. You are his father in every sense of the word. You tell him that, for that is the truth. And I know better than anyone how you like the truth."

"I cannot leave you," argued Juniper as dust flooded the corridor. "Billycan, you still don't know the whole truth. The serum given to you was a cure for the drugs you were given in the lab—not a truth serum, as I told the others."

"I knew it was something like that. I didn't think I'd suddenly turned good." Billycan smiled. "It's ironic. The one time in your life that you lied, you lied for me. Thank you."

"That's not all. Lenore, the rat who saved you from the lab all those years ago, she was your mother—*our* mother. On her deathbed she told me about you. I have the proof back in Nightshade. Your matching lab tags—mother, offspring, both marked 111. Billycan, I am your brother."

Billycan nodded as he reflected. "She looked like you . . . the same fur. . . . You always reminded me of her. Now I know why."

"Yes," said Juniper, "same mahogany fur and same eyes, my father used to say."

Billycan's eyes began to burn. He remembered her so clearly, always watching him with a hopeful, tender expression. "Lenore," he whispered. Suddenly he grinned. "The rat who's late may wind up with a frightful fate."

"That's what she always said," said Juniper.

Looking up at the quaking ceiling, Billycan put a paw on Juniper's shoulder. "Never was there a time, brother, when those words were more fitting." Vincent started to moan. "Go, hurry now!" said Billycan. He turned to leave. The corridor to Nightshade began to shake, rumbling over their heads.

Billycan suddenly turned back. "Juniper, wait! There's something you need to know about that rat you sent to see me—Elvi!" He shouted as loud as he could over the clamor. "Don't trust her. She's not who she says she is! She seeks revenge—on you!"

"What?" called Juniper. "Billycan, I can't hear you. We must leave before the corridor caves in!"

"Do not trust Elvi!" Billycan yelled again. He could not hear his brother's reply. Billycan gave Juniper one last look and then vanished into the dark.

CHAPTER EIGHTEEN

Spirit of a Lion

EVERYONE GATHERED IN the Council Chamber. Vincent, his leg broken in several places, stood uncomfortably on the crutches Virden had fashioned for him. He looked around at his friends. Everyone was banged-up, scratched, bruised—battle-worn, but in good spirits. "Today's the big day, then," he said, nudging Carn's shoulder. Carn and Oleander nodded. "I'm sure Telula and Cotton are already waiting for you two in the alley."

"Bats are never tardy," said Juniper with a chuckle. "We'd best send you on your way."

"Dresden said someone from his colony will report to you once a week," said Carn, "telling you everything we've discovered about the scientists' diaries."

"There's so much to learn," said Oleander. "Cobweb and Montague have been organizing the scientists' papers by date, trying to make sense of it all. One can only guess what will be revealed." She hesitated for a moment. "Not surprisingly, they've found more than a few white hairs scattered among the papers."

"You're right," said Juniper, "that's not surprising at all."

No one spoke for a moment, still baffled by what had happened in the Catacombs—the fury of the white rat, which seemed to explode upon everything evil that night.

"I'm still concerned about the snakes," said Juniper, changing the subject. "I want to trust them, but they don't call them snakes for nothing."

"We'll be fine," said Carn. "Besides, we'll have Thicket and Stono at our heels, watching our every move." He smiled excitedly. "I can't wait to see them!"

Clover squeezed Oleander's paw. "We'll see you soon," she said. "We'll join you at the manor as soon as Vincent's well enough to travel."

"Good," whispered Oleander, glancing at Carn. "Someone has to help me keep *Corn* from getting into more trouble." The girls giggled. Both Carn and Vincent flushed a warm indigo, unsure of which one of them was being poked fun at.

"Get used to it," said Vincent.

Carn snorted. "Already am."

Juniper gave Oleander a hug. "Thank you for all your help. Give your father and the others our best." He turned to Carn and embraced him, slapping him on the back. "Don't let this one get away," he whispered.

"Not a chance," said Carn.

Mother Gallo and Juniper sat in the Council Chamber with Texi and Elvi, who sat across from them.

"Texi," said Mother Gallo, "you're very lucky things turned out the way they did."

Texi's eyes were puffy from crying. "I know. I'm so sorry. I understand now what could have happened to Julius and the others. My sisters promised me they'd be good. I didn't think they would attack the way they did." Ashamed, she looked away. "I didn't think at all..."

"It's not just what could have happened to Julius or the others," said Mother Gallo. "It's what could have happened to you. We could have lost *you*."

Texi looked up, her chin quivering. "I don't understand. Why would you care about what happened to me?"

"My dear, how little you think of yourself," said Mother Gallo. "It breaks my heart to know you thought your sisters were looking out for you, and not us. It worries me dreadfully."

"They told me they were wrong to treat me so poorly all those years. Bitsy told me they were all going to make up for it and treat me like a *real* sister."

"Texi, think clearly now. How would *you* treat a real sister?" asked Juniper.

"Well... I'd be kind to her. I do things with her, like read books and play games and stay up all night talking." She smiled feebly. "That's how I would treat a sister."

"I know how your sisters treated you," said Juniper, "but tell me, how did they treat each other?"

Furrowing her brow, Texi thought about all ten of her older sisters. A thought struck her. "They were terrible to one another. They bickered and fought all the time. They stole things from each other. They were hateful."

"So then tell me, who are your real sisters now?"

"Well...Mother Gallo," she said. "And Elvi...and of course Clover."

"All right, then." Juniper smiled. "I think you understand what a real sister is. Many times, it has little to do with blood." His face turned serious. "Now Texi, as much as we'd like to forget all of this ever happened, we can't, not just yet. We want to be able to trust you, but we have to be assured that nothing like this will ever happen again." He nodded at Elvi, who put an arm around Texi. "Elvi has offered to take you under her wing, to watch over you, to be that sister you never had."

"You know how Elvi feels about you," said Mother Gallo, "and with the life lessons she's acquired, you'll learn a great deal."

"You will be on probation," said Juniper, "under Elvi's constant supervision. You will share quarters with her, have your meals with her, assist her with her many duties around Nightshade, but most of all you'll learn from her. We think after a while we'll be able to trust you again and you'll get a much better sense of who you are. You need some confidence, Texi, a sense of worth. You need to realize *you* are important, too, to everyone in Nightshade, and all those unkind words you endured from your sisters—that you're slow-witted—well, that's utter drivel. You are smart. You only need to realize it."

"That's my *punishment?*" asked Texi, surprised. "It doesn't sound very harsh."

"It's not meant to be, Texi," said Mother Gallo.

"Don't you worry, dearest," said Elvi, patting her paw. "I will be your friend, your mentor, and your sister. I will teach you everything I know. I will give you the same confidence I learned growing up in Tosca. By the time I'm through with you, why, you'll have the spirit of a lion!" She laughed. "What a pair we'll make. No one will be able to stop us." She smiled broadly at Mother Gallo and Juniper. "No one."

The city was sleeping. Mother Gallo held Nomi in her arms, singing softly as she drifted off. The boys had fallen asleep—all but one.

"Papa," said Julius as they rocked in the chair, "is Billycan really, truly my father?"

"Yes, Julius, he *is* your father."

"Is he a bad rat like everyone says?"

"No, son, he was a broken rat. When he was a little boy like you, he was hurt very, very badly, and no one ever bothered to fix him. But he's all better now—he's good."

"I thought so," said Julius. "I *knew* he was my father."

"Oh, I see," replied Juniper, "and how do you feel about that?"

Julius looked at Juniper. "It's all right with me."

"Well, that's nice to hear," said Juniper. "I'm sure Billycan would be very pleased to know that."

"Papa, where is he now?"

"I have a suspicion where he might have gone, but then again, who can be sure? I can tell you this, though. I know he thinks about you every day and dreams of you every night."

"Will he ever come back here?"

"That's something I wonder about, myself. I've a feeling that if your father ever does come back we may never know it. Either way, you will *always* be his son, no matter how near or far he may be, and you will always be part of him."

Julius smiled at that. He suddenly sat up and looked at Juniper, worried. "Are you still my papa?"

Juniper settled back in his chair as Julius rested his head on his chest. "Yes, son, I will *always* be your papa."

CHAPTER NINETEEN
Of Fish and Family

A WARM BREEZE HIT his whiskers as Billycan looked out over the open waters of Hellgate Sea. It was an unusually hot day, even for Tosca, but the heat felt good on his bones.

Taking in a deep breath of salty air, he closed his eyes. He thought of Julius, safe at home—his son, his entirely remarkable boy, who would have the life he never did. He thought of Juniper, the one who released him from the chains of hatred that had bound him for so long—his brother, his friend.

As the sun glinted off the gently rolling waves, Billycan wondered how much time he had left in this world. He supposed it didn't really matter. He was alive for now, and when it was time to go, many years from now or perhaps only a single day, he was not afraid. Perhaps he'd be reunited with Dorf, no longer trapped inside their small, cramped cages, finally free. No more smell of bleach.

The soft wind blowing across the sand reminded Billycan of his mother, Lenore, and the night they'd escaped from the lab...that same gentle breeze . . . the wind blowing through their coats . . . the feel of her soft fur something he had never forgotten, even in his darkest of hours. If she had left him in the lab, so much would have changed. Killdeer would still have defeated the High Ministry—Billycan was certain of that—using other rats to serve his purpose and taking many lives along the way.

If his mother had been caught that night, there would have been no Barcus, no Juniper, and because of that, no Nightshade City.

Billycan slowly exhaled and opened his eyes. He took in all the beauty before him, beauty he never would have noticed before.

Fish, he thought. Yes indeed, fish sounded good for lunch.

He smiled and dived into the sea.